THE OFFICE OF GARDENS AND PONDS

D1149137

Didier Decoin

THE OFFICE OF GARDENS AND PONDS

Translated from the French by
Euan Cameron

MACLEHOSE PRESS
QUERCUS · LONDON

First published as *Le Bureau des jardins et des étangs*
by Editions Stock, Paris, in 2017

First published in Great Britain in 2019 by MacLehose Press

This paperback edition published in 2020 by

MacLehose Press
An imprint of Quercus Publishing Ltd
Carmelite House
50 Victoria Embankment
London EC4Y 0DZ

An Hachette UK company

1 3 5 7 9 10 8 6 4 2

Designed and typeset in Bembo by Patty Rennie
Printed and bound in Great Britain by Clays Ltd, Elcograf S.p.A.

Once there was a man burning incense.
He noticed that the fragrance was neither
coming nor going;
It neither appeared nor disappeared.
This trifling incident led him to gain
Enlightenment.

SHAKYAMUNI BUDDHA

For Jean-Marc Roberts

MIYUKI'S JOURNEY

HEIAN KYŌ

KII MOUNTAINS

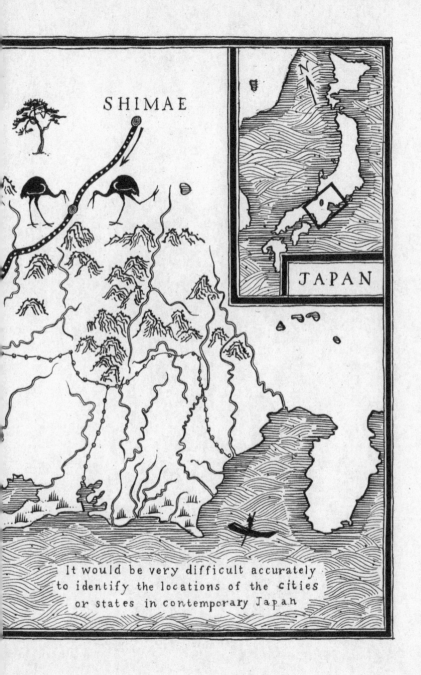

SHIMAE

JAPAN

It would be very difficult accurately
to identify the locations of the cities
or states in contemporary Japan

FOLLOWING A LONG CONFINEMENT and strict observance of the eating restrictions associated with bereavement, and after she had polished Katsuro's body with a sacred fabric that was intended to absorb any impurities, Amakusa Miyuki undertook the ritual that would purify her from the stain of her husband's death. But since it was inconceivable that the young widow should immerse herself in the very same river in which Katsuro had just drowned, the Shinto priest merely pursed his lips and flourished the branch of a pine tree over her, the lowest boughs of which had been moistened by the waters of the Kusagawa. Then he assured her that she could now resume her life and show her gratitude to the gods who would not fail to grant her courage and strength.

Miyuki knew perfectly well what lay behind the priest's words of comfort: he hoped that despite the precariousness of her situation, exacerbated by the death of Katsuro, she would provide him with a concrete expression of the recognition she owed to the *kami*.*

---

* Divinities of the Shinto religion. The *kami* represent nature (mountains, trees, wind, sea, etc.) as well as the spirits of the dead.

But although Miyuki felt some gratitude towards the gods for having washed away her stains, she could not forgive them for having allowed the River Kusagawa, which after all was no less of a god itself, to rob her of her husband.

The alms she donated were therefore modest, comprising white radishes, a bunch of garlic bulbs and some sticky rice cakes. Skilfully wrapped in a linen cloth, the offering, due mainly to the considerable proportions of certain radishes, was of a size that implied a much larger gift. The priest was unsuspecting, and went happily on his way.

After which, Miyuki forced herself to clean and tidy the house. Not that she was a very orderly person. She was more the sort who prefers to leave things lying around, even deliberately scattering them about. In any case, Katsuro and she had very few possessions. Finding them strewn here and there, particularly in places where they should not be, afforded them a fleeting illusion of opulence. "Is this rice bowl new?" Katsuro would ask. "Did you buy it recently?" Miyuki would put her hand to her mouth to conceal her smile. "It's always been on the shelf, the sixth bowl from the back – it belonged to your mother, don't you remember?" When it had rolled around on the straw mat after Miyuki had knocked it over (and she had forgotten to pick it up straight away), the bowl had simply come to a stop and turned upside down in a shaft of sunlight, taking on reflections that Katsuro did not recognise, and this was why he had not immediately identified it.

Miyuki supposed that wealthy people always lived in the midst of constant clutter, just like those landscapes in which it was the turmoil that made them look beautiful. And so the River

Kusagawa was never more elating to contemplate than after a heavy downpour, when the mountain tributaries filled it with muddy brown waters, full of pieces of bark, moss, watercress flowers and rotting leaves swirling about, all black and shrivelled; then the Kusagawa lost its shimmering appearance and became covered in concentric circles and spirals of foam that made it look like the whirlpools of the Naruto Strait, in the Inland Sea. Rich people, Miyuki thought, must be swamped in the same way by the countless waves of gifts which their friends (countless too, of course) gave them, and by all the dazzling trifles that they bought from travelling salesmen without counting the cost, without even asking themselves whether they would ever use them. They always needed more space to make room for their trinkets, to stack up their kitchen implements, hang their fabrics, line up their ointments, and to store all those riches whose names Miyuki sometimes did not even know.

It was an endless race, a relentless competition between people and things. The ultimate in opulence would be reached when the house burst like a ripe fruit from the pressure of the useless things that had been stuffed into it. Miyuki had never witnessed such a spectacle, but Katsuro had told her that on his trips to Heian Kyō he had seen beggars searching through the rubble of fine residences where the walls appeared to have been blown out from the inside.

In the house that Katsuro had built with his own hands – one room with a mud floor, another with a bare wooden floor and, beneath the thatched roof, an attic that was reached by a ladder, all of a modest size for he had had to choose between putting up walls or catching fish – there was mainly fishing equipment. It was used for everything: the nets put up to dry in front of the windows took the place of curtains, when folded they served as bedding, in the evenings they used the hollow wooden floats as headrests, and the tools for cleaning Katsuro's fishponds were the same as those used by Miyuki to prepare their meals.

The fisherman and his wife's one luxury was the salt pot. It was merely a copy of Chinese pottery from the Tang dynasty, a piece of brown glazed earthenware roughly decorated with peonies and lotuses, but Miyuki attributed supernatural powers to it: she had inherited it from her mother, who in turn had been given it by a grandmother who maintained that it had always been in the family. The pot had thus passed through several generations without suffering a single scratch, which made it miraculous.

Although it took only a few hours to tidy the house, Miyuki needed two hours to scrub it clean. The work carried out inside it was to blame: fishing and the breeding of magnificent fish, mainly carp. When he returned from the river, Katsuro never paused to strip off his clothing which was coated with a slimy silt that spattered onto the walls with every hurried movement he made; he had one thing on his mind: to rescue as quickly as possible the carp that were flapping about in their wicker nets, lest they lost any scales or tore off a barb – in which case they would lose all their value in the eyes of the imperial stewards – and to release them into the fishpond dug specially for them at the front of the house: a pool scooped out of the earth, not very deep, and filled to the brim with water that Miyuki, while her husband was away, had enriched with the larvae of insects, algae and seeds

4

from aquatic plants. This done, Katsuro would spend several days at a stretch sitting on his heels and observing the behaviour of his catch, watching in particular for those fish that he had first considered worthy of the ponds of the Imperial City, searching for signs that they were not simply the most attractive ones, but were also healthy enough to survive the long journey to the capital.

Katsuro was not very talkative. And when he did express himself, it was more by allusion than by assertion, thereby affording those he was talking to the pleasure of having to guess the distant perspectives of an incomplete thought.

On the day of her husband's death, once the five or six carp he had caught had been placed in the fishpond, Miyuki was squatting, as Katsuro used to do, by the edge of the pool, allowing herself to be hypnotised by the fish circling anxiously like prisoners discovering the boundaries of their gaol.

If she was capable of appreciating the beauty of certain carp, or at least the energy and sprightliness of their movements, she had not the least idea of what criteria Katsuro adopted to gauge their resilience. This was why, not wishing to deceive the villagers, and above all not to delude herself, she had got to her feet, brushed herself down, and, turning her back to the pond, had taken refuge in her house – the last one to the south of the hamlet, recognisable from the shells embedded in its thatch, their pearly sides facing the sky to reflect the light of the sun and to frighten away the crows that nested in the camphor trees.

The villagers were relieved to learn that Miyuki was forcing herself to scrape the mud from her floor and wash down her walls.

5

They had feared that she might make herself a tourniquet with a cord and a stick, and use it to strangle herself so that she could join Katsuro in the *yomi kuni*.* It was not that she was too young to die – at the age of twenty-seven, she had reached the average life expectancy for a peasant woman and could consider herself happy with the portion of existence that had been assigned to her – but that she had shared certain of Katsuro's secrets and now there was no-one apart from her to maintain the privileged relationship the village had with the Imperial Court at Heian Kyō: the provision of special carp to serve as living ornaments in the temple ponds, in exchange for which the inhabitants of this collection of rickety humpbacked huts known as Shimae benefited from a virtual exemption of taxes, not to mention the small gifts from Watanabe Nagusa,† the Director of the Office of Gardens and Ponds, which Katsuro never failed to bring back for them.

Now, it so happened, Watanabe had just sent three officials to place an order for some new carp to replace those which had not survived the winter.

One morning – it was a few days after Katsuro's death – the emissaries from the Office of Gardens and Ponds had appeared out of the humid mist which, after heavy rain during the night, hung over the edge of the forest like a curtain.

On their previous visits they had come on foot, which had been extremely costly to the people of Shimae, because, exhausted by their journey, the carp buyers had lingered for a fortnight, living off the villagers, their appetites and taste for sake increasing

---

* The world of the dead, according to Shinto mythology.
† In Japan the surname is traditionally placed in front of the first name.

6

as they recovered strength. But this time they had arrived on horseback, accompanied by an equerry bearing the silk banner in the colours of the Emperor, and they had abandoned the comfortable, loose-fitting *kariginu*[*] for warriors' uniforms with the metal plates protecting their chests and their backs jangling like old, cracked bells. Their sudden appearance had frightened the few women who had gathered on the threshing floor to plait the rice straw and had put them to flight.

In his capacity as the village's senior magistrate, Natsume had come out to meet the three riders and to greet them with the deference due to representatives of the imperial throne; but as he put his hands together and bowed as low as his stiff neck permitted, he wondered how the Emperor, reputed to be the most refined prince of his time, could tolerate such unattractiveness in the men responsible for making his wishes known throughout the provinces: swaying listlessly on their black lacquered wood saddles, their heads nodding beneath helmets extended by their neck-guards, their armour green with the moss that had clung to them as they rode through the forests, the emissaries resembled enormous woodlice with bellies swollen by waxy and nauseous substances. But perhaps His Imperial Majesty had never set eyes on them: some second-class deputy to a counsellor of the fifth minor lower rank had placed their names on a list (and nobody would ever know why the deputy had selected these names rather than any others), he had presented them to an inspector of the fourth minor upper rank, who had, over time, passed them on to the top of the hierarchy, whence they

---

[*] An article of clothing midway between a cape and the coat that the nobility wore for hunting.

7

had gradually come back down again finally to fall into the hands of Watanabe Nagusa, who had approved them with an impatient brushstroke – and of all this, as with so many other decisions affecting the sixty-eight provinces, the Emperor had known nothing.

The imperial messengers were very upset to hear of Katsuro's death. They had grimaced, groaned and emitted noises from their throats, shuddered with displeasure and jangled their breastplates. To calm them, it had been necessary for Natsume to introduce them to Miyuki. They had gazed at her in silence, rolling their small black eyes above wooden masks bristling with false devil's teeth that covered the lower part of their faces.

While Miyuki bowed, bending so low that her forehead touched the dusty ground, the village chief reassured the emissaries: the fisherman's widow would serve them as scrupulously as Katsuro had done. Then, to mollify them fully, Natsume gave them a meal of buckwheat noodles, seaweed and fish accompanied by vegetables pickled with sediment of sake, before taking them along to the waterfall whence they continued on the road to Heian Kyō.

Then he came back to converse with Miyuki.

"Your husband was dead when they found him, but fortunately the carp that he had already managed to catch are very much alive," – he gave Miyuki a kindly look, as though she were responsible for the thriving health of the fish – "and the ambassadors paid me many compliments."

"Those fat grasshoppers are ambassadors? They're nothing but minor officials who are so poorly regarded at Court that they

8

are despatched to the depths of the provinces when a simple letter would have sufficed."

Was she suggesting that she would have known how to read this letter? She had a nerve, that was for sure. But since Natsume himself could not read, he did not raise the matter, preferring not to venture into any area that risked his humiliation.

For a silent moment, his reticence making it appear that he was pondering Miyuki's words, he watched the carp swimming lazily in their fishpond.

"Sending three horsemen costs considerably more than sending a simple letter bearer," he observed. "I see in this a sign that the Office of Gardens and Ponds attaches particular importance to this order and to its satisfactory completion. You will leave for Heian Kyō as soon as possible."

"Yes," she said with unexpected compliance. "Yes. By tomorrow if you wish."

He gave a growl of satisfaction. The notion that Katsuro's death could have made Miyuki impervious to many things, even to setting out on the journey to Heian Kyō, for example, had not occurred to him. He had no idea of the grief that had consumed her, leaving her an empty husk, grey as ash.

To all intents and purposes, Natsume had never looked at this woman, this widow, as she should properly be referred to now. She was too emaciated to be the sort of mistress he liked; in only a short time, grief had hollowed out her cheeks and accentuated her slender, windswept figure. But perhaps he could take her home and give her to his son who had still not found a wife to his liking and who appreciated sad women. He used to say that although the tears were salty, the majority of grief-stricken women gave off a pleasant aroma of very sweet fruit. And if Hara (that was his son's name) did not want the carp fisherman's widow, Natsume could always try to fatten her up for his own pleasure; this would be an altogether more enjoyable task since Miyuki's attractions – her *future* attractions, he corrected himself, thinking of the fattening process that he would first have to impose on her – were clearly accompanied by a spontaneous and exquisite submission.

"How many fish will you deliver to the Court? At least twenty or so?"

"Carp are not demanding," Miyuki said, "but they need plenty of water. The pots in which Katsuro carried them could not hold much, so the fewer fish there are, the less they will suffer."

She did not dare add that her shoulders, which would bear the weight of the bamboo pole from which the pots would hang, were not as strong as those of her husband: the amount of water to be carried would be the only concession she could negotiate if the pain of conveying the fish was greater than she thought she could endure.

"Twenty fish," Natsume repeated. "It's the least the village can do."

Had he not been certain of finding the carp he wanted there, Katsuro would never have gone so far down the river. But the magnificent fish were plentiful in this part of the Kusagawa, just past the Shuzenji weir, where they were easier to catch after they had withstood the strong currents upstream created by the waterfall and while they were giving themselves a sort of breather, almost drifting on the surface of the water.

For as experienced a fisherman as Katsuro, it was enough for him to dip his hands in the water, fingers spread wide, and wait for a carp to come and rub its nose against his open palms. All Katsuro had to do was close his fingers, pressing them lightly against the gills, to relax the fish, which had stiffened into a sort of terrified erection on contact with the man. Its fins continued to flutter, but, suddenly soft and submissive, its flesh surrendered to the hand that was touching it. Then Katsuro hurried to remove the carp from its river and place it carefully in one of the rice straw nets made watertight by an application of mud.

Lined with grassy banks where buttercups grew, meandering between a double screen of wild cherry trees, persimmons, reeds and blue pines, the path leading to Katsuro's fishing grounds appeared at first glance to be a very pleasant walk. But the fisherman was not deceived, he knew that it was a perilous path that could quickly be turned into a gully by the rainstorms, and that the streams of water created faults that made stepping there akin to walking into a trap. It was one thing when Katsuro walked down towards the river, because his nets were empty and he could concentrate fully on where he planted his feet; but it was quite another matter on the return journey when he had to look far ahead of himself to keep the pole balanced across his shoulders with the baskets overflowing with water and fish; the slightest jolt roused the carp from their torpor and they became frantic, some of them even managing to throw themselves out of the nets despite the plaited, wide-meshed lotus stalks with which the fisherman had covered them.

On two occasions, Katsuro was injured.

The first time, it had been only a sprain. Ignoring the pain, and after breaking his pole to make crutches for himself, he had been able to get back to the village. But he had had to leave his nets behind, concealing them beneath the long, fresh grasses that had been flattened by the rain and looked as though they were made of green lacquer. As he hobbled towards Shimae, he heard, behind him, the rustle of wild animals from the forest that were bound to discover his fish and eat them.

The second accident was more serious: he had broken an ankle. This time, with or without crutches, he was unable to get to his feet. He had to make up his mind to haul himself along on his stomach, dragging his broken, swollen and burning ankle as it bumped over the rough track and made him cry out in distress. As well as the torture that crawling inflicted on his foot, the flesh on his knees, thighs and stomach was also scratched. Quivering with fever and pain, Katsuro had then tried to clamber up the other side of the path, the one where the verges, soaked by the frequent overflowing of the river, were less secure. Initially he had felt relief when he smelled the damp freshness of the mud soothing his burning body. But then he had crawled into an area where the ground was eroded, and the absence of vegetation caused sudden subsidence in the clay-like mud. Even though this forced him to tumble down towards the river and actually get his face wet, Katsuro was not afraid of the landslides that he encountered: the worst ones were hidden beneath apparently smooth and compact areas where the Kusagawa had created hidden faults that threatened to collapse under his weight. And this is what happened, just before a bend in the river.

A white heron watched impassively as the man, slimy with

mud and contorted with pain, squirmed and gasped for breath, and then, suddenly, disappeared in a commotion of water and silt.

One of his hands had remained above the water, clutching at the sky, desperately grasping for something to hold on to. His fingers had found the remnants of the riverbank, they had clutched at the mud and thrust deep into it, but the sodden clay had slipped between his knuckles; his hand, held up for a second towards the sky, had fallen back and then, almost gracefully, without a splash, it was as if it had dissolved into the river.

At that moment, the white heron's neck had quivered; but this should not be seen as a kind of gesture of compassion for the fisherman on the part of the bird, no, the death of a man and the swallowing reflex of a great wading bird renowned for bringing misfortune was pure coincidence.

OF THESE EVENTS THAT had taken place at Shimae on the twenty-fourth day of the third moon, the seventy-three families of the village remembered especially that Miyuki had shown a restraint and dignity that surprised everyone.

Fishermen's wives had a reputation for complaining. When they were not berating their husbands or railing against the stewards, they criticised the wickerwork, the quality of which, they said, deteriorated by the year. As a result, the Kusagawa current wore out the fishing tackle two or three times faster than it had done in the past – whereas, in actual fact, it was these women's inability to plait the nets that was the cause.

From the back of their throats they drew tearful voices to reproach their husbands for fish that were too small, for clothes that were always damp and rotted more quickly than those of the peasants, for nets full of holes that allowed their best catches to escape. Or else they moaned about the lack of eagerness on the part of the imperial stewards to order new carp to restock the ponds of Heian Kyō.

Yet it was not the stewards they should have blamed, but Katsuro alone, who provided fish of such exceptional longevity that the Office of Gardens and Ponds had considered bestowing on him the honour of Master of Carp; but as this title had never existed (at least, the secretaries of the Office had found no trace of one in any official document), Watanabe became discouraged when he reflected on the complexity of the many procedures that would need to be followed if the creation of this new honorary function were to be ratified. Furthermore, Katsuro asked for nothing. He went from temple to temple with his buckets full of carp, chose the most temperate pond, emptied his fish into it, observed their acclimatisation for a few days (squatting motionless on the bank, as he did at Shimae, except that here he did not have a wife to bring him rice and cover his shoulders with a straw coat when the night grew cold), made his recommendations about how to feed them and catch them without frightening them in order to distribute them to other pools, for when panic-stricken the carp could lose their glints of glossy leather, of polished bronze.

As they made their way to Miyuki's house to inform her that Katsuro had drowned, the villagers were expecting a distressing scene. The poor woman would cling to them and utter terrible curses against the *kami* of the river who had taken her husband from her, and against Natsume and his councillors who had encouraged the trade in carp and had always urged Katsuro to catch ever stronger and more magnificent fish, and perhaps, in her extreme grief, Miyuki might go so far as to curse the Emperor himself who insisted that his ornamental ponds should always be pulsating with carp, even though His Majesty probably never took the time to go and laze by a pool to admire the fish.

But no, Miyuki had allowed the villagers to go on talking, telling her about the death of her husband – what they knew of it, which was very little – and she had merely inclined her head to one side as though she found it hard to believe what they were telling her.

When they had finished, she let out a strangled cry and fell to the ground.

It was odd, the way she slumped down: she seemed to coil into herself the closer her shoulders came to the floor. Her cry remained suspended above her body's descending spiral. A fraction of a second later – and this shows how fleeting her cry had been – nothing further issued from Miyuki's lips beyond a barely audible exhalation. Then there was the sudden dull thud of her forehead hitting the ground, like the sound of a wooden bowl that is dropped from a height and spills its contents as it falls.

Miyuki's thoughts had scattered like the thousands of grains of rice that form a solid ball, warm and fragrant, in the bowl. Gathering up those grains one by one to put them back in the bowl is too tiresome a task. When such a thing happens, it is better to sweep them up or throw a pail of water over the floor. This is what the brain of the fainting Miyuki did: under the impact of the blow, it sent all the grains of rice that made up her conscious energy (memory, emotion, awareness of the outside world) to the back of beyond, limiting her activity purely to vital functions.

Deprived of sensation, Miyuki lay motionless on the mud floor. The men had lifted her up and laid her on her net. She was light. Natsume had noticed a damp patch spreading over Miyuki's gown, level with her pubis. Leaning over her, he had recognised the smell of urine. He wondered whether he should speak to the others about it. But he thought that this could be humiliating for Miyuki. He also remembered that, when it dried, material soaked in urine gave off an odour more or less like that of fish, and he reckoned that no-one would be surprised if the clothing of a carp fisherman's widow smelled of fish. So he said nothing.

In the middle of the night, Miyuki had been woken from her dazed state following her loss of consciousness by the hollow clicking sound made by the mercenaries; Natsume had enlisted ten or so to protect Shimae in the event of possible raids from Chinese pirates. The noise was made by the twanging of the strings of their bows following the custom at the Imperial Palace where it was forbidden to raise one's voice during the night or call out the hour.

Now the time had just passed from the hour of the Wild Boar to that of the Rat.* The moon was full, shedding a cool light that cast shadows like patches of gleaming black ink. It was as though they had just been brushed in.

Miyuki had opened her eyes. She had immediately seen Katsuro's body, which the fishermen had laid across an open chest to allow it to dry, in such a way that the murky water that continued to seep from his clothing and his hair would not contaminate the mud floor – a pointless precaution, to tell the truth, because the moment that Katsuro's corpse had crossed the threshold, the impurity of death was said to have infected the entire house,

---

* In other words, it was almost midnight.

17

the objects (not many of them, as we have stated) it contained, the animals (mainly the ducks that Katsuro had brought back from the Kusagawa in the past and that had made their dwelling there), and above all the villagers, those who had brought back his remains, those who would gather for the funeral vigil, as well as all those who would have to enter the house during the prescribed forty-nine days of mourning.

Custom decreed that Miyuki should place at the disposal of visitors a receptacle full of salt which they could sprinkle over themselves for purification; but she had no idea what type of receptacle would be suitable (bowl, pot, bucket? Why not a large lotus leaf that would remind people of the river where Katsuro had lost his life?); in any case, she had hardly any salt left and did not have the means to buy enough to satisfy the demands of the ritual. She sensed that life without her husband was going to be a succession of troublesome questions that she would have to try to answer on her own. She was immediately annoyed with herself for this fit of selfishness, remembering that Katsuro's fate was scarcely more enviable than her own, at least in those early hours of his death that belonged to the indeterminate period when the souls of the dead persisted in wanting to return to the life they had left and, being unable to do so, developed an anxiety that bordered on despair. Thereafter, everything depended on which religion was in possession of the truth. If the path of truth were Shintoist, Katsuro would descend to the domain of the dead, which is a reflection of the world of the living, with mountains, valleys, meadows and forests, but infinitely darker, and, taking his place, perhaps, among the family ancestors, he would keep watch over Miyuki until she joined him – it was not the worst of hypotheses. If the truth were Buddhist, the time spent wandering between the dissolution of his former life and the acquisition of another existence would be fairly brief, and Katsuro would not suffer long from the disconcerting sensation of having lost his shape, his substance and his feelings.

Someone had brought a stone bowl filled with clear water, as well as a bamboo ladle so that Miyuki could wash and purify her husband's body.

In three days' time, the carp fisherman's corpse would be burned on a pyre built outside the village. The bones would be withdrawn from the embers, starting with those of the feet and ending with those of the skull, and they would be placed in the funerary urn in the same sequence – in this way the dead person would be spared the discomfort and ridicule of being laid upside down. Then the posthumous name of Katsuro would be inscribed on a tablet which Miyuki would put on the shelf of the Spirits. The urn would remain in the house for forty-nine days, it would be filled with offerings of flowers, food, incense and candle lights, libations would be poured in its honour, and then it would be buried and there would be no further mention of the carp fisherman.

Miyuki had gently stroked Katsuro's body, unable to prevent herself asking him in a quiet voice whether the water she was pouring over his flesh was not too cold, whether she was putting her wet hand there in the place where he loved to be fondled – she no longer had her husband's little grunts of pleasure to guide her, as her fingers pressed and played freely.

The mud that encased the fisherman made him look like

pottery, like a tall earthenware jar in which the cracks fade and close beneath the moist palm that is rubbing it. Miyuki took the opportunity when no-one was looking to place her lips for one last time on the long shaft of his penis, which had grown cold.

The earthy taste surprised her. When he was alive, when it swelled inside Miyuki's mouth, Katsuro's penis had tasted of raw fish, of warm young bamboo shoots, and of fresh almonds when she finally released its juices. Now it was insipid and muddy to her tongue, like the pools of the temples of Heian Kyō when the Office of Gardens and Ponds had them drained for cleaning.

Miyuki had loved this man. Not that he was a very good lover – but what did she know, after all, since she had experienced no-one but him? He used to upset her by the way he silently loomed up behind her and took her by the shoulders, his nails scratching her flesh, his strong breath enveloping her neck, a smell of ripe fruit and poorly tanned leather, his knee pushing against her lower back to open her tunic and expose a portion of naked flesh against which he would then rub his organ as if he were furtively making omelette rolls. He did not derive his pleasure without her, but in front of her, and differently.

Once Katsuro had left for the river, Miyuki would go back to bed to relive every phase of the semblance of predatory behaviour that had just been inflicted on her – the silent approach, the lunge, the grasp, the stripping, the devouring, the gratification, the flight into the night; this feeling of having been attacked by a wild animal was often enough to satisfy her, the sides of her nose would flare, quiver and turn blue, her breathing wheezed and grew quicker, beads of sweat formed between her breasts, her bosom was an invitation to bite; she let out a brief, hoarse cry, the skin on her face seemed to tighten, she choked, and she would suddenly release herself, her back arching, and allow a long whistling sound to stream out between her lips; it was her way of coming, one that resembled the gentle flow of the Kusagawa over its bed of wet grass.

It also seemed to her that her husband's body had become larger. Perhaps it was due to the release of death, after all, even though this release did not form part of the nine stages of the transformation of the corpse as taught by the monks.

On the night of the vigil over the remains, Miyuki had disguised herself as a bird: with her neck stretched forward and her arms held away from her body, she had walked in circles around the room, taking quick, short steps, and had bowed low to the other women before hopping from one side to the other; she had let out the piercing cry, *krooh*, *krooh*, *krooh*, the nasal trumpeting call of the ash-coloured crane, to help Katsuro's soul – his soul which was believed to behave like a bird – to fly away to the *takama-no-hara*, the high plain of paradise.

But Katsuro believed in neither gods nor portents. Nothing had ever stopped him from putting out his nets, whereas other fishermen remained confined to their homes on the pretext that it was an ill-fated day or that there was some religious constraint they had to obey. As far as constraints were concerned, the only ones Katsuro knew about were the fierce floods of the Kusagawa that kept the carp at the bottom of the riverbed.

He was not the sort to ask questions. Neither of himself nor of anyone else. He had often said yes, sometimes no, but he had scarcely ever asked either where or when, or how or why.

And yet, in his early youth, he had certainly displayed the same curiosity as any other child; as he grew older, however, he had gradually become convinced that there was no point in getting to the bottom of things since there was nothing he could do to change matters. His thoughts had become as steady as the rocks that emerged in the lower part of the river, impervious equally to weariness, to discouragement, to apathy – so many emotions that would eventually come to sap the energy of a carp fisherman more effectively than the water that gradually wore away the crumbling part of the banks of the Kusagawa.

Katsuro had never asked the oracles whether any particular night would be more auspicious for catching carp: they would either be there, or they would not, that was all there was to it. The colour and shape of the moon might have an influence on women's moods, but not on the presence of fish either upstream or downstream from the Shuzenji weir.

Miyuki showed no interest in omens either, even though some greedy monks had sought her out to tell her that her journey was taking place under unfavourable auspices, and that they were fortunately able to remedy this by enclosing in a cloth bag strips of hemp on which they proposed inscribing the names of all the sanctuaries that she would encounter during the course of her long road to the pools of the Heian Kyō temples. According to them it was a powerful talisman, as efficacious on the outward route as on the return. All it would cost Miyuki would be a few bottles of sake and a meal consisting of *mochi** seasoned with

* A dish made of glutinous rice.

22

a mixture of salt and fillet of loach, and garnished with a generous portion of those oyster mushrooms that are reputed to prolong life.

This was not a feast, merely one of those good meals that she had often prepared for Katsuro, and yet she turned down their offer: there was no question of eating into the nest egg that Natsume had given her on behalf of the villagers who had paid Miyuki a lump sum to cover the transportation of the carp and their acclimatisation in the sacred ponds. After this final delivery, the villagers would no doubt appoint another fisherman to replace Katsuro, and it would be very unlikely that the new supplier would need Miyuki's help to carry his fish to Heian Kyō – he would take responsibility for the assignment himself, for the job was only profitable if you were in charge of both catching the carp and delivering them to the temples of the Imperial City.

On her return from Heian Kyō, Miyuki should therefore reconsider what her life had been until then.

She would become a farmer without land, the most underprivileged of the peasant classes. Who would provide her livelihood from now on? Would she lend her arms to grind the millet? Or would she go and wear herself out in Lord Shigenobu's rice field, which, in addition to the benefit of then being exempted from land tax, would apparently provide the opportunity from time to time of catching one of those wild ducks that Shigenobu encouraged to nest on his land because they plucked out the weeds as they devoured the insects that lived off the rice. Miyuki's only certainty was that she would not die of hunger: upstream from the Shuzenji weir, the Kusagawa was covered for

23

much of the year with bindweed with pointed leaves, soft to eat and delicately flavoured.

If it had been up to her alone, she would have left at once – the transportation of the fish was cumbersome enough for her not to go to the trouble of packing another bag. All she would take with her would be a coarse article of clothing made from wisteria fibres, a few mouthfuls of *narezushi** and some rice cakes, which would be enough to sustain her as she walked. Once dusk fell, and on days when it rained heavily and the stormy atmosphere was likely to turn the water in the fishing baskets green, she would stop at one or other of those inns that are strung out along the road to Heian Kyō, and that are increasingly numerous in the provinces of Totomi and Mikawa.

She remembered how Katsuro's eyes gleamed whenever he spoke of these taverns. And sometimes he even laughed about them. He had his favourites: the Inn of the Six Crystals, the Inn of the First Plucking (so named in an allusion to the harvesting of the fruit of the persimmon tree – at least, that was what Katsuro maintained, but then his voice would falter, and Miyuki preferred to look away), the Inn of the Red Dragonfly or the Inn of the Two Moons in the Water.

Before leaving Shimae, Miyuki had to prepare as safe as possible a habitat for her carp.

For the journey to the Imperial City, she planned to keep as close as possible to rivers and streams, only deviating from them

---

* Fish gutted and preserved in fermented rice to prevent it decaying. The rice coating was discarded before the fish was eaten.

when she had no choice. It would make her journey longer, but it guaranteed that the carp would have a supply of fresh water, even if their baskets happened to be damaged in the event of an accident. In any case, despite all the care that Miyuki would devote to their waterproofing, nothing could prevent the baskets from losing a certain amount of water. To provide them with maximum impermeability, and to soothe the carp, which prefer the dark, Katsuro used to caulk each basket with a heavy silt, apply a strip of coarse material to the inside and outside, and end by coating it with a generous amount of clay that he could simply knead with his wet hands whenever excessive sunshine or wind caused cracks to appear. But this did not stop the water leaking from the containers when the carp, bored with their cramped and unstable homes, became restless, or when a pronounced swaying of the yoke (which could be caused by stumbling and recovering a little too hastily) created waves, some of which overflowed.

When she had prepared the baskets, Miyuki chose the carp she would put into them. First of all, she picked out the ones whose scales formed the most uniform and harmonious patterns, with noses neither too long nor too short or squat, symmetrical fins and a perfectly consistent colour from nose to tail. Following this first selection, she took two black carp (one a metallic, shiny black, the other velvety and matt) and two fish of a more sallow yellow colour, but whose growth and longevity were often exceptional, then two deep bronze ones that had a sheen like flowing brown honey, and she rounded off her selection with two carp that were almost devoid of scales and looked as though they were sheathed in leather.

To provide them with as much space as was essential, Miyuki had decided to take only relatively small carp, carp that were two summers old, a little less than one *shaku** and weighing about one *kin*.†

She caught them by hand, as patient and skilful as Katsuro, a procedure that was like a caress.

She had waited until nightfall to undress and walk down to the pool, her toes curled like small hooks so as not to slip on the slimy riverbed. Unable to swim, and immersed in the water up to her waist, she risked drowning if she were to trip or fall. She had started by stepping cautiously along the banks of the fishpond, her knees, her thighs, her pubis rippling the black water, blurring the reflection of the moon that receded before her. The water was icy cold. Darkness hid the fish, but she could detect their presence from their light brushes against her skin, from the slight flutter of their fins on her legs, and she felt as though she were walking amid a flight of cold butterflies.

As she had seen her husband do, she scraped a part of her body with her nails, removing tiny particles of skin which, when they dissolved, would be accepted by the carp as a natural component of the pool water. In this way Katsuro gradually became familiar to the fish to the point where they would come of their own accord and rest their bellies in the hollow of his hand, something that never failed to enthral the clerks of the Office of Gardens and Ponds.

⊙ ⊙ ⊙

---

* Just over 30 centimetres, or about one foot.
† 675 grams, or one pound and eight ounces.

26

So that her carp could grow accustomed to the confined space of what would be their home for many moons, Miyuki waited for almost three days before she set out.

She compared her journey to Heian Kyō to those summer days that begin with the contours of the landscape masked by sheets of mist which are eventually burned off by the sun – at least until the storm clouds rise once more on the horizon at the hour of the Dog.* Since Katsuro's death, Miyuki had lived in a fog that muffled sound and diluted colours. But she sensed that this opacity would be shattered as soon as she set off, and that she would then see the world as it really was, with its positive aspects and its harmful sides. Then, once she had delivered her fish, when they were gliding around in the pools of the temples, her life would flatten out again and she would return to obscurity.

"Well," said a voice.

She looked up. Natsume had arrived and he was gazing down at her.

"Are you taking a bath?" he said. "Really?"

She told him that she was taming her fish. At least, she was trying to. The carp would have only her as their reference point, they had to grow accustomed to the scent of her diluted in the water in the baskets.

"I don't know whether they'll come," Natsume said, pointing towards the village square, which was still empty.

He was alluding to the villagers' ritual of gathering around Katsuro and accompanying him to the edge of the forest. Once they were there, the fisherman and the villagers used to

---

* From seven o'clock to nine o'clock in the evening.

27

exchange blessings, expressing hopes that Katsuro and his carp would arrive safe and sound at Heian Kyō, and that he would then return to Shimae without being robbed of the promissory notes from the Office of Gardens and Ponds in payment for his fish, three-quarters of which would be passed over to the village before he and Miyuki went to exchange the remainder in an imperial warehouse for sacks of rice and bundles of hemp and silk.

Like a chicken contemplating a handful of grain, Miyuki bobbed her head up and down, adding to her small pecks a series of shrill *oh! oh! oh!* sounds, and she said she did not deserve to be escorted because she was not even sure that she would succeed in walking half the distance.

If she failed, the entire village would be dishonoured for failing to supply fish to the temples of Heian Kyō, and never again would the Office of Gardens and Ponds send emissaries asking for carp to be delivered. Shimae would lose not only its reputation, but also the greater part of the subsidies on which its inhabitants depended. Of course, certain priors who were keen on ornamental fish would probably continue to obtain their supplies from the fishermen of Shimae, but one could not compare the custom of unfussy, surly monks with the demanding but so very sophisticated clientele of the Office of Gardens and Ponds.

Stocking the pools of Heian Kyō was such a privilege that the lakeside residents of Yumiike, and the people from the Sumida and Shinano rivers, never stopped pestering the director, Watanabe, to give the job to them instead of maintaining his steady reliance on the people of Shimae. Miyuki thought she could hear the grumbles of satisfaction from the fishermen of Koguriyama, Asakusa or Niigata when they had learned of the death of Katsuro.

"How many fish did you decide to take in the end?" Natsume said.

"I have four baskets, two fish in each basket, so eight carp."

"Did I not ask you to allow for at least twenty?"

As he did whenever he became angry, he let out a shriek. A flight of swallows, imagining they had heard a fox, flew noisily out of a clump of trees.

Miyuki bowed humbly to Natsume and explained that each carp needed a large amount of clean water. Twenty fish would produce too much faeces, and this would risk them poisoning themselves. She added that eight was a beneficial number, a symbol of abundance and good luck.

"And yet your husband certainly carried twenty or so, did he not? Come now, I did not pick on this number by chance!"

"Katsuro could carry much bigger baskets than the ones I shall take. Katsuro was such a strong man, so resilient," she added with a smile – a smile that the village chief did not notice because she was still bowed down, and all that Natsume could see of her was the parting at the nape of her neck between two bunches of glossy black hair.

Having placed an offering of flowers and food in the little shrine that had been set up in front of her house, which contained a few modest mementos of her own ancestors as well as those of her husband, Miyuki balanced on her left shoulder the long pole loaded with two wicker containers at each end.

Alerted by the sudden swaying of the yoke, the carp began to swim around their mobile prison – in a spiralling motion, they swam up from the bottom, rising to the surface in concentric circles before dropping down again. This one movement through the water was enough to cause the pole to vibrate. This pulsating sound seemed to generate two musical notes, one coming from the front end of the bamboo, the other from the rear; at the moment that the sounds merged, at the exact point where the pole rested on Miyuki's shoulder, they blended into one another in a single perfect note.

The most minute alteration to this sound would raise the alarm, indicating that the bamboo rod was slipping either forwards or backwards, whereupon Miyuki had to adjust its balance quickly.

She walked through the village, Natsume scampering beside her. In spite of the wisps of smoke that rose vertically from the chimneys, the houses seemed deserted and the main thoroughfare and alleyways all remained empty.

Tarnished by the death of her husband and by the fact that she had not scrupulously abided by the restriction that stemmed from it (she should have remained at home in seclusion for thirty days), Miyuki could not help contaminating with her impurity all those who came close to her. She realised that the villagers had chosen to avoid her rather than be obliged to stay indoors for several days in order to purify themselves from an inevitable stigma. The one brought about by the death of a human being was among the most serious.

"Suppose the people at the Office of Gardens and Ponds

were to pay you the sum I agreed with their messengers," Natsume began, "on condition that the carp that you deliver are still as shiny, agile and graceful as they are here . . ."

"No, no," Miyuki said. "I've already told you: the fish will not all arrive at Heian Kyō in good condition. I may not be able to release even a single one into the sacred ponds."

Did not Katsuro himself, despite all the care he lavished on them, lose several fish on each journey? It took only a storm for the water in the baskets to become murky and foul-smelling. Then the fish would descend as far as they could, their large, soft lips nibbling at the base of their prison as if trying to find a way out and flee the polluted waters. And then they began floating on their sides, and that was how they died.

At the outskirts of the village, Natsume, too breathless to continue, sat on the stump of a tree. With the same gesture he used to chase away flies, he indicated to Miyuki that she should walk on. But perhaps, after all, it was a gesture of blessing.

Beyond the last house, the one that was used as a communal barn and was not covered with thatch but with cypress bark, thirty-six plots of land subdivided into small portions formed a chessboard of very small squares, each of varying shades of green depending on whether rice, millet or other cereals were being grown there. Natsume waited until Miyuki's outline had passed the thirty-sixth square of the board and had melted into the mist ascending in swirls from the drainage ditches, then he left his tree stump and returned to the village square, shouting out in a husky voice that the die had been cast, that the fisherman's widow, gallantly striding forth on her two small legs, had set off on the road to Heian Kyō, the bamboo of her long pole glinting in the rising sun each time it swayed.

Water rails, flying low, passed by, their cry sounding just like that of a piglet being slaughtered.

LIKE ALL IMPORTANT OFFICIALS, the Director of the Office of Gardens and Ponds, Watanabe Nagusa, was granted the privilege of living at Susaku Oji, on the Avenue of the Red Bird, the best-known thoroughfare in Heian Kyō.

The main entrance to his residence gave onto Tomi and Rakkaku streets, but the chief parts of the property – the house and its outbuildings, the vegetable patch and especially the garden with its pond fed from a headrace – overlooked Susaku Oji. Thanks to this location, Watanabe avoided the hustle and bustle of the great thoroughfare that divided the Imperial City in two sections, and also the cloud of ochre dust that permanently hung over it.

The Avenue of the Red Bird consisted of three lanes, one for men, one for the stream of vehicles going up and down, and one restricted to women. Since his house bordered the women's lane, Watanabe was occasionally obliged to wait before being able to cross over and join the men's lane. This was the case that morning, when he had to allow a slow procession of gossiping women, who were on their way to pay homage to Ebisu,

33

the hairy, barbaric and ebullient fish-god, to pass by. Then, the Director of the Office of Gardens and Ponds had to wait patiently yet again for a seemingly unending stream of ox carts, escorted by fifty or so riders.

Fortunately, Watanabe did not have far to walk along the Avenue of the Red Bird before passing through the Suzakumon, the southern gate, inside the triumphal wall of the Great Palace.

In addition to the Inner Palace, which housed the imperial residence, the *dairi*, the Great Palace, very much a city within a city, contained all the ceremonial and administrative buildings directly related to the person of the Emperor, among them the Office of Gardens and Ponds, which was situated in a pavilion inspired by Chinese architecture: a stone-built foundation with a staircase on either side, surmounted by a wooden structure surrounded by pillars painted in a matt red, and with a curved roof covered in glazed tiles.

In actual fact, the Office of Gardens and Ponds had not officially existed since 896, the date when, like the Office of Oil and that of Tableware, it had been incorporated into the Office of the Emperor's Table; but the position of director had been maintained and, for just over a century after the Office had been absorbed, there had always been a senior official of the upper sixth rank major to continue to exercise unrestricted jurisdiction over the flowers, vegetable gardens and waterways.

With its copious workforce – forty cooks, as well as twice that number of assistants, agents and couriers, and not forgetting a particular deity: the God of the Stoves – the Office of the Emperor's Table was endowed with substantial importance and prestige; but even though he was occasionally requested to

34

prepare offerings for sanctuaries, its administrator did not have the same familiarity with the gods as Watanabe did: because the ponds formed part of the sacred domain of the temples, the Director of the Office of Gardens and Ponds was, for his part, in close and constant contact with the Buddhist and Shintoist monks who attended the gods.

Hunched over, due to back pain that resisted all recitations of sutras and even aromatic reed baths – it was only in the presence of the Emperor that the old man succeeded in standing straight without wincing too much – Watanabe made his way across several small quadrangles of white sand and finely combed gravel, scattered with grey boulders over which mosses crept. Connected by covered passageways, these courtyards were all alike, forming a kind of *cloisonné* partition: the clay walls had been designed in such a way that, when the sun was at its zenith, out of deference to the Emperor, there would no longer be any shadows cast over the *dairi*, thereby giving it the unreal appearance of a palace floating in the dazzling sky.

The onset of autumn meant that it was necessary to prepare for days, and especially nights, of extreme cold, and the Palace staff had arranged for the installation of large *hibachi** to heat – in actual fact, simply to warm up – the glacial atmosphere that, in winter, would grip the pavilions of the Great Palace. At any given moment, Watanabe was obliged to step to one side, against the wall, to avoid not just the servants carrying the braziers, but

---

* A kind of brazier consisting of a large porcelain or wooden bowl, decorated with paintings and/or inlay, and containing a metal receptacle to collect the embers.

35

more particularly the clouds of ashes and soot they spilled in their wake.

And so, angrily dusting himself down, Watanabe entered the first of the three chambers allocated to the defunct but still active Office of Gardens and Ponds.

Kusakabe Atsuhito, the youngest and most dedicated of the six officials who assisted Watanabe, got immediately to his feet and, as he did so, bowed very low, thus transforming a simple gesture of respect into a dance movement.

It was during a night-time banquet given by the Emperor at the Pavilion of Kindness and Happiness that Watanabe had been deeply moved by the grace of Kusakabe as he danced in a ballet, playing the role of a fisherman discovering a feather dress of indescribable splendour that a heavenly creature had left on the branch of a pine tree on Miho beach; and Kusakabe Atsuhito had been so much more sylph-like, more fervent and radiant than the dancer who played the princess, that Watanabe, who cherished beauty in all its forms, had straight away schemed to take him on as an assistant.

"I'm sorry to be late," Watanabe said, "but it is becoming so difficult to make one's way in Heian Kyō. More and more folk in the streets, and fewer and fewer faces one recognises – there are certainly many people in the city who have come from goodness knows where and who should not be here, and I certainly intend to draw His Majesty's attention to this matter."

It was a way of reminding people that he still enjoyed the privilege of being able to approach the Emperor. Kusakabe did not fail to make another bow.

"We waited as long as we could for you, Watanabe-*sensei*.* But it is such a pity that you missed the visit of the priest from the Rokkaku temple!"

"The one who lives in the small hut beside the pond?"

"The very same," the young official said. "He came to complain about the carp that the Office promised to deliver to him, which he had not seen a glimpse of."

Kusakabe Atsuhito accompanied his words with a sort of open-lipped pout, imitating the prominent lips of the carp, which made his colleagues laugh and perturbed the Director more than he would have wished.

"When did our emissaries return from the village of Shimae?" Watanabe said; and since his subordinates stared at him without replying, he scolded them, "Come now, open the registers! Look it up! Seek it out! The holy man in the hut deserves an answer!"

For the Director, life was made up of a collection of fragments that fitted together like the stitches of a tapestry. If one of those stitches, however tiny, should happen to come away from the canvas, the whole tapestry would be in danger of unravelling. This way of seeing things gave Watanabe not a moment's respite: his time was spent keeping a close watch on the threads, on the lookout for the slightest snag.

Kusakabe fiddled with the screws of the small side cabinet in a chest of drawers made of lacquered elm. He took out a scroll that he unwound until he found what he was looking for.

---

* It is customary to add the honorary suffix -*sensei* to the name of someone who is a professor, a doctor, a scholar, or anyone who is in a senior position within an organisation or a group. For someone of lesser importance, the suffix -*san* is used.

37

"Here it is," he said. "The three emissaries returned to Heian Kyō on the first moon of the fourth month. The report indicates that on arrival at Shimae they learned of the death of our supplier of carp, the fisherman Katsuro; however, the head of the village arranged for the widow of this Katsuro to take his place and to deliver the fish to us within a reasonable deadline."

"Reasonable?" the Director said.

"About thirty days, that's what the people in Shimae suggested."

"Did the widow agree to this herself or was it the village head who negotiated on her behalf?"

Kusakabe held the scroll up to the daylight and frowned as though he was finding it difficult to decipher the text – which was indeed the case, the scribe having opened the tip of his brush too widely: by applying it to the end of each character, he had run out of ink, and the line was completed by a web of strokes not connected to the main body of the character, which grew ever more thin and grey, the rich blackness of the calligraphy restored only with the next character.

"The scroll does not tell us," Kusakabe said, bending double as though he bore responsibility for this oversight.

The Director of the Office of Gardens and Ponds could scarcely conceal his disapproval; but this, of course, was not aimed at Kusakabe, and he directed his wrathful gaze at another official.

"Do we know how many carp this widow Katsuro is by way of delivering to us?"

"The Office's order was for twenty or so fish. That is roughly the number of carp that the fisherman emptied into our ponds on each of his visits."

"His wife will never match that, of course. She is probably elderly and unsteady on her legs."

As much to show his contempt for the fisherman's wife as to circulate the heavy air that festered in the room, Watanabe unfolded and flourished the large fan he kept in the pleat of his coat.

"As soon as she has released her wretched carp," he said, "I shall inform her that we do not intend to renew our agreement with her village."

"Should I prepare a document to that effect, *sensei*?"

Watanabe affirmed this with a nod of the head. As this concerned the cancellation of a deal made with peasants who were certainly too uncultivated ever to have been aware of the importance of the Office of Gardens and Ponds, Watanabe had no intention of burdening himself with customs that these people would not understand. Moreover, he declared that it was pointless to inscribe the termination of the contract on *washi** which was becoming more costly by the day, particularly since the factory established on the River Shikugawa was producing new types of paper made from the bark of the mulberry tree, the surface of which was so silky that the ladies-in-waiting at the Imperial Court would have no other on which to write their journals: a wooden board would be sufficient to notify the village of Shimae that the Office of Gardens and Ponds had no further need of their services.

"Should we thank them for favours provided in the past, *sensei*?"

_____
* The specific name for Japanese (*wa*) paper (*shi*).

39

Watanabe Nagusa did not reply. He would have shrugged, but from his coccyx to his shoulder-blades his back was really too painful.

Being let down by his body in this way was all the more exasperating since, in certain lights, his face still looked the part, thanks in particular to the frothy plumage of his very white hair and, beneath his half-moon eyelids, his restlessly shifting gaze, possessed of a febrile determination that rejected, that repelled the weariness and debility of old age.

NEITHER KATSURO'S FAMILY, NOR Miyuki's – of whom only her sister and her uncles remained, the rest of the clan having been slaughtered during bloody raids by rebel hordes – were wealthy enough to afford the cost of a Shinto wedding. It was obligatory to provide a donation towards the upkeep of the sanctuary, to remunerate the priest and the *miko** in their white kimonos and scarlet trousers, to buy the red lacquer cups from which the married couple would drink the golden sake, as well as a sasaki branch with delicate pink blossom that would be left on the altar at the conclusion of the ceremony.

Instead, Katsuro and Miyuki had chosen to marry by "nocturnal intrusion", a form of union that was all the more widespread because it cost nothing: all the suitor had to do for their union to become official was to spend several nights in succession in his "fiancée's" bedroom and copulate with her.

Having made sure that Miyuki had no professed lover, Katsuro had accosted her on the pretext of a dream that he had had about a trap for catching carp. Up until then, he explained, he

---

* Female assistants of the celebrant and guardians of Shinto shrines.

41

had made do with submerging interwoven branches into which those carp seeking somewhere to hide would thread their way. But they then found themselves so trapped that, in order to free them, he had to untwist his branches, one by one, and all of a sudden, the small branches would divide and fan open, and the carp would seize the opportunity to escape.

Miyuki had not understood why the agility of fugitive fish and the frustrations of the man who fished for them should be relevant to her. And it was only out of politeness that she had sniggered behind her hands held up over her mouth in a shell shape, as though she had never heard anything so funny as this story of carp intent on regaining their freedom.

Katsuro then explained to her the idea he had had of a kind of funnel made of supple rushes, with a sort of lid contrived in such a way that the fish, once inside, could not get out again.

"That should work," Miyuki acknowledged as she leaned over the drawing that he had traced in the dust.

Modesty obliged her to temper her admiration for the ingeniousness of the trap, but she thought no less of it.

"Oh, I know what I'm doing!" Katsuro said. "But weaving this kind of trap requires fingers that are slender and nimble. You have such fingers. That is why I thought you might agree to make three of these traps for me. Could we say two small ones and one big one?"

Katsuro was perfectly able to weave the rushes himself, but he used the excuse of making sure that Miyuki's work was progressing so that he could creep into her home at night.

The disastrous state of public finances had led to the virtual disappearance of money, and the people made do with barter.

Straw sandals were exchanged for rice, sake for wads of indigo paper, venison for waterproof parasols. And so Katsuro, in return for the traps that she was going to make for him, had offered Miyuki a lacquer comb, nine measures of rice and three of the largest fish he could catch in the River Kusagawa. Miyuki agreed to these conditions without hesitation, for the transaction seemed clearly to her advantage.

It was recommended that a man preparing to perform a nocturnal intrusion should be more or less naked when he slipped into the house in which his intended slept, not in order to seduce her more swiftly, but so as not to be mistaken for a villain: thieves actually went about their work wrapped in several layers of clothing to protect themselves against any thrashings with sticks.

By way of compensation for his nudity, the lover was also advised to conceal his face under a cloth to avoid showing his embarrassment in the event that, once inside the house, he might be rejected by the woman he desired.

Finally, he was urged to urinate over the sliding door separating the bedroom of his beloved from the rest of the dwelling to lubricate the groove and prevent it from creaking.

But Katsuro had no need to concern himself with the door: since the death of her parents, Miyuki had lived alone in a crooked hut, and everyone knew how she longed for a nocturnal visit that would make her officially recognised as a lawful wife. Far from counting on a discreet intrusion, she dreamed of *taiko* drummers twirling their sticks over the white hide of their enormous drums to announce to the sleeping village the sudden arrival of Katsuro both in her home and in her life.

Every evening, she thought she heard the heavy, powerful and majestic roll of ritual drums beating out the steps of the man who was coming to be with her. But it was merely the thumping of her heart that she mistook for that of the giant *taiko*.

Marriage by means of nocturnal intrusion presupposed that a relation of the fiancée, usually her mother or her brother, would stand at the entrance to the abode to inform the visitor about the layout of the house and provide him with a lit lantern so that he could find his way. Knowing that Miyuki no longer had either a brother or a mother, Katsuro arrived bearing his own lantern made of iron with a bird motif. As for finding his way around the house, it was very easy for him since the dwelling consisted of just one small room with a mud floor, above which was an alcove for sleeping, attached to an outhouse where some chickens and a couple of pigs lived.

He found Miyuki up there, squatting on her heels in the alcove, which was hung with an assortment of curtains – not having the money to acquire enough of the same material, she had had to make do with disparate offcuts, some of the same colour, others printed or embroidered with symbolic designs.

Even though the weather was not yet very warm, that evening she wore only a light white *yukata* with wisteria branches stencilled on it.

"It's me," Katsuro said, bowing very low. "Me, Nakamura Katsuro."

"Katsuro," she said. "You who have been out of doors, Katsuro, is it still raining?"

She could have found out just by listening. But was not

worrying about whether it was raining a good opening gambit when you were scarcely acquainted with one another?

All she knew about Katsuro could be summed up in a few words: he was almost twice her age, he had never been married and he made his living as a fisherman – he even made a fairly good living whenever the Office of Gardens and Ponds in the Imperial City ordered carp from him, something that occurred two or three times a year; at those moments he enjoyed a surge of esteem on the part of the inhabitants of Shimae, for the economy of the village partly depended on the provision of ornamental fish for the temples of Heian Kyō.

"The rain has stopped," Katsuro said. "But the mist has risen."

Cold showers on warm earth, it could not be otherwise.

"I am ashamed," Miyuki whispered, "that there was no-one from my family to welcome you, to provide you with a lantern. You must have had to find your way on your own."

She was as upset as she would have been had Katsuro been obliged to find his way through a house consisting of a labyrinth of corridors leading to countless rooms.

He squinted in order to see her better, because, out of modesty, she had moved away from the pool of light provided by the lantern. He wanted to arrange the lighting differently, but once more she concealed her face, framed as it was by the gleaming blackness of her oiled hair, piled on top of her head and tied with a red ribbon. Then there was a gust of wind, and the rising moon broke free from a cluster of clouds. It lit up the alcove. The fisherman blew out the now unnecessary lantern and lay down beside Miyuki.

Rummaging among the folds of Katsuro's kimono, she

45

uncovered areas of naked flesh that she began to stroke with the tips of her fingers, with her lips, her tongue and with a sweep of her hair, sleek and cool as the feathers of a crow. Drawing her mouth close to the opening of the wide sleeves of the *haori*[*] that he wore over his kimono, she took hold of the fisherman's fingers, nibbled them and sucked at them, coating them in a saliva so smooth that they became as slippery as if he had stuck them in a pot of honey, to the extent that he was then incapable of picking anything up.

And Miyuki could not stop laughing when she observed that she had disarmed him as effectively as if she had bound his hands together.

Katsuro moaned as a bulge formed beneath the material of his kimono, a bulge that Miyuki seized, kneaded, massaged, squashed and crushed. With the fondling, Katsuro's penis and testicles became one single mound that rolled around beneath the grip of her hand. Miyuki felt as though she was manipulating a small monkey that was curling up its paws.

Katsuro toppled over onto his stomach, withdrawing his painful organ from the pressure she was inflicting on it. Miyuki stretched out her arms and began to crawl over Katsuro's body, her hands running up and down his back while her lips kissed in succession the back of his knees, his thighs, and the cleft in his bottom. Then her mouth slid in little jumps from one vertebra to the next, as far as the hollow of his neck, the place where beads of sweat formed, where the fisherman's excitement was concentrated before it spread all over his body.

---

* A sort of jacket.

46

Miyuki grabbed her lover by the ears, forced him to look at her, and breathed over his tense, closed eyelids to make him open his eyes; he partly complied, revealing two slits of black lacquer, then she slipped her tongue over his nose, releasing a powerful, organic, salty scent into his nostrils, and he moaned once more, his imprisoned hands crushed beneath Miyuki's knees.

She continued crawling over him. It was the turn of her breasts to brush against Katsuro's face. They were small, round, full and supple; they skipped over the obstacles of the fisherman's chin, his nose and the arch of his eyebrows, exposing small furrows in his hair, like the tracks of hares through millet fields.

Then it was her slightly rough bush that rasped against his chest, and her open-lipped genitals that slid over the man's face, immersing it in warm balms, sticky and musky.

He moaned for a third time while Miyuki, a lock of whose hair had come adrift (she grabbed it and held it between her teeth in the way that courtesans do), spread her thighs wider and impaled herself on Katsuro's nose. On contact with this pistil of warm flesh, cyprine tears appeared on the labia minora of her vagina; sliding onto the fisherman's cheeks, they were trapped on the stubble of his beard, and his face became starry-eyed and began to sparkle as it did when he walked through the curtain of foam of the waterfall at the Shuzenji weir.

Later, they washed their sweat away and scrubbed each other clean, purifying themselves by throwing over each other buckets of water that had been left to cool on the ashes in the hearth, rubbing one another with pumice stones; their skin turned red and they laughed.

47

Just before dawn, as tradition decreed, Katsuro left Miyuki's house.

For several nights running, unbeknown to the villagers, the fisherman let himself into Miyuki's home. He showered her with tender kisses and received them in return; Miyuki was expert in lavishing intimate touches with her mouth and her tongue, while Katsuro possessed fingers each of which, as a consequence of having knotted fishing nets, seemed to be endowed with an astonishing life of its own. Afterwards, he slipped away, without anyone having seen him.

This continued until the day when his blurred features, his red eyes, his slower movements and his tendency to fall asleep anywhere and at any time, alerted other fishermen who confided their concerns to Natsume.

After bowing low to the village chief, Yagoro, who was master of the sturgeons that had inhabited the rivers for one hundred and forty million years, just as Katsuro was master of the carp, spoke out.

"He is starting to look like a ghost," he said. "His complexion is the colour of ash, but beneath his eyes he is crimson as a plum, and, when you come across him in the morning, his breath is as strong as a man with a dry mouth, an exhausted man, a man drained of his substance."

"Spectres are the dark part of our soul," Natsume observed. "Perhaps that is why this one hides in the *shirikodama*:* ghosts

---

* Japanese folklore. The *shirikodama* is supposed to be a ball that is buried in the flesh close to the human anus, and is coveted by the *kappa*, small aquatic demons of the rivers and lakes. In order to take possession of a man's *shirikodama*, the *kappa* first tries to drown its victim before ripping open his rectum.

are going about their business in there, among the darkness and the stench."

"I myself," said Akinaru, the best eel fisherman in the whole Kusagawa basin, "have never succeeded in finding my *shirikodama*. I've got nothing in that area, nothing but a stinking hole."

"But I don't believe that Katsuro has been transformed into a spectre," Natsume said, unconcerned about Akinaru's troubles with his *shirikodama*.

"Oh, no?" Yagoro said. "Then how do you explain his having changed so much, and so quickly too?"

"Barely one moon," Akinaru said.

"Has one of you ever followed him?" Natsume enquired.

"Follow him where? He's scarcely left his home since the Kusagawa burst its banks and became all muddy – the carp don't like that, and neither does Katsuro."

"And at night?"

"At night . . .?"

"Well!" Natsume said, narrowing his eyes in a malicious way. "Suppose Katsuro's in love?"

Akinaru and Yagoro looked at one another. Nowadays, they were elderly men. They had not thought about love for a long time. Yagoro's third wife had been snatched from him during an invasion of pirates, and Akinaru had lost his penis after being bitten by a silurid. The notion that Katsuro might run through the moonlight in search of a woman had not occurred to them, and it struck them as incongruous even though the village chief himself had voiced the idea.

◎ ◎ ◎

49

Although it had not been celebrated according to the Shinto rite and there had been no festivities, the community of Shimae simply gave their consent to Katsuro and Miyuki's marriage.

Miyuki brought no dowry, but, according to custom, she took responsibility for Katsuro's welfare: it was she who now provided his clothing, prepared his meals, cultivated their two plots of rice and took care of his nets and fishing gear.

SHE WAS IN THE forest immediately. The grey wisps of morning mist clung to the brambles and the shrubs with thin branches studded with waxy white flowers that were like rows of little votive candles. She could hear the sound of deer making their way stealthily in the darkness and the gnashing of their teeth on the bark of the ash trees as they nibbled down each trunk.

Rays from the rising sun fell across Miyuki's neck and shoulders, caressing them with plentiful shafts of warm light.

The path she was following was made of ash-coloured earth and formed a sort of ledge above a winding scar – probably once the bed of a stream that the summer droughts had dried out. Curiously, despite the absence of water, a number of dragonflies frolicked above clusters of dwarf bamboo shoots, a sign that pools of water survived beneath some of the stones.

Gnarled roots had gouged out the path on either side of the vanished stream. Fearful of tripping and losing her balance, Miyuki advanced with very small steps, her gaze fixed on the rocky outcrops, her head forward, her body bent double like that convict who had passed through Shimae one day, his neck locked in a heavy wooden cangue that prevented him from putting his

51

hands to his face where flies swarmed, drawn by his tears. Miyuki had been one of the compassionate women who had pressed balls of rice into his starving mouth from which a fetid froth dribbled.

If she could no longer claim to be Katsuro's wife, at least Miyuki remained a woman of Shimae. This was the identity under which she would continue to live, both publicly and in private.

And just as she had scrupulously fulfilled everything that was ordained to assure Katsuro's crossing into the other world, so she hoped that when it was her turn to die, the inhabitants of Shimae would postpone their labours in order to observe the ritual of the dead and accompany her to the borders of the Beyond; the reality of this Beyond concerning them no more, incidentally, than it troubled Miyuki.

But, now, the invisible thread that linked Miyuki to Shimae was becoming more strained and more fragile with every step that took her away from her village. She had only just begun her journey, and yet it seemed to her that certain features of Shimae were already fading from her memory. The variety of colours, in particular, were giving way to vast, flat, monochrome hues, as though the images of her immediate past were being submerged beneath the spreading mists, swept away by drifts of quicksand. The moist green fragrance of the paddy fields, the smell of fresh wet plants and of earth saturated with water, and the fluffy, muffled aroma of cooked rice that came steaming from the houses, the grey smoke rising from the cow dung, the glossy red of the cherry trees after the autumn rain – she could identify these things, she could describe them, but they were now no more than immaterial evocations, imitations.

Whatever it was about Katsuro that endured – his spirit, his soul, his ghost – was it responsible for this numbing of Miyuki's memory? Did he believe that he was protecting her against a nostalgia that might make her lose the fighting spirit that she would need to carry the carp to the ponds of the Heian Kyō temples?

Whether among other people or when they were alone, Katsuro had always tried to speak and act for both of them. It seemed that most of Miyuki's life had been spent waiting for the man who had married her. Like most of the women of Shimae, she woke early to carry out the household tasks that kept her busy until the hour of the Horse* was past. Afterwards, she devoted herself to the fish, feeding and taking care of the carp that Katsuro bred, and repairing those parts of the pond that had been damaged by an excess of sun or cold.

On exceptionally hot days, she allowed little Hakuba, the son of the potter, to come and cool down in the pond; in return, the boy brought clay of a particularly pliable and good quality and coated the walls of the fishpond with it, to make them more waterproof. Hakuba was too small to tackle the Kusagawa, but the ease with which he moved among the fish in the pond, the way he touched and stroked them, had appealed to Katsuro, who saw in him a potential successor – that is, if the Office of Gardens and Ponds continued to do business with him. Hakuba's hands would eventually be big enough, and his fingers long enough, to enable him to place them around a carp's body to move them from one habitat to another. On that day, Katsuro would give

---

* From eleven o'clock in the morning to one o'clock in the afternoon.

53

him his first cup of sake to drink, and the fisherman and his wife would finish the flask, talking about young Hakuba as though he was their son.

When evening fell, Miyuki would position herself at the doorway of her house, squatting on her heels, her gaze fixed on the end of the path along which Katsuro would return from the river.

As soon as she recognised the figure of her husband and his animal-like suppleness that enabled him to carry his baskets full of fish with perfect balance, Miyuki rose to her feet, shook off the dust on her clothing from her remaining still for so long, allowed her lips to open wide with happiness for an instant, then she would retract her smile (it would not have been proper to reveal her teeth and her gums in the very centre of the village) and merely offer Katsuro the vision of her mouth, barely open, but as appetising as a tender and juicy fruit.

The first days were exhausting. In addition to the fact that progress was difficult through the sodden forest and its dense, tangled vegetation that struggled for light, Miyuki had to endure the crushing weight of the yoke on her shoulders. The bruising was all the more painful because the swaying of the long bamboo pole was unpredictable: even when she thought she had balanced her load and relieved the pressure on her shoulders and against her neck, she would have to adopt a new position to ascend a steep path or to slow down over uneven ground. The swaying of the baskets and the shifting of their weight would cause the pole to slide forwards or backwards and the knots on the bamboo grazed her skin until it bled.

She walked in this way until the visibility was so diminished that the trees all around her blurred into a dark, unbroken wall.

As the darkness swept through the undergrowth and concealed possible hazards on her path, Miyuki grew increasingly anxious at the thought of stumbling, falling over and losing her fish. The carp were sufficiently shiny for her to be able to spot them if they were wriggling around on the ground, but what would be the point of putting them back in their baskets if all their water had been lost when she fell?

She would have no alternative but to put them out of their misery.

When, for one reason or another, Katsuro was obliged to destroy one of his carp, and as long as the fish was not too big, he would stick a finger in its mouth and inflict a sharp blow, which produced a clean break in the fish's neck. But Miyuki was not sure she could be as skilful as her husband, quite apart from the fact that her fingers were not as long as Katsuro's. She told herself that she would do just as well to be very careful not to put her sandals in the opening of any *tanuki*'s* hole or between two roots lurking in the dark.

As she continued on her way, lifting her knees to step over obstacles that probably only existed in her imagination, the carp awoke to their nocturnal life.

Through observing them in their natural habitat as well as in captivity, Katsuro had learned a great deal about their behaviour

---

* A mammal whose features resemble those of a water rat, a dog and a bear cub. Reputed to be able to transform itself into almost anything, this mischievous little animal, said to be very fond of sake, is the hero of numerous Japanese legends.

and had passed on his knowledge to Miyuki. She knew that this fish prefers to feed at dusk. Being very lazy, the carp stuffs itself on animal or vegetal prey that it flushes out by burrowing into the silt directly beneath its nose; but it is too lethargic to pursue the pupa of an insect or a small speck of algae that a fluctuation of current has just removed from its barbels: for every one worm lost in the mud, ten more are found; carp's oath.

Masses of tiny xylophagous insects' larvae fell from the trees into the baskets as Miyuki weaved her way between them, brushing against their bark. Having drowned, they congregated on the bottom of the baskets, and the carp could not imagine a more appetising feast. Miyuki improved it by sprinkling into the water bits of spinach and waterlily leaves that she had poached before leaving Shimae, and by adding freshly ground garlic, which Katsuro believed improved the energy of his fish.

Their barbels all aquiver, their noses in the silt with which Miyuki had generously filled their baskets, the fish feasted. Miyuki could not see them, but she could feel the long bamboo pole vibrating under their impact and she was aware of the splashing of the water created by the fast ripple of pectoral fins and the more measured movement of the pole caused by their unfurled tail-fins.

Since twilight was falling and it was beginning to rain, Miyuki dedicated the carps' delight to the memory of Katsuro.

The night was totally dark when the fisherman's wife finally emerged from the forest.

Before her lay an area strewn with pine needles, pieces of bark, dead moss and greyish-blue deposits that made the place resemble a shore at low tide.

Scarcely had she left the protection of the large trees than she was directly assailed by the rain. It seemed to have chosen her as a target, for, as far as she could judge through her drenched eyes, the downpour was less violent one step ahead of her; but Miyuki had only to make this step for the rain to double in intensity, remaining immediately above her, and thrashing her neck with tentacles of icy water.

Disturbed by the beating of the rain and the gusts of wind that ruffled the water in their prisons, the fish crammed themselves together over the thin layer of mud at the bottom of their baskets. Lined up side by side, they rolled their large eyes with yellow irises scattered with black dots, clearly upset at this interruption to their feasting. It was three days before the new moon, the period when the carp is at its greediest.

After climbing a steep path, on her right, beyond a dogwood hedge, Miyuki made out a small house. It was built of grey wood with a roof made from thick bundles of rice straw dotted with wild iris, sedums and clumps of fescue grass. The yellow glow of oil lamps flickered behind the few translucent paper windows.

The Hut of Just Retribution – that was the name of the establishment – was this one of the inns that Katsuro had been fond of?

Miyuki had hoped to break her journey at an inn where he might have left a sufficiently good impression for the owner, who was frequently also the administrator of a nearby monastery (as it happened, a bell could be heard ringing in the mist), to be charitable enough to offer a young widow a bowl of rice and a night under cover.

And even if Katsuro's custom had not earned her any privileges, Miyuki would have taken it as a good omen to have spent a few hours at an inn where her husband had taken refreshment, where he had slept, where he may have laughed in his sleep – the fisherman sometimes used to dream that he could fly, all he had to do was stretch out his arm to feel the elasticity of the air and he only had to lean into it to raise himself above the world, to propel himself from rooftop to rooftop in perfect contentment, and he would laugh like a child.

In order to reach the Hut of Just Retribution, Miyuki had to follow a narrow, slippery path that skirted a huge lake overgrown with lotuses. Some boats moored to large stones enabled one to make a more direct crossing, but Miyuki could not imagine herself navigating through the lotuses that covered almost the entire surface of the water. What would happen if her pole were caught in their tangle of plump roots? And suppose the sweet, skulking smell of the lake made the carp so restless that they jumped out of their baskets? Murky in the daylight, the stretch of water had darkened at nightfall, and it was now glassy, black and dense as calligrapher's ink.

Like most inns, the Hut of Just Retribution was long and narrow, the reception area situated at the front and the rooms grouped together at the back.

Halfway down the corridor that ran through the whole building, the kitchen marked the junction between the two areas. A couple of women were busy there, preparing food for the travellers that the inn would welcome that evening. They came out from their lean-to area to see what Miyuki was carrying, and when they saw the carp they started to prance about, making a sort of yapping noise, and the elder of the two grabbed a knife that she pretended to sharpen on a bluestone.

"No, no," Miyuki said sharply, "you mustn't touch them: these fish are not to be eaten. I am taking them to Heian Kyō to serve as ornaments in the temple ponds. I am travelling on behalf of Watanabe-*sensei*, the Director of the Office of Gardens and Ponds."

When she pronounced the name of Watanabe, Miyuki bowed as low as her long and cumbersome bamboo pole allowed. The elderly cook and her assistant did likewise.

"I remember I once prepared a meal – some mushrooms, I recall it perfectly – for a man who was also transporting fish for the temples of the Imperial City."

"That was my husband," Miyuki said. "It was Katsuro."

Her wish had been granted. Chance had led her to this inn where Katsuro had slept. Perhaps his dreams still inhabited the premises.

A hot spring gushed beneath the inn. The steaming water filled a natural bowl before flowing over a row of smooth, grey volcanic rocks until it rejoined a stream that ran parallel to the lake. Several monks were immersed in the hot water, their round and impassive faces turned towards the garden of the inn.

Akiyoshi Sadako, the *okamisan** in charge of the premises, suggested to Miyuki that she join the monks and relax from the strain of the journey by taking a bath.

---

* Manageress, administrator, receptionist.

Despite the good this would have done her, Miyuki declined the offer: the sight of the elderly cook sharpening her knife as she eyed the baskets had been enough to persuade her that as long as her journey lasted, it would be best never, under any circumstances, to be separated from her carp.

Having heard the news that there were pirates roaming around the region, the administrator recommended that Miyuki accompany the monks who were planning to set off from the inn very early the next morning for the Isle of Enoshima.

"You can make your way under their protection as far as the mouth of the Katasegawa, where you can take the road to Heian Kyō. All you will have to do then is to attach yourself to a group of pilgrims."

"The monks will expect me to make a donation for their having escorted me. But I have nothing apart from a little pickled rice, just enough to give me the strength to carry the yoke to my journey's end."

"Oh, I'm sure they would accept being remunerated with . . . well, they're men first and foremost and . . . they'll certainly, you know what I mean . . ."

Her lips slightly parted, Miyuki stared at the *okamisan*.

"Are you not a rice stacker?" the latter said.

And since Miyuki still said nothing, she added with a giggle:

"Do you really not know what a rice stacker is?"

"Of course, I do," Miyuki said. "We have rice fields in Shimae, our rice is plentiful and very tasty, and even though I do – I mean *I did* – spend more time attending to my husband's fishing, keeping the pond clean and looking after the fish, I often stacked

60

the rice. And I have never hidden my armpits from the other women," she added, to indicate that she spared no effort to raise the pestle high, certainly high enough to reveal the underside of her arms.

"Here," the manageress corrected her, "the rice stackers do not husk the rice. In actual fact, the rice has nothing to do with their work. If we refer to them in this way, it's because their task consists in letting slide between their joined hands certain shafts of flesh that, in a certain way, can make one think of pestles . . ."

Akiyoshi Sadako paused and smiled, lowering her eyelids modestly.

Miyuki closed her eyes too, wondering whether the fingers of a rice stacker had ever fondled, caressed and kneaded Katsuro's swelling and burning penis. Of course they had, she thought. Whenever he returned from the Imperial City, Katsuro had on him the means to remunerate a few rice stackers generously over several nights in succession. The Hut of Just Retribution was aptly named.

"Well, now do you understand?"

"Oh yes," Miyuki whispered. "Yes, but . . ."

". . . but of course, you're not one of those prostitutes. A pity, because if you had been, you would have been given a warm welcome. And as for me, I wouldn't have charged you for the night you're about to spend here."

Akiyoshi Sadako led Miyuki through a world of gates and wooden screens, oil-papers, curtains and lowered blinds, behind which the rain could be heard pattering over the garden along with, in the gap between showers, the chirp of crickets.

61

Hurrying along, Miyuki followed in the *okamisan*'s footsteps, taking care not to spill a drop of water from her baskets.

At one point, as she stepped through a doorway, she tripped on something soft. It was a young girl's dress, a greyish-beige *kazami*, lying in a heap like an exhausted animal. Miyuki's clogs were caught up in it, and it was as if, after tapping along loudly and clearly on a paved surface, they had suddenly become bogged down in a clayey hole. Propelled forward, Miyuki instinctively reached for her yoke, jolting it and causing the buckets to sway. At that moment, a carp was rising to the surface. Propelled by the heaving of the water, it slipped out and fell to the floor with a dull thud that was immediately followed by a wild drumming: the terrified fish was flapping its tail on the ground, trying to give itself the necessary momentum to jump high enough to regain its basket.

Then the carp stiffened and stopped struggling.

"No!" Miyuki wailed. "Don't die, I beg you, by Ebisu, the god of fishermen, I beseech you!"

"Ebisu clasps a sea bream to him," the manageress said. "Sometimes it's a tuna, sometimes a cod or a bass, but without meaning to demoralise you, I've never heard anyone say that fat old Ebisu would be interested in a carp."

Miyuki's eyes grew as dark and moist as two distressed little black fish.

"Don't cry," the *okamisan* said. "All is not yet lost. But Ebisu, as well as being obese, has the reputation of being deaf in both ears, so we shall have to make quite a din if we want him to take any notice."

And Akiyoshi Sadako began to stamp violently on the floor with her clogs.

Was it the shaking of the floor that persuaded Ebisu? The fact remains that the vibration of the oak boards roused the carp from the deadly state of lethargy into which it had sunk. It arched its body and started flapping its tail and its fins. Immediately, Miyuki made a shell with her hands and slipped them beneath the fish's body, lifting it up gently and placing it on the bed of wet clay at the very bottom of the basket.

"Do carp close their eyes when they sleep?" Akiyoshi Sadako said.

Miyuki let out a little laugh. This question had bothered her greatly at the beginning of her marriage to Katsuro. She could have asked him what he thought, and he would probably have willingly told her what he knew about carp, but she was frightened he might think her one of those simple women who do not know the facts of life: certainly, strictly speaking, carp do not really have much to do with the facts of life, at least not with present-day facts, and thousands and thousands of people die without ever having seen a single one of these fish, without even having deciphered the brushstrokes with which one writes their name, but Katsuro the fisherman was not like those thousands and thousands of people; nothing was more familiar to him than carp, so much so that he sometimes had the impression that the heart that beat in his chest must have the shape, the size and the flesh of one of these fish.

Miyuki remembered the nights at Shimae when, for hours at a stretch, she squatted by the side of the pool, taking advantage of the moon's reflections to observe the carp that floated around here and there.

"In actual fact, Sadako-*san*, if these fish have no eyelids, how could they close their eyes?"

63

She did have eyelids herself, and they were growing increasingly heavy. She gulped down some piping hot taro soup while the *okamisan* laid out a straw mattress on the floor of the women's dormitory, a quiet room with its space deliberately reduced by the provision of flimsy sliding partitions.

"I suggest you sleep directly beneath the window," Akiyoshi Sadako said. "We call it the window of spiritual enlightenment."

The *okamisan* pointed to the small round window halfway up the wall overlooking the garden, a wall where the paper had become sufficiently porous to let in the smell of rain-drenched plants.

For the first time since dawn, Miyuki could at last relieve her shoulders from the weight and chafing of the bamboo.

As she watched Akiyoshi Sadako unfolding and laying out her bed, it occurred to Miyuki that she had never yet spent a night away from her home in a strange place. Despite her weariness, she was not sure that she would fall asleep easily. To soothe herself, she contemplated the slow course of the moon and the stars through the oil-paper that sealed the window.

What could Katsuro have been thinking about, she wondered, when he stretched out on his bed? Did he go over in his mind everything that had happened during the day, or was he already planning for the days ahead? When he was nearing the end of his journey on the road from Heian Kyō, did he count the time that separated him from Miyuki with the same degree of impatience with which she herself counted down the hours until at times she grew breathless? Or did he linger on his return, with a nostalgic smile on his lips, remembering the good times spent with the rice stackers?

64

Oh, why did he not hurry home, why did he stay hanging around daydreaming? In what way could the women of pleasure from the inns satisfy him better than Miyuki? She never refused him anything, any type of activity, any position, any caress. It was enough that he should return from Heian Kyō, weary and shivering under his old straw coat that had not been waterproof for years, and bringing with him new, surprising, amazing ideas about lovers' practices.

Having nothing else to offer him, she agreed to embraces that tore her apart and crushed her, exchanges of fluids that sometimes disgusted her.

BALANCING THE BAMBOO POLE on her painful shoulder, Miyuki strode past the men lounging in the corridor of the inn.

They slept fully dressed, their chins resting on their chests, their thighs spread, their squat arms acting as props to prevent their plump, beetle-shaped bodies from toppling over. Most of them wore bowl-shaped helmets made of panels held together by rivets. Some of the helmets were decorated with metal fins that were meant to deflect lateral sabre blows, but to judge by the reddish scars on their bloated faces, the fins were more decorative than effective. At the top of the bowl there was a circular opening for the *bushi*'s* long hair.

For this is what they were: rural *bushi*, *bushi* from unproductive regions, from sparse forests or muddy rice fields, who had deserted their unrewarding moorlands to be hired by more fortunate, wealthier peasants.

Their eyes were invisible behind the visors that were just effective enough to prevent rain or splashes of blood from blurring their vision.

---

* Warrior. The samurai would originate from the *bushi*.

66

Slipping through the half-open doorway, the morning mist from the lagoon had seeped into the corridor. But it did not stop Miyuki from recognising Akiyoshi Sadako, who was going around on her knees, from one warrior to another, gently shaking each of them awake.

The *bushi* responded with groans or by lashing out indiscriminately. When one of them struck her in the face, Sadako curled herself into a ball like a hedgehog. When she re-emerged, the lower part of her face was pink from a mixture of blood and dribble.

As she wiped herself with the back of her sleeve, the *okamisan* explained that these men defended the properties, the family and the person of Yasukuni Masahide, a wealthy local landowner who had on several occasions been the victim of a raid by the pirates who infested the inland Sea of Seto. As the Hut of Just Retribution belonged to this man, Akiyoshi Sadako was automatically placed under the protection of his *bushi*.

Now, during the night, she said, at about the hour of the Tiger,* some pirates aboard a raft made from bulrushes had crossed the lagoon in the direction of the inn. But before they could launch their assault, the *bushi* had sprung out of the forest to repel them. The arrows had flown and swirled around the *katana* swords. According to the rules, execution quickly followed the confrontation, and nine of the assailants' heads had rolled down among the reeds of the lagoon. And the gang had fled without a murmur.

After which, naturally, the *bushi* had taken to drink to

---

* From three o'clock to five o'clock in the morning.

celebrate their victory, and they were now blind drunk; their bowels had emptied without their realising, and a stench of excrement lingered in the place, wafted by the light breeze that drifted beneath the thatched roof.

"I didn't hear any of that," Miyuki said.

"You were probably too worn out by your journey. Contrary to belief, fatigue does not just dull our limbs. Our senses also lose their capabilities. Because the tongue does not wriggle around in the mouth so much, it can be unaware of certain tastes. We had a horse dealer staying here who was in such a state of exhaustion that he was no longer able to tell the difference between sweetness and bitterness.

"As for their overstrained eyes, they don't have the strength to move or look around, they just see straight ahead like those warriors who, if they have put on their helmets correctly, cannot see to either side.

"The sense of smell is not spared. When our breathing slows down due to extreme weariness, our sighs of languidness cause us to expel the air almost as quickly as we inhale it, and we are left incapable of enjoying all those elusive moods with which it is imbued. I knew a woman, Akazome Rinshi, a lady who was reaching the end of her life admittedly, who was so weak that she could only breathe with extreme difficulty, which meant that the insides of her nostrils had gradually grown closer together until they became blocked, rather like snails that seal their shells when the wind changes. She perished in a fire at her home, poor lady, because she was unable to smell the smoke in time. And why should it be any different for one's own ears, why should lying prostrate have spared them?"

In the same gentle and solemn tone that she had just used to explain the effects of fatigue, the *okamisan* reminded Miyuki of her suggestion that she set off for the River Katasegawa in the company of the monks going to Enoshima on pilgrimage.

But despite the risks that she was taking in travelling without an escort in a region where pirates lurked and whose ferocity would be inflamed by the defeat they had suffered during the night, Miyuki persisted in declining the offer. Even if they did not make her pay for their protection, the monks might delay her by stopping in front of every *hokora** at the side of the road, at the foot of every tree, every rock, every stream, every foxhole that they suspected of being the sanctuary of a *kami*. With eight hundred thousand gods reigning over Japan at the time, even a humble sandal made of rice straw left by the side of the path might be the dwelling of a spirit.

Akiyoshi Sadako did not insist. She thanked Miyuki for having stopped at the Hut of Just Retribution. With her hands pressed to her knees, and her eyes lowered, she bowed from the waist and maintained this position for several seconds.

No-one had ever said goodbye to her in this way before, and Miyuki wondered in her confusion how she should react. Because the *okamisan*, after standing erect, bowed down to her once more, Miyuki bowed low in return.

The more fluid and gracious Sadako's salutation, the more her own struck Miyuki as stiff and awkward. However, the manageress of the inn did not have a bamboo pole cutting into her shoulder, laden at each end with heavy baskets filled with

---

* Miniature sanctuary dedicated to a *kami*.

carp, with the clay that lined them and the water they contained.

Dipping into the wad of papers that Natsume had provided her with for her expenses along the way, Miyuki held out a promissory note.

"Negotiable in any rice warehouse," she pointed out.

But Akiyoshi Sadako, bowing low over and over again (this time she almost touched the floor with her forehead), refused to be paid: even though it had failed, the attack by the pirates constituted serious harm to her customers, an offence to the peace of mind that travellers who stopped at the Hut of Just Retribution were meant to enjoy and for which the *okamisan* and her staff – which was limited to the elderly cook and a servant who maintained the garden and pond – were responsible. As the cook and the odd-job man had been killed by the pirates during the attack, it fell to Akiyoshi Sadako to assume sole responsibility for the inconvenience her guests had suffered.

Miyuki left the inn by the sunken path that ran alongside the lotus pond. She took the opportunity to renew some of the carps' water in the lake nearby.

Just as she was preparing to hoist up the baskets, now filled with liquid containing tiny animals and vegetal debris, she suddenly saw rising up in front of her, in the damp grey light of the dawn, the figure of an abnormally tall creature: a body puffed up with self-importance, with long, spindly limbs, which appeared to be wrapped in a large black and white cloak that the creature kept opening and closing as if to ventilate its chest.

The face, if one could so describe this slender frowning

aspect, studded with two brown eyes and a head capped with a sort of grainy red skullcap, swayed at the top of an elongated neck that resembled a long, frail arm supporting the creature's head.

It was only when she observed the panic among her carp that Miyuki became aware that this thing that, literally and figuratively, was looking down on her did not belong to the human race.

The fish, for their part, had immediately recognised a large white crane, and they had begun to swim in circles in their baskets, their tails and fins beating the surface of the water to make it frothy and blur the predator's vision.

Miyuki had only ever seen cranes in flight, when they flew very high above Shimae, uttering cries so penetrating that they could be heard long before anyone could see them. Their appearance was supposed to bring happiness, prosperity and long life. The villagers came out onto their doorsteps and, as they chanted prayers, they gazed at the cranes until the whiteness of the birds fused into that of the clouds.

Miyuki's initial instinct was to protect her carp from the wading bird, which was clearly intent on jabbing its greyish beak into the flesh of the fish. The bird's wing feathers were quivering with greed, while from its throat there came a whistling, buzzing, rattling noise.

Miyuki remembered the story that Katsuro had told her – which caused her hands to shake even now – concerning a sort of duel he had had with a couple of cranes just as he was about to release three carp into the pond of a small Shinto sanctuary in Harima province beside the Inland Sea, the carp having been

71

rejected by the Office of Gardens and Ponds as unworthy of the temples of Heian Kyō. The huge birds had begun what Katsuro had at first taken to be a nuptial dance. He was not particularly worried as the birds remained some distance away. In actual fact, they had no need to approach their adversary: it was enough for them to stretch out their necks to stab at him with their beaks, or to unfurl their enormous wings in order to strike without leaving themselves open to assault.

The crane that was in front of Miyuki had not yet taken up an attacking position. If she had known how to read its small eyes, Miyuki would have realised that the white bird, rather than trying to harm her, was looking for a way of skirting around her to gain access to the fish. Hence this recital of shrill cries that the crane, its head tossed back and its beak pointing skywards, must have thought were sufficiently terrifying to persuade this young woman to abandon her carp and flee.

Then, realising that its attempt at intimidation was not having the desired effect, the bird began to circle around Miyuki, its wings wide open, alternating jerked leaps and sudden bounds.

This kind of dance reminded Miyuki of the children of Shimae, on nights of the full moon, when they presented shadow plays on the outer walls of the village houses: the children and the bird shared the same innate grace and, at the same time, a similar incoherence, the children not knowing why they were projecting the shadow of a bull followed by that of a rat, and the bird alternating for no reason between hostile attitudes and attractive, charming poses.

Miyuki was about to beat a retreat when another crane suddenly loomed up behind her.

This one glided in noiselessly, level with the reeds, its neck straight and tilted forward, its long legs stretched out behind its body. Then, as it was about to land, black, claw-like fingers appeared at the end of its feet, while its wings, raised in a vault like wind-filled sails, slowed its flight.

Scarcely had the bird touched down with a loud cry and folded back its wings than the first crane, losing interest in Miyuki, welcomed its fellow creature with greetings that consisted of genuflexions, sidesteps and skips, elongation of its wings and clacking of its beak. To which the new arrival responded with bowing and scraping that was performed with legs folded and wings raised, and with graceful leaps, stopping occasionally to pick up bits of dead wood that it tossed up into the air.

Their saraband was so wild, their black and white calligraphy so complex, that Miyuki could foresee the moment when she would no longer be able to protect her carp. The dance of the cranes already formed part of a territory from which she would soon be excluded.

So Miyuki decided that she, too, would dance.

She did not have the conceit to identify with the magnificent birds – despite her youth, she knew she was much more ungainly, clumsy and sluggish – but she just wanted to slip into their farandole in the hope of remaining close to her carp and so be in a better position to defend them.

Gently rolling the bamboo pole down her back, from her neck to her waist, Miyuki lowered the baskets until they touched the ground. Then, with her arms outstretched and her neck arched, letting out hoarse, trumpet-like cries, she began to leap around, jumping to and fro over her baskets as though to signify to the two cranes that they were her territory and her property.

The strange cackling noises and the syncopated poses she adopted bewildered the birds. To begin with they had paid her no attention, seeing her as one of those creatures with whom their tribe maintained only loose associations, except in the palaces of Heian Kyō where ladies in the Emperor's entourage tried to make captive cranes mimic the dance steps of humans, whereas the *ninchō*,* on the other hand, taught young dancers to imitate the body language and hieratic attitudes of cranes. But after Miyuki's ballet, the cranes, slightly disoriented, no longer knew to which realm she belonged: could she be a bird, a bird that had lost its feathers, a bird that was ugly and repulsive, but a bird, nonetheless?

There was one way of knowing: if this creature were able to fly, then, without properly being a crane (and she was very far from being one, and not simply because she lacked a long, pointed beak), she at least belonged to the realm of birds.

The two cranes suddenly began running and beating their wings. They quickly reached sufficient speed for a final thrust of their wings to allow them to take flight. Feet and neck stretched out horizontally, their bodies lengthened, wings against wings, letting themselves be carried away on a gentle, invisible fluid.

Miyuki followed them enviously, but only with her eyes: in addition to the forty-five kilos of human flesh that rooted her to the ground, there was also the weight of the water and the carp to consider.

---

* Officials in charge of dances performed in the presence of the Emperor whenever there was a ritual related to the cult of ancestors.

After a farewell wave to the cranes, she bent down to pick up her bamboo pole, balanced it on her shoulders and set off.

The last vision that she took away from the Hut of Just Retribution was that of two intensely pink spheres floating on the pond and bumping into each other with the muffled sound of a buckskin leather ball which *kemari* players, using only their feet, try to keep in the air as long as possible.

These shrivelled balls were none other than the decapitated heads of the cook and the odd-job man, which were gently knocking into each other among the lotuses.

Miyuki wondered whether Akiyoshi Sadako knew that the heads of her servants were floating on the pond. It was unhealthy, she reckoned, to let them soak in water that they were bound to contaminate, and with it the avenue of lotuses, and all the fish, and the multitude of water insects, the larvae of dragonflies and caddis worms, the water stick insects, the pond skaters, the diving beetles, the waterboatmen and other surface water bugs. Miyuki, of course, did not know their real names, for her they were simply tiny insects, but Katsuro often brought some back into the house, unintentionally, trapped in the folds of his clothing. On summer evenings, when it was too hot to sleep, the fisherman and his wife enjoyed watching them swim on the surface of the pond. When the moon was reflected in it, they made bets as to whether this or that creature would reach the reflection first. They called it the game of the princess. One night when he happened to be in Heian Kyō, in fact, and was walking past the walls of the Imperial Palace, Katsuro had heard the voice of a courtesan singing the story of Princess

Kaguya,* an inhabitant of the moon whose father had sent her to Earth to shelter her from a war that was raging in the sky. Kaguya found herself hidden in the centre of a bamboo plant. An elderly peasant who made his living from harvesting bamboo had cut the shoot in which the princess, who resembled a baby the size of a little finger, was waiting to be rescued. After many misadventures, though not without having made the old peasant and his wife very happy, Kaguya had managed to return to her native moon – and it was this homecoming that was symbolised by the insects swimming haltingly towards the moon's reflection.

With her heart in her mouth and trying not to tremble for fear of knocking the baskets and disturbing her carp, whose jerky swimming proved that they had not yet recovered from the terror the two cranes had instilled in them, Miyuki forced herself to retrieve the decapitated heads.

She was afraid of confronting the coagulated stare of their still open eyes, and she tried to make them swivel round so that she could see only their necks. But the heads were floating like balloons and the slightest impulse caused them to spin over several times. And, by a terrible irony, the empty stares consistently stopped in front of Miyuki. After several unsuccessful attempts, she simply turned her eyes away and, groping about like a blind person, she managed to grab the two heads by their hair and extract them from the pond.

They gave off a sickening smell, the result of their being tossed about in murky water and of the bacteria that had begun

---

* From *Taketori no monogatari*, an anonymous Japanese tale from the 9th century.

the process of decomposition. This stench impregnated Miyuki's fingers and, leaning over the pond, she snatched a few lotus flowers and squeezed their stalks to release the sweet-smelling sap and wipe her hands with it.

IT WAS AT THE end of this new day that she set off along the footpath that, twisting this way and that through forests of cedar trees and bamboo plantations, ascended to one of the highest points of the Kii range.

She did not know the name of this peak, it could equally well be Mount Shakka, Mount Odaigahara or Mount Sano, but it did not matter to her what the mountain was called. In this respect she was like Katsuro, who refused to clutter his memory with every place name and preferred to retain only those that were useful for his journey, that is to say the names of inns along with particular features in the landscape that prevented him from getting lost and going around in circles, were he to be caught in the mist.

This was why Miyuki focused all her attention on the parts of the journey where the smell of sulphur from the hot springs was strongest. To find her bearings more easily, she made a mental note of the intensity of the smell and associated it with sounds such as the roar of a mountain stream or the cries of a group of macaques warming themselves in pools where hot springs steamed: were a thick mist to overtake her, she would simply be guided by the chatter of monkeys or the sound of a rushing stream in order to discover again the fumes of a given spring and thereby manage to find her way among the vast mountains.

On his way out and on the way home, crossing the Kii range was the part of the journey that worried Katsuro the most. Not so much on account of the effort the ascent required as because of the countless pilgrims that filled the paths leading to the sacred sanctuaries of Kumano. The fisherman had nothing against these staunch believers, apart from the fact that they walked in large groups and occupied the most passable section of the route, one which was paved with overlapping stones, as though setting off in search of the gods meant they took precedent over other users of the narrow path. As he wore himself out transporting his load of carp destined for temples where the Emperor and his court prayed, did Katsuro too not deserve to be on the higher ground?

The mass of pilgrims gave Miyuki a sense of security. After the events that had brought bloodshed to the Hut of Just Retribution, she felt safe in the midst of this long line of men and women who, without favouring her with a glance or paying any attention to her at all, made her feel a part of their group. To keep her baskets away from the disorderly stream of walkers, she had frequently been tempted to extricate herself from the column and slip away by climbing up the verges, but the sides of the path were too steep, and the uneven stone slabs worn away by the tread of hundreds of pilgrims' straw sandals had become as slippery as ice and had invariably channelled the walkers back into the central groove.

Miyuki felt reassured by the somewhat acrid aromas that emanated from the group of devout travellers; they reminded

79

her of Katsuro's smell when he returned from the river, shaking himself to get rid of the sweat that dripped down his face and darkened his *kosode** at the level of his armpits. Glad of this chance to be reminded of her husband, she let herself be lulled by the background noise from the crowd, a trampling sound punctuated by onomatopoeia and interjections dominated by the pronounced rotundity of the ō syllable and the *k*s that clicked like storks' beaks.

She who knew nothing of the world beyond her village was astonished by all the mottled brown and green clothes, by the scarlet of the baggy trousers tied at the ankle, the undergarments dyed in sappanwood, the mauve-, yellow- and plum-coloured dresses, the delicate, flimsy tunics, those silky materials that shimmer in the lightest breeze, or alternatively are stiff and shiny, as though coated in wax, all giving the illusion of a jewellery box that had been thrown from the top of the mountain, causing masses of jewels to cascade down the slope.

The peaks were emerging from the spirals of vapour created by the contact of the morning dew with ground that had been dampened by the networks of warm underground streams, which could be heard gurgling beneath the earth.

There was not a single plot of her village, however insignificant, over which Miyuki had not set foot on many occasions. Unlike these Kii mountains and all the landscapes through which she had walked since her departure, Shimae was so familiar to

---

* Originally an undergarment, it gradually became, rather like our T-shirts today which it resembled, an easy-to-wear article of clothing used by the people for virtually all situations in daily life.

her that she felt at home in every hidden recess; there was no alleyway, no thatched roof, no field of white radishes or water celery, no garden of mulberry bushes, no rice field that she did not know, so that when Katsuro asked her in the evening what she had done during the day, she could reply in all honesty that she had not stirred, whereas in reality she had not stopped coming and going.

In Shimae, everything was *here*, there was no *over there*.

Whereas on the mountain she had no reference point, there was nothing familiar apart from her recollections of Katsuro, or at least his ghost – for it was very much a ghost she was dealing with now, this Katsuro of her reminiscences had no consistency, no life of his own. Miyuki manipulated his image along the pilgrim path in the same way that she did these tiny black flies – or, rather, very brilliant flies – that sometimes became embedded in her field of vision, and which she batted away simply by moving her eyes.

As she passed by a stream, Miyuki changed the water in the baskets.

When he described his trips to Heian Kyō, Katsuro never failed to emphasise the care he took in changing the water; for the fish, already disoriented by the narrowness and the rocking motion of their prison, suffered from the numbing effect of the warming of the liquid in which they were confined.

But when Miyuki had replaced the stale water, her carp began to behave in a very strange way; they started to swim in circles, bumping into one another as though they were drunk or blind.

Miyuki then remembered that only water from rivers and ponds agreed with the carp, the water that came from unknown sources was too unpredictable, and full of indiscernible substances that could affect them like poisons.

Miyuki sat on a tree stump and, dipping her hand into the baskets, lightly brushed the backs and sides of her fish with the tips of her fingers, hoping to soothe them with her touch.

Heavy clouds were gathering in the sky, knitting into one another.

The pilgrims continued to stream along, quickening their pace. Two of them had stopped not far from Miyuki to relieve their bladders. They were elderly, and the cold mountain air had swollen their gnarled fingers, so they took a long time to undo their red silk trousers, all the while discussing the proximity of a sanctuary where it would be sensible to shelter should the weather become really threatening.

One of those urinating, a man with a long, narrow face, and thick black lips that made him look like a horse, smiled at Miyuki.

"Would you like to come with us?" he said. "We're going to spend the night in a sanctuary. The monks there are Buddhists, but they worship the *kami* too. And they don't despise women in the least."

"Besides," his companion said, "the first three people who left the secular world in order to become Buddhists, were they not women?"

"Possibly," said Miyuki. "But I cannot say."

"We will plead on your behalf and we would certainly have no difficulty in getting you admitted."

"Furthermore," the horse-faced man said, glancing at the baskets in which the carp were continuing their saraband, "we could carry your load – it's not very far from here to the sanctuary, but the path becomes quite narrow."

"Thank you," Miyuki said. "But I have promised myself not to be separated from them."

With each other's help, the two men had finally succeeded in unfastening their trousers. Their urine shot out, thick and yellow, spreading over the stone slabs like two small streams running into each other. The earth absorbed it immediately, leaving only wisps of steam. With groans of satisfaction, the horse-faced man and his companion dressed again.

Although Miyuki was not depending on the rain to renew the water in the baskets completely, she hoped that it would at least help dilute the harmful particles that were responsible for the feverish state of the carp. But the clouds, increasingly massive, took on a purplish lividness that portended far more than a heavy shower, and she was suddenly frightened of exposing her fish to this further trauma that would not fail to end with enormous raindrops beating down on them.

The pilgrims repeated their suggestion that she accompany them to the Buddhist sanctuary.

The idea of taking shelter was tempting, but Miyuki wanted to give herself the freedom of making her own way if, for one reason or another, the place did not appeal to her. She could visualise Katsuro's expressions, his manner of knitting his eyebrows when he described his nights spent in certain temples, notably those where the monks pampered young boys on the pretext of educating them. The fisherman was not offended by the equivocal relationships the monks had with these adolescents, but he regretted that the holy men, for all their devotion to the young, did not give guests who were passing the care and attention that they expected to find: the novices were stuffed with stacks of sticky rice cakes and crushed ice flavoured with cane syrup and black sugar, whereas the travellers had to be content with hastily peeled and boiled vegetables.

"I'm obliged to walk slowly because of the fish," Miyuki said to the pilgrims. "Go ahead, I'll catch you up."

She allowed herself to be left behind by the horse-faced man and his companion. To begin with, they turned their heads from time to time to make sure she was following them, urging her on with a great many gestures, but, after a while, they continued on their way without troubling themselves about her anymore.

Miyuki was soon on her own. Long filaments of clouds hovered in the tangle of pine trees. And when the sky fell like a lid, the light faded away so that Miyuki, who was sitting on a tree stump beside a stone lantern, had the impression that night had already come.

Animals began to screech in the undergrowth. The monkeys were the noisiest. Miyuki wondered whether the creatures were calling for rain or whether, because of the din they were making, they were trying to intimidate it into staying away.

The storm burst. Brief but violent. For a while, all that could be heard was the clatter of raindrops beating down on the forest. The path had become a stream.

When the moon rose over the valleys, disappearing then reappearing behind the jagged mountain peaks according to the flight of the clouds, Miyuki could at last see the outline of the sanctuary the pilgrims had mentioned.

It was a temple of modest dimensions with a stream flowing nearby; a small, rather dark temple with floors built one on top of the other, to the east of a mountainside village, in a cedar wood with a dry, rather camphorated smell that contrasted with the sugary, very pleasant scent of the forest after the rain.

Three or four squat figures emerged from the temple and began to skip about among the cedars. They were child monks carrying torches which they used to light the stone lanterns scattered in the undergrowth. Every time they bent over a lantern, the sleeves of their garments came apart from their bodies like the wings of fireflies, which the lights they were carrying resembled as they walked among the trees.

Miyuki had not seen fireflies since that spring night when Katsuro had allowed her to follow him as far as the Kusagawa. As they were drawing near to the river, a few bright green sparkles had begun to frolic around the fisherman and his wife. And then the number of fireflies increased, more and more of them at every step, until they formed clouds of light. Beside the river, there were thousands of them glittering on the damp grass and sparkling in the bushes. Their cool glimmers throbbed rhythmically, as though directed by the same beating heart. Miyuki could not remember ever having seen anything so beautiful. Katsuro had explained to her that fireflies epitomised the brevity of existence, since, once they were fully grown, they had only three or four weeks left to live – and this longevity was the privilege of females alone; the males died earlier still.

"Katsuro," Miyuki had said, "do you think you will die before me too?"

"Oh, of course," the fisherman had calmly replied. "Just as my father died before my mother. It's the logical nature of things, is it not?"

Whirling her arms around, Miyuki had slapped him.

"Our logic is not the logic of fireflies!" she had said, as she struck him with smacks that made more noise than they did harm.

He had laughed. Then he had grabbed his wife's hands in his and had soothed them by stroking them with the tip of his thumb, as he would do whenever he trapped a panic-stricken bird.

"Neither the logic of fireflies, nor that of men: there's no logic at all, Miyuki, no logic, no gods, fate does everything, and it does it well."

The fisherman had added that, for most people, fireflies were one of the final manifestations of the souls of the dead before they lost themselves in the world of the deceased, proof of the stubbornness of the dead in clinging to any form of life at all, even that of a short-lived firefly. He, Katsuro, did not believe in this nonsense. With a quick movement of his hand, he had then captured one of these insects and had held it in front of Miyuki: in the hollow of the fisherman's hand the firefly had stopped shining and had once more become a dark, dried-up little creature. And so stiff that it might just as well have been dead.

The young monks were not romping about aimlessly as Miyuki had at first thought. When she observed them more closely, she saw that they were lighting certain lanterns and disregarding others. As she drew nearer, she realised that those they were leaving out were not lanterns, but tombstones, hundreds of memorial slabs that many generations of believers had erected on the side of the mountain.

It so happened that certain temples which were primitive and rustic – yet blessed with pleasant surroundings – in time attracted other wandering monks who settled in them for a while, enlarged them, embellished them and dignified them to the point of endowing them sometimes with a *sorin*** or with coloured wood reliefs.

This was the case with the temple before which Miyuki now stood.

It was dedicated to the Buddha Fudo Myoo, known as the Immutable, the Unshakeable, whom nothing could perturb, a protector with a wrathful expression encircled by an aura of fire. Protruding from thick lips twisted into a perpetual angry glower were two canine teeth, the right one directed at the sky like an invitation to raise oneself up, the left one pointing downwards to stigmatise the wrongs borne of illusions.

Because he saw everything as it really was, Fudo Myoo was not susceptible to hesitation or to doubt or to embarrassment. Unlike a wisp of straw such as Miyuki, the Buddha Fudo was an irresistible force, he swept everything before him and there was nothing that could stop him. His ability to focus all his determination in the folds of his plump forehead, the cracks of his eyebrows, the crow's feet of his bulging eyes, the furrows of the base of his flat nose, not to mention his two fangs that became

---

* An arrow made of stone, wood or bronze that was split into several symbolic parts and erected on top of a Japanese pagoda.

covered in dribble at the slightest fit of annoyance, was enough to dissuade any opponent from defying him.

Fudo Myoo was said to guide the souls of the dead and to preside, for the sake of their eternal lives, over a ceremony that should be held seven days after death. Putting her hands together and bowing before the statue until she almost touched the ground with her forehead, Miyuki offered her apologies for not having respected the seven-day ritual after her husband's death; because of her preparations for her journey to Heian Kyō she had not known which way to turn, but since Fudo Myoo kept watch over the vast throng of the departed, perhaps he would agree, in spite of everything, to bless and protect Katsuro's soul?

At that moment, a monkey swinging in the tree above Miyuki caused a branch to snap. Miyuki looked up and, as she moved, an unexpected scent filled her nostrils.

Cool and dark, the aroma, one composed of pinewood, peppery mint and iris root, came from an oblong cavity about two and a half metres high in the trunk of a sugi* tree many hundreds of years old.

Having wedged her baskets against a tree stump, Miyuki reached up as far as she could and managed to dip her hand into the crack with its sticky edges that were smooth and rounded like the rims of a scar. Her fingers encountered a mass of leaves that had fallen from the old tree. Of course, this was what was giving off the powerful, delicious smell that had almost made her dizzy; Miyuki could not stop herself thinking, however, that the scent that seeped from the tree and hung over her like a flimsy veil was

---

* *Cryptomeria japonica.*

88

Fudo Myoo's response to the prayer she had made to him to keep watch over Katsuro's soul.

Then, with her mind at rest, she secured the bamboo pole across her shoulders and set off towards the sanctuary.

The sanctuary was made up of two buildings joined together by a long L-shaped passageway covered in cypress bark.

A pilgrims' house provided a refectory and a communal dormitory. Inside, Miyuki discovered the horse-faced man and his companion, who were eating a dinner of herbs and wild plants from the mountains. She hurried over to their low table and bowed.

"I didn't really think that you would spend the night all alone. The mountain, the rain and the night are not suitable for a young lady. By the way," the horse-faced man said, "my name is Akito."

"And I'm Genkishi. Please sit here," his travelling companion said as he made space for Miyuki.

She squatted on her heels between the two men. Akito looked about him with a puzzled expression.

"But tell me, *ojōsan*,[*] I don't see your fish . . .?"

"Oh," said Miyuki. "I thought it better to leave them in the half-light of the dormitory rather than expose them to the greed of the guests. They're nice plump carp and they might entice certain appetites."

"How mistrustful you are!" Genkishi smiled. "You watch over them as though you were guarding a treasure. Yet they are

---

* Young lady.

89

only fish. The rivers are full of them, around here. What is it that's so special about yours?"

"Nothing, except that it was my husband who took them from the River Kusagawa. Katsuro was the best carp fisherman in the province of Shimotsuke. I don't mean the most skilful, because there's not much merit in catching fish that are generally placid. But Katsuro's gaze could cut through the deep water like a sword, he could see through the silt, he could sense what lay beneath the stones; merely by thinking, he could turn them over and flush out the carp he wanted, and that would be the one he caught, that one and no other. I've seen Katsuro come back from the river exhausted, muddy, soaking, and sometimes bleeding, but never disappointed with his fishing. Oh no, never ever! These carp that are travelling with me are the last ones he caught. Afterwards, he departed from this world."

And Miyuki told them about Katsuro's death, a death that had no witnesses but that she had imagined from the few indications found by the villagers on the banks of the Kusagawa – the long scratch marks that the fisherman's hands had scraped into the mud at the place where he had drowned, the traces of where he had crawled along, the subsidence on the riverbank when he had fought to escape the suction of the mud, and some feathers of a white heron, paradoxically a symbol of long life.

Miyuki could not ever remember having strung together so many sentences, especially in front of strangers. If she had had to talk about herself, she would certainly have had nothing to say; but this was to do with Katsuro, and the words came naturally, they collected and fizzed around in her head like young fish that are still only the size of needles.

The two pilgrims looked at one another and made noises in their throats as though they were stifling coughs. This incidental hoarseness expressed their sudden mistrust of Miyuki: she told her story well, certainly, but instead of dwelling at length on how the fisherman had drowned, why had she not alluded briefly to the purification rituals that she should have undertaken to remove the stain acquired through contact with her husband's corpse? Had not this young woman, so reckless that she was unbothered about where she would spend the night (where would she have sheltered from the rain had the horse-faced man and his companion not encouraged her to follow them to the sanctuary?), been just as negligent at the time of Katsuro's death, and did she not now risk transmitting the impurity, which might still stain her, to them?

Their wariness, however, did not prevent them, once their frugal meal was over, from escorting Miyuki to the women's dormitory, and ensuring that neither she nor her carp lacked for anything. The horse-faced man was even considerate enough to offer her a few little cakes which were spiral-shaped like shells.

"For you, *ojōsan*, in case you are hungry during the night."

"But you can start eating them straight away," Genkishi said. "Because they're delicious, and you have scarcely eaten anything this evening."

Miyuki thanked the two men for the care they were taking of her. She set down her baskets on either side of her mat and lay down.

As the pilgrims disappeared down the corridor, Miyuki thought she heard soft laughter. For a second, she wondered

91

whether they were making fun of her; but not finding anything about her appearance or her behaviour that could have given rise to humour, she persuaded herself that no-one had laughed and that she had been deceived by a noise coming from outside – the crescendo of rain on the leaves, perhaps.

All around her, sleeping women were breathing loudly. They were mostly elderly ladies who had come to pray to the divinities to obtain in the Beyond a generous portion of what had been refused them in this world. The climb up to the sanctuary had wearied them, and their scrawny, bent bodies, dark mounds on the pale cotton of the mats, called to mind a tangle of gnarled branches that had snapped and been blown to the ground by the wind. They gave off a dull stench of sugary sap, of broken twigs and soggy bark.

Miyuki tucked into the cakes the pilgrims had given her. They were filled with a thick paste of small red beans boiled in sugar cane. Katsuro occasionally brought some back from his trips, he always bought them at the same place, from a dark, narrow stall straddling a bridge that spanned a river. But although Katsuro's delicacies had filled Miyuki with extra energy, the cakes the pilgrims had given her made her irresistibly drowsy. As she was raising another shell-shaped mouthful to her lips, she could feel her eyes closing, and nothing in the world would enable her to open them again before the end of the night. Just as she had as a small child, she smiled and drifted off, unable to resist the sleepiness that came over her. The cake slipped from her fingers and rolled down as far as her thighs where it crumbled into a fine powder. It was not impossible that a small rodent could then have slipped into the folds of Miyuki's clothes and, making the most of the bonanza, feasted while she was in a deep sleep, unaware of the storm that raged, drumming on the walls of the sanctuary, rolling, roaring and submerging the sky in dazzling streaks.

THE SILENCE AFTER THE storm woke Miyuki. Though the sky was still dark, she had the sense that it was later than the surrounding gloom led her to believe. The chatter of the birds was already drowning out the background noise of the river. She recognised the singing of the white sparrows, the *hohokekyo* of the nightingales perched in the plum trees, and the bush warbler that began each of its soliloquies with a long drawn-out syllable, a *kuuu* that reminded Miyuki of the barking manner in which the emissaries from the Office of Gardens and Ponds had addressed the villagers.

The mist that glided over the sanctuary diffused the morning light, but not so much so that Miyuki, getting to her feet to see how her carp were faring, could fail to notice that six of them had disappeared. As lightning strikes a tree and cleaves it in two, a spasm shook her from head to toe. She yelled. Her cry – in the opinion of the elderly women still lying listlessly in the fetid dankness – was more frightening than the thunder had been.

Miyuki sped away through the sanctuary at a run. Distraught, she bumped off the walls like a moth trapped in a lantern.

94

Nothing worse than this could have happened. Without the carp that were to be put into the Heian Kyō ponds, not only did Miyuki's journey no longer have any purpose, but her failure would also sully the honour of the people of Shimae for years to come.

She had never felt herself so alone when confronted with an event of such gravity. There had been Katsuro's death, of course, but she had relied then on the support of the entire village, and, even when it had become motionless, blind and dumb, the body of the fisherman had still been physically present – she had been able to speak to him, imagining the replies he would have given, going even so far as to imitate his fine, always somewhat hesitant voice, which rose and rippled like the river when the wind blew upstream.

She needed to have someone who could witness her confusion, someone who would listen to her carefully, even though this person, only vaguely understanding what it was about, might have nothing to say to her in the first place.

She summoned Genkishi and Akito to her aid. In her dismay, she had forgotten that the two pilgrims had planned to set off again at the hour of the Tiger; they must now be tackling the first bends on the hill overlooking the sanctuary.

Akito had indeed invited her to walk with them as far as the next sanctuary, but he had made a point of clarifying that Genkishi and he would walk at a steady pace, and he was not sure that a small person like Miyuki could keep up with them, especially with her heavy yoke.

"It will be a very early departure and it would be unwise to delay," Genkishi had said. "For, as soon as the sun rises, the earth, made hard by the cold of the night, will quickly turn into slippery mud, and we have to make sure we reach the pass before the ascent becomes too perilous."

"Which it will be, in any case," Akito had said, nodding solemnly and gazing at Miyuki as though he could already see her lying crushed at the bottom of a ravine.

The corridors were deserted, no glimmer of light fluttered through the oil-paper of the sliding doors, the monastery was plunged in silence save for the long, low reverberation of an enormous cylindrical bell, the *tsuki-za**of which rang out when struck by an external clapper made of a beam of wood hung on ropes. Despite the fullness of its tone, the bell's soothing, vibrating note echoed over the mountain in waves, richer when the sound dipped into a valley, sharper if it rose towards the peaks.

At its call, the guests of the sanctuary, except for the elderly ladies in the dormitory, had gathered in the building used for worship. If anyone could help Miyuki find her vanished carp, it was there that she would find them. And if there was no-one to help her, she would make do with one of those amulets that the sanctuary sold, which were supposed to dispense the three powers: *shugo* (protection), *chibyō* (healing) and above all *genze riyaku*, which is to say the procurement of immediate benefits in the present world. By "immediate benefit", Miyuki meant the recovery of her carp.

Yes, the recovery, for they could not have escaped on their own: even if one imagined that, in their distress at the storm,

---

* The reinforced section of the bell that is struck by the wooden beam.

96

they had panicked to such a degree that they had leaped out of their basket, they would have landed on the hard-earth floor where, their bodies tensed and arched, they would have suffocated, their gills turning a shade of blue, then black, and they would have died right there.

Miyuki ran along the covered path that connected the domestic part of the sanctuary to the religious buildings. In the openings between the pillars that supported the roof of the passageway, she encountered the smell of earth newly doused by rain as well as the more acidic one of mist from the mountains, its heavy grey coils thrumming the walls like waves.

As she ran, Miyuki remembered that before she bowed down at the altar she would have to erase any impure thoughts prompted by desire (for was not the fierce longing to retrieve her carp one of those desires disapproved of by the buddhas?) or by anger (she furiously resented the unknown plunderer, be it man or beast, as it was not impossible that her thief could have been a pack of monkeys that had spirited away, almost from under her nose, the six finest of her eight fish).

She also knew that she could expect no favour, no indulgence, no miraculous intervention by the buddhas. It was in their nature to remain deaf to this kind of prayer, obstinately deaf – though the *kami* were scarcely more obliging. For these superior creatures, this human being was a mere scrap, a flimsy particle that had come adrift from its support, from that existence to which she adhered so feebly that it required only a breath of wind to separate her from it. Now that Katsuro, the living being who had been closest to her – so close that their

97

two personalities sometimes became confused so that Miyuki, forgetting the polite and modest language of women, would employ specifically masculine turns of phrase that made her husband scold her, *you are talking as though a thousand stinking toads were hopping around in your mouth!* – now that he frequented a world she could not enter, a world she could not even imagine, Miyuki must rely on herself alone. Katsuro would remain forever unmoved by her most fervent prayers, her most languid sighs, her most sensual poses.

Slipping between the worshippers, Miyuki drew close to the altar. Lit only by four oil lamps whose small flames rose and fell with the breathing of the congregation, the altar shone softly with its red and gold cloths, and the sparkle of the coals on which the incense sticks were lit.

The statue of the Buddha was kept in the shade, as though in his compassion the Wakeful One feared that the gold leaf that overlaid its plump and pot-bellied avatar might be taken as a provocation in the eyes of the exhausted, frozen, sometimes emaciated pilgrims who hovered around its feet, gazing greedily at the altar offerings, however modest: pure water, bowls containing a little mound of boiled round rice, or a few beans.

More familiar with the Shinto rites than with Buddhist prayers, Miyuki watched her neighbours and imitated them to avoid any indiscretion. She raised her joined hands above her head, brought them slowly to the level of her throat, and then her heart, and, having knelt, she bowed low until she touched the ground with her forehead. On the first occasion, she thought she detected a faecal smell just by her nose. Her nostrils quivered, and she inhaled a subtle aroma that reminded her of the long, low shed where the few cattle that belonged collectively to the residents of Shimae were kept. They were small animals, solidly built, with tightly knit, very soft coats and, beneath a smooth hide, a backbone that was almost too delicate for cattle that were required to pull heavy loads.

Neither Katsuro nor his wife owned a rice field, nor even a vegetable patch. Katsuro was too absorbed in fishing to till the land, and Miyuki was too busy with the upkeep of the tackle and the carp pond. Furthermore, keen to make herself useful to the community, she had collaborated with the girls who tended the cattle, and in particular collected the animals' dung and urine which were diluted in a bucket before being used to fertilise the cultivated plots. Since Miyuki's arms and hips were sturdier than those of the girls, it was frequently she who carried the bucket over the fields, extracting the sludgy mixture with the help of a long-handled spoon to spread it over the tops of the plants, watching it trickle down the stem to the root and using a piece of straw to correct its flow if a node made it deviate from its path.

Miyuki had never found the handling of this mixture repugnant: if the diluting had been carried out with the scrupulous respect for ratios recommended by the Elders, and if the brew had been left to settle overnight, enabling the most volatile elements to evaporate, the smell from the bucket was rather sweet, almost sugary. And when Miyuki had to recruit new girls, she always minimised the unpleasant smell of the work by assuring them that the countless number of small flowers that the cattle fed on during the spring gave their dung the scent of gum benzoin.

Like a bout of nausea that returns, she felt a wave of nostalgia when she recalled this detail of her normal life. She was angry with herself for not having appreciated its true value.

But was this its only value?

She had lived the dreary, exhausting and wretched life of very many thousands of Japanese women, but with two exceptions. Unlike her parents, who had died trying to flee the massacres inflicted by the warriors of a provincial governor rebelling against the Emperor – this uprising had occurred at the same time as the violent earthquakes and bloody forays carried out by pirates who came from Goryeo* – Miyuki had not experienced suffering, she had never felt the sharp pain of being beaten with sticks or the burning lash of a whip; the only scars that showed on her body were those made by Nature, from a stone when she had tripped, from a low branch she had run into when fleeing, from the bite of a panic-stricken animal, from a fall on a patch of ice, from a prickly bush she had got too close to, and afterwards she would comfort herself, and even smile, believing that she had been subjected to a reprimand from a *kami* whose privacy she had unwittingly disturbed.

The other exception to the dreariness of her existence had been Katsuro's love, the love that he had given her, that she had given him in return.

Miyuki remembered the itinerant storytellers who, on summer evenings, having squashed the cicadas whose noise interfered with their tales, would sit in the centre of the main square and

---

* The Korean peninsula.

recite horrifying stories about lovers separated by fates each more cruel and unjust than the last; and the people of Shimae, wearing garments with long sleeves, would drench them with their tears. The only ones to nudge each other and burst out laughing were Miyuki and Katsuro, because they were convinced that no human wilfulness could separate them – only Death could do that, of course, but even when the thought of him crossed their minds, he was faceless and therefore might as well not have existed. They would hide their giggles behind their hands, and they shook with laughter to such a point that the villagers thought they were weeping. And the storytellers began to miss the cicadas who, although just as noisy as this young couple, were at least not so shrill.

Miyuki felt glad she had been happy, even though, truthfully speaking, she did not know what the word happiness (*shiawase*, she called it) entailed. She would have been incapable of providing a definition save by differentiating it from its countless opposites (grief, suffering, injury, torment, embarrassment, shame, disgust, repulsion, disappointment, extreme weariness, exhaustion, weakness, deceitfulness, distress, despair, pain, boredom) that were the daily lot of sensitive human beings.

But happiness had passed. Not only would she never see Katsuro again, but perhaps she would not see Shimae again either: after the unforgiveable loss of her carp, how would she dare return to her village? What would she say to Natsume? What excuses could she give to the inhabitants who had placed their trust in her?

Was it not best to continue on her route to Heian Kyō, to report to the Office of Gardens and Ponds and wait for the

Director Watanabe to decide how she should be punished?

Would she be assigned to washing and preparing the beheaded corpses of enemies, prior to their presentation to the Emperor, which would be a respectable way of atoning for her incompetence? If, on the other hand, this expiation seemed inadequate, perhaps she would be allowed to commit *jigai*, the only truly honourable way out of an unacceptable situation. This ritual suicide was mainly the prerogative of women of the nobility, or the wives and daughters of warriors, but it sometimes happened that ordinary servants who were found to be guilty of a serious error would choose *jigai* in the hope of reinstating themselves in the eyes of their masters. By severing her jugular vein or by perforating her carotid artery with the blade of a *kaiken*,* Miyuki would prove her loyalty to the Office of Gardens and Ponds, and above all to her compatriots in Shimae.

This form of death was supposed to be quick and, unlike *seppuku*, it did not call for the assistance of a friend armed with a sword to cut short the unbearable suffering of the person committing suicide by decapitating him. For a woman, the only precaution required was that, after sitting down on her heels, she should have her legs bound together to avoid any indecency when she toppled over at the moment of death.

But if she took this decision – which scarcely bothered her now that Katsuro was no longer in this world – Miyuki would be faced with a difficulty she did not know how to resolve: she did not own a *kaiken*, and, obviously, she had no means of acquiring one.

---

* A type of dagger, about fifteen centimetres long, which samurai wives carried in the sleeves of their kimono.

As she remained in her prostrate position, she raised her eyes, gazing around in the hope of seeing a *kaiken* blade gleaming softly among the things that the pilgrims had rid themselves of when they had opted to return to monastic life.

But the only offerings laid upon the altar were the ritual bowls of water, the flowers, the incense, the light, the food and the music that was symbolised by a small shell placed upon a dome of rice.

At that moment, there was a thunderclap in the mountains. The sanctuary bell rang out even though it had not been touched by the clapper.

And then she saw them: shoved against the foot of the altar, protruding from the hem of the red and gold cloth that covered it, the six heads of her stolen carp, their fine cheeks still plump, their long backbones resembling six white combs, denuded, without a single morsel of flesh remaining on them, but still covered by scaly skins dulled by death, like coats of thin, stiff leather.

Miyuki felt a wave of nausea rise up inside her, and she pressed the palms of her hands to her lips. Her head fell forward, hitting the ground with a heavy thud.

Stolen, killed, carved up, devoured . . .

This must have been the work of men, for, had it been animals, they would have eaten the heads and broken the little pearly skeletons.

Togawa Shinobu was a relatively young Buddhist monk, but his face, severely pockmarked by the smallpox that he had contracted at the age of nine, already bore the loose features of an old man. During his illness, he had spent many long days between life and death, the suppuration of his pustules giving off a stench so unbearable that his own mother could not remain in the room where he lay, almost naked, so sensitive had his body become to the slightest heat. Miraculously, he had survived, thanks to the intercession of a protecting spirit, one of the seven gods of happiness to whom he had afterwards dedicated his life in gratitude. Having entered the religious life, Togawa Shinobu had climbed the ladder of priestly hierarchy until he became the *zasu**of this sanctuary which, although Buddhist, was considered to be one of the pilgrimage landmarks of the three Shinto divinities of the Kumano region.

He welcomed Miyuki to the Pavilion of Dreams, a small octagonal building that took its name from a prince whose virtues had enabled him to have a dream in which a heavenly being had come down and revealed to him the meaning of a sutra that until then had been thought to be indecipherable.

At the centre of a room occupying the inner area of the pavilion, screens marked off a space furnished only with cushions. Through the oiled paper, one could make out the nearby mass of mountains and the forests that covered them.

Togawa Shinobu invited Miyuki to sit down (out of humility, to show her respect, she avoided sitting on a cushion) and explain herself.

While she related the purpose of her journey, emphasising the fact that failure would not merely be a dishonour for her but that it would also be most detrimental to the inhabitants of

---

* Literally, Father Abbot, the title given to the head of a Buddhist monastery.

Shimae (she lowered her head to conceal the tears that threatened to slip down her cheeks), the temple master recalled the sutra of Gonjikinyo, according to which, *"even if the eyes of all the buddhas of the past, the present and the future were to pop out of their sockets and fall to earth, no woman in the entire universe could become a buddha"*. Some of them might succeed in coming close to illumination, but, in order to reach the very last stage, they would have to be reincarnated as men.

With his head tilted to one side, the *zasu* gazed at Miyuki, and thought that it would be a pity if her rebirth were to be in a male body. Togawa Shinobu was not one of those religious men who dote on young monks; he preferred nuns, and, what is more, he could frequently be seen making his way along the stony path that led to the nearby building where they lived, busily washing and mending the monks' robes, preparing meals, and looking after everything connected with the upkeep of the temple, which is why His Reverence had confided to his disciples that he hoped that in his next rebirth he would be a woman or a farm animal, the two best ways, to his mind, of being useful to men.

As though numbed by his contemplation of Miyuki, Togawa Shinobu had stopped listening to what she was saying. He shook himself, doing his best to reconnect his train of thought, trying to remember the reason this woman had given for asking him for justice. And why did she present herself to him in such slovenly clothing? Should she not have combed and tied her hair, and washed her face? Was she in such an emotional state that she had to gasp as though she had had to run to him from the foot of the mountain?

"It's true they were tasty," she was saying, "but I shouldn't have eaten all of them."

"What are you talking about?" asked His Reverence, shaking himself again.

"Those little cakes, of course. The spiral-shaped cakes that Genkishi-*san* and Akito-*san* gave me yesterday evening."

Even though she had come to the conclusion that it was probably they who had stolen her carp, she still showed them the respect that, in her view, was owed by as insignificant a person as a fisherman's widow to two pilgrims from the sanctuaries of Kumano.

"And where did they come from, these biscuits?"

"From the temple kitchens. That's what they implied."

"They lied to you!" Togawa said. "Owing to a lack of red bean paste, which we have not had for two moons, our kitchen has been unable to prepare anything like that. I suspect your gentlemen made the cakes themselves and filled them with a powerful soporific substance, with the intention of causing the pilgrims they chanced to meet to fall asleep so that they could be robbed more easily."

To clarify the matter, Togawa Shinobu sent two novices to check the contents of the chest where the medicaments were kept. The young monks soon returned: two small silk bags, one containing tiny bunches of black nightshade seeds, and the other monkshood roots, had disappeared.

"It is now virtually certain that your travelling companions drugged you and stole your carp," His Reverence said. "Having killed them, they probably cooked them using the oil lamps that are lit before the altar at night. Then they ate them. May they be no more satisfied by them than they would be if they were to spend this incarnation and the thousands to come gulping down the cool mountain air. As for you, young lady, calm yourself. Your distress will not solve anything. The carp are not going to reappear and return to their clay pots just because you are moaning and soaking your sleeves with tears. But tell me, even though things are not as you would wish them to be, have you decided to continue on your journey?"

"If only I had a reason for resuming the journey! But now, why should I go to Heian Kyō empty-handed?"

"For the reason that you have left your village, you have walked a great deal and you have clambered up this mountain."

"But that had a purpose, and now there is none."

"There is always a purpose in continuing to act as you should," said Togawa Shinobu. "Even when you think there is no longer any reason to do so. My desire is to help you become aware of this truth."

"But what would I say to the Director of the Office for Gardens and Ponds? What excuse could I give to Watanabe Nagusa?"

"None. Don't apologise. If they blame you, even wrongly, say nothing, if they punish you, even wrongly, don't weep. But perhaps," he added with a malicious smile, "perhaps you will still be able to fulfil the mission with which you have been entrusted."

"But how, how? Eight carp, there were so few of them as it was. My husband, Katsuro, used to deliver twenty or more each time. And I, only eight! I had expected to make a second trip, and even a third, if Watanabe, the Director, wanted . . ."

"Heed my advice: follow the slope that runs along the side of the mountain, walk northwards. Soon you will reach a river. It is called the Yodogawa. Its waters are supposed to be full of fish. Many fishermen frequent its banks, and it would be very surprising if none of them was able to catch a few fine carp for you."

"Fine carp? The most beautiful fish in your Yodogawa could never match any of those in our river. Ours are the longest, the heaviest, the shapeliest, the strongest. Their scales are like fans that are neither fully open nor fully closed. Such delicacy, such harmony! It would not be diminishing the merits of my husband to say that the waters of the Kusagawa, his river, were as rich as he was poor."

"You're talking about your fisherman as though . . ."

"Yes, yes," Miyuki interrupted eagerly, forgetful of the respect she should show to the master of the sanctuary. "You guess correctly: Katsuro is dead, borne away like the blossoms of a plum tree on a windy day. However, even if its blossoms have been blown away and trodden upon, the plum tree that bore them will flower again the following spring – but when, and in what world, will the soul of my husband be reborn?"

Togawa Shinobu's lips, which were not very plump to begin with, grew even thinner – it was his manner of smiling, the kindly smile he bestowed on children and the elderly.

"I do not have the answer, young lady. I could probably suggest hypotheses, even expectations, but nothing that is certain. Even the most infallible of certainties is precarious, changeable, questionable. What appears in the morning rain to be true may prove to be an illusion once the cloud has passed. What I do believe is that the soul – what you call the soul – does not leap from one body into another: it is intimately bound to the being to whom it has given life, in such a way that the extinction of the flesh necessarily involves that of the soul with which it is connected."

"He did not say it quite so well, but this was also what Katsuro thought," she murmured; and she saw once more the sort of dry and dark lentil – all that remained of the firefly that had lost its light, and then its life – in the palm of the fisherman's large hand.

"While your husband was alive," the master of the sanctuary continued, "all his actions were like so many small seeds that established his karma. Now the karma, for its part, continues after our lives have ended, and the seeds that form it – because they are deeds that derive from the person who has performed them, and are therefore external to them – continue to grow when the life of this person ceases. Consider the grains of a plant that fly off in the wind: they derive from this plant, but they are not this plant because they have become separated from it, and, by falling and burying themselves in the ground, they give life to a plant other than the one from which they were blown away. Were they endowed with thought, they would not remember anything, and neither would they expect anything. Without any memory of their past, without premonition of their future, they would float on the present moment like a blade of straw over the immensity of the sea. The world that appears coherent to you is only the intricacy, the entanglement of all these karmas. Were it not constantly challenged by the consequences of these billions and billions of actions, the world would not exist."

The sky, which had appeared to brighten at daybreak, was now filled again with clouds.

"Well," Togawa Shinobu said (the master had a voice that tended to become shriller as he tried to make it more solemn than it actually was), "what have you decided? Will you go to the Imperial City? Or will you take the road back to Shimae?"

IT TOOK MIYUKI MANY hours to descend the mountain.

She did not have to walk as cautiously as she had on previous days, of course: the loss of the remaining two fish would not alter her position very much as far as the Office of Gardens and Ponds or Natsume and the people of her village were concerned. But the surviving carp had been caught by Katsuro, it was he who had begun to acclimatise them in the pool at Shimae, who had stroked them, who had bathed with them, and they had eventually become bold enough to rub themselves against his thighs. They represented the last physical trace of Katsuro on this earth, and it was this trace that Miyuki wanted to preserve whatever it might cost her.

She reached the valley at the hour of the Rooster.* Like flocks of sheep that return to the shelter of the stable at dusk, groups of dark, bulging clouds, swollen with rain and thunderbolts – long streaks of light could sometimes be seen snaking through their woolly exterior – descended from the peaks more and more swiftly.

---

* From five o'clock to seven o'clock in the evening.

Where the sheer rock gave way to wooded slopes, beneath the last layer of Japanese cedars, there flowed a river. Probably the one mentioned by Togawa Shinobu.

Miyuki decided to climb up towards the source of the Yodogawa, if it was indeed this river, keeping her distance from the riverbed to avoid her shadow shimmering on its waters. After all, she had to reckon – yet another nugget of information she had gleaned from Katsuro, one of those stories that he kept for their long evenings – with the *kappa*, a small aquatic creature with a body covered in greenish scales, an absurd combination of a monkey and a frog. The vile reputation of the *kappa* came from its ability to climb out of rivers and ponds and move about on the ground, thanks to a cavity filled with a supply of water at the top of its skull. From this advantage, no-one was shielded from its cruel actions not the least of which, when it allowed itself the pleasure of hunting a man, was to dig its claw-like and webbed hands into its victim's anus in order to climb up to their liver, which it tore out and feasted upon; the *kappa*'s appetite even included young children, whom it consumed after drowning them. But what this monster preferred to everything else was the cucumber. Katsuro would never walk along a riverbank without having wisely equipped himself with a few fine cucumbers to divert the craving of the *kappa*.

All the same, Miyuki did not believe that *kappa* existed. Katsuro had been making harmless fun of her with his story about cucumbers. She had laughed about it then, she laughed about it now. Since it was growing dark and no-one could see her, she did not feel obliged to put her hand over her mouth, and she found it wonderful to be able to laugh with her mouth wide open with nothing intervening between her outbursts of laughter and the humidity of the night that advanced in waves.

Then her clogs stumbled upon something soft lying across the path. Miyuki bent down. It was a corpse, one belonging to a young man, very handsome, with a perfect oval face, its deathly pallor accentuated by the flashes of lightning that were now making a riotous entrance. He had a small mouth, two almost almond-shaped eyes that death had not closed, and a thin tuft of beard on the tip of his chin. His scarcely ruffled clothing gave off a sweet scent of mud and river algae. At first sight, he bore no wound to hint at the cause of his death. Stretched out in a position of abandon, devoid of any tension, his calm air and posture, as relaxed as if he were lying on a comfortable bed and not on the bare earth, gave the impression that death was simply his normal state.

Merely stumbling on the corpse was enough to have inflicted a stain on Miyuki's soul, a stain she had exacerbated by stooping over the dead man until she almost touched him. She decided that, having gone this far, she had little to lose by turning the body over to see whether an examination of his back might better inform her as to the reasons for his demise.

She set her baskets on the ground and wedged them with large stones. Then, bending down once more, she tipped the body over – on its side to begin with, then onto its belly. She noticed that the cords holding up his baggy white silk trousers had been untied, revealing an *ōguchi** that had slipped down to his ankles – or that somebody had pulled down that far. This

---

* Garment that served as underpants, frequently red in colour.

113

second hypothesis seemed the more likely, because the young man's anus had been torn and lashed as though with a blade. The already darkened red of the coagulated blood that smeared his buttocks and the tops of his thighs contrasted with the silky scarlet of the *ōguchi*.

There was no question that this was the appalling work of a *kappa* that had used its sharp, rounded beak to remove the flesh and force its way to the liver.

Miyuki stood aside to be sick. Then she raised her head to the sky, eagerly imbibing the cataracts of rain to take away the bitter taste of her vomit.

Kneeling beside the young man's corpse, she whispered to him, pausing whenever a rumble of thunder pierced the night, that the same gods who insisted that she should purify herself from the stain she had contracted because of him, should punish her more strictly still were she to abandon him as he was, without doing anything to facilitate his access to the afterlife. For the gods had already shown her how cruel they could be by taking the person who mattered to her more than anyone else in the world, more than the gods themselves, and by allowing Akito, the horse-faced man, and Genkishi, his accomplice, to steal six of her eight carp and devour them.

And so she made up her mind to do everything possible, to go as far as she could in such circumstances; although the young man, dead though he was, should understand that she, on her own, could not perform the rituals that ensured the liberation and flight of his soul; she had neither the knowledge of the sacred formulae to be uttered, nor the essential religious accessories, nor, above all, the legitimacy.

The first thing she did was to move the corpse aside to prevent it being violated still further by animals that might emerge from the river – and not just the *kappa*.

She slipped one arm beneath the dead man's neck, and the other under his knees, and she attempted to lift him. But he was too heavy for her, and she was obliged to abandon that plan.

It was then that a *kaiken*, which he must have been concealing up his sleeve, fell from the young man's clothing. The metal case fitted the narrow shape of the weapon; it was decorated with birds, while the engravings on the blade were of delicate grasses dancing in the breeze.

This discovery plunged Miyuki into confusion: had the gods read her thoughts when she had yearned for a *kaiken*? If they were now sending her this object she had so desired, was it not so that she should use it for the purpose for which it was conceived – the *jigai*, female suicide by severance of the jugular vein?

However, the discovery of this *kaiken* did not resolve two vital questions: where exactly was the vein on Miyuki's neck that she should cut to comply with the ritual? And, as far as she knew, this type of suicide was the privilege of ladies of the nobility and the wives of heroic warriors; she had never heard it said that the widow of a simple fisherman could perform it.

At that moment, she saw a low, narrow boat gliding along the Yodogawa.

The boat appeared to be drifting, but this was an illusion as the evening light was dimmed by the storm clouds that hung over the river. In fact, three men dressed in straw raincoats were thrusting long poles into the riverbed, energetically driving the boat against the current.

Miyuki flattened herself behind the corpse. She feared that these men, if they saw her, might approach her. If they did, they would discover the dead man, which would necessarily oblige them to subject her to a close interrogation.

She would be punished for having concealed the truth – a truth that she knew nothing about, but her judges would take this ignorance as proof of a rebellious and dissimulating nature. She felt as though she could already feel her neck clasped in a cangue that she would have to endure for several moons at a stretch. Grazed by the rubbing of the heavy wooden clamp and the chafing on her collarbones, her shoulders would be bruised for life. The dimensions of this instrument of torture being calculated to prevent convicts from putting their hands to their mouths, Miyuki would be obliged to beg for the smallest handful of rice, the tiniest drop of water. If she wanted to survive, that is, for if she chose not to ask for anything from anyone, if she set off on her own through the forest (it seemed to her that Japan was nothing but one immense forest: ever since her departure from Shimae, she had only occasionally left the shelter of trees), then she would eventually waste away from exhaustion just as surely as if she had performed the *jigai*.

Dying did not horrify her. If it were to happen, her only regret would be not to enjoy the splendours of this autumn. It was her favourite season: the days were still mild, it only grew cold in the evenings, and, even then, it was not a biting cold, merely a suppressed coolness that made one want to snuggle up rather than wrap oneself in heavy coats. And where better to curl up than in the nooks and crannies that Katsuro created, just for her, with his warm body? She huddled up to him, with delicate little groans like those made by the cats that roamed Shimae and that, drawn by the smell of fish, occasionally plucked up the courage to venture inside the fisherman's house.

But Katsuro had drowned, and the charms of autumn would fade with him.

The boat drew up alongside the bank. The eldest of the mariners, who appeared to be in charge, a short man with a curious chin, at the end of which flowed a stream of long yellowish hairs, jumped ashore. For a moment, he stood swaying on his crooked legs, as though confused by stepping from the fluctuations of the water onto the stability of dry land.

"*Otome*,"* he said, looking at the corpse behind which Miyuki was trying to conceal herself by scraping frantically at the soil made soft by the storm. "You had better show yourself. I know you are there, *otome*, I saw you before you hid yourself."

Miyuki uttered a pitiful moan.

"I also know that you have nothing to do with this dead person," the man continued. "Really, you have no reason to be frightened of us."

He drew closer, waddling on his bowed legs.

"Of course I had nothing to do with it," Miyuki said, as she remained prudently hidden. "But who would believe me?"

"This dead man belonged to the retinue of Kintaro, the servant of the samurai Minamoto no Yorimitsu, himself a loyal supporter of the regent Fujiwara no Michinaga, our venerable minister of Supreme Affairs."

---

* Young lady.

117

These names, which the man with the ugly legs articulated with deep respect – did he not go so far as to emphasise each syllable with a bow of the head? – meant nothing to Miyuki. The boatman seemed shocked by such ignorance.

"What world do you live in, *otome*?" he said. "You should know at least that the confrontations between the Minamoto clan and that of the Taira are growing more and more frequent. One day, they will no longer even have truces, and their war will set the entire empire ablaze. If the empire still exists, that is. Already, this morning, at sunrise, it must have been between the hour of the Tiger and that of the Rabbit,* bandits in the pay of the Tairas killed this young man whom you think you have made into a shield. Why did they execute him? For the simple reason that on his back he was wearing the white *nobori*† embossed with gentian flowers and bamboo leaves, the emblem of the Minamotos. But for our part," he added, pointing to the two other mariners who remained on the boat, "this murder does not concern us any more than it concerns you: we are merely humble fishermen. By trailing this young man, it is his master, Kintaro, we are really following. Purely to get to the bottom of the story, do you understand?"

"What story?" Miyuki said.

"Oh, a rumour that's going around that, when he was still a child, but a child of exceptional strength, Kintaro fought with a giant carp. That was a long time ago, and today this incredible fish, if it ever existed, is bound to be dead. Besides, it's not the carp that interests us, my friends and me, but the river in

---

* Around five o'clock in the morning.
† A Japanese banner in the shape of a long, narrow, vertical flag.

which Kintaro was supposed to have challenged it, straddling the fish and mastering it by thrusting his arms into its gills up to his elbows. After all, this river may harbour creatures of the same kind. But this can be of no interest to you, *otome*!"

Miyuki then showed herself, suddenly standing over the corpse, her eyes open wide, her mouth rounded.

"On the contrary, it is of great interest: I was the wife of Nakamura Katsuro."

"Ah," the boatman said, knitting his eyebrows. He had not the least idea who Nakamura Katsuro could be, and he did not appear at all concerned about redressing this gap in his knowledge.

"He, too, was a fisherman," Miyuki said. "A great fisherman. Perhaps the greatest. Most of the carp that spawn today in the ponds of the temples in Heian Kyō are descended from fish caught by Katsuro in the Kusagawa, our river."

Okano Mitsutada, for this was the name of the owner of the fishing boat, frowned again. Yes, he had heard tell of an exceptional fisherman living at the far western end of the island of Honshu, near the ring of small volcanoes known as Abu, in the region of San'in – the dark side of the mountain – overlooking the Sea of Japan. But he had never known the name of this fisherman. Perhaps it had been mentioned to him without his paying attention. He, Okano Mitsutada, did not catch ornamental fish: the fish he caught were meant to be eaten, so it mattered little whether they were good to look at, his customers were only interested in their weight and flavour.

"If you are going to Heian Kyō, why don't you come with us?" the fisherman suggested. "Even travelling up river, the shortest way is by water. And it's the safest for sure. Certainly, you're no longer very far from the Imperial City, but even a short distance can hold dangers for an unprotected young woman."

"I thank you for your offer," Miyuki said, "but I can't travel with the three of you, because I contracted a stain when I drew close to the young man. And not satisfied with being close to him, I touched him, I smelled him, I turned him over, and it was when I saw the wound between his thighs that I realised he had been the victim of a *kappa*."

Okano gnashed his teeth and slapped his thighs with the flat of his hand; it was his way of laughing and was not dissimilar to the gloomy excitement of vultures discovering rotten flesh.

"You realised nothing of the sort, *otome*: the Tairas tore his anus to make people think he had been attacked by a *kappa* and thereby escape vengeance from the Minamotos."

He strode along the bank, leaving footprints in the sand that had been softened by the rain.

"Instead of taking me with you," Miyuki said, "perhaps you could still do me a great favour, Okano-*san*."

She gestured towards her baskets, inviting the fisherman to draw near. He came over and bent down. He whistled, then called to his companions:

"Come and look, both of you, it's not every day you see such fish."

"I had eight of them, which even then was nowhere near enough to propagate the ponds of the temples of Heian Kyō, where the carp were badly affected by the long summer drought, and now there are only two left after robbers stole the others from me. Since you are fishermen, could you not catch a few carp to replace the stolen ones?"

Okano and his men looked at one another.

"To tell you the truth," the fisherman said, "our fish would be far less beautiful than yours. Not as plump, the scales not as neat, less shiny, the fins damaged by the shocks they received when they were spawned."

"I would tell them that my carp have suffered from the journey – oh! I beg you, Okano-*san* . . ."

The fisherman and his two companions squatted down a little way away. The shower spattered their straw coats which bulged from their backs like tortoise shells. They talked among themselves for a moment, glancing furtively at Miyuki.

Okano Mitsutada returned to her at last. His companions agreed to catch fish for her, he told her, but they demanded remuneration of one *koku*[*] of rice for each fish.

"You see how honest we are, *otome*: we cannot say in advance whether the fish that we shall take from the water will be beautiful enough for the temples of Heian Kyō, so you shall only pay for those you judge worthy of the sacred ponds."

In formulating her request, Miyuki had in fact considered whether it would be right to give Okano and his crew a reward, but she had scarcely anything left from her supply of *narezushi* and rice cakes.

"I have nothing to give you," she murmured. "No rice to offer you in exchange."

The three men exchanged knowing, almost amused, glances as though they had been expecting this inconvenience and had an alternative means of compensation in mind.

---

[*] A unit of measurement corresponding to the amount of rice eaten by one person in a year.

Okano Mitsutada allowed a particularly loud roll of thunder to pass, waited patiently for the birds that had been scattered by the din to return to their nests in the pine trees, the cherry trees and the willows bent by the wind, then he said,

"Listen to me, *otome*, there exists a method of your procuring as many *koku* of rice as you require, and not just rice but also lengths of silk, incense, salted fish and even heavy necklaces of copper coins threaded like pearls with a hole in the middle."

"What is it, this method?"

The fisherman pointed to some buildings on the opposite shore that rose up from a reed bed ruffled by the gusts of wind. Thrown together by the long lashings of the storm, the clatter of the reeds mingled with the pathetic cry of the *higurashi* cicadas.

Okano Mitsutada had to speak loudly to prevail over the turmoil of the elements.

"Climb on board, I'm going to take you to the other side of the river, to the Inn of the Two Moons in the Water. Once you are there, ask for the old *obasan*,* the old madam with green lips, and offer her your services."

"As a rice stacker?" Miyuki guessed.

"We say *yūjo* here. But it's the same thing. The old woman with green lips has a gift for attracting customers. And she's the wiliest when it comes to business matters. Before becoming a madam, she was the best *yūjo* in the whole of Yodogawa. Oh, she won't spare you, but after a few days under her rule, you'll be wealthy enough to persuade any fisherman, me or anyone else, to catch all the carp in the Yodo and its tributaries for you."

---

* Aunt. The nickname given to the madam in a brothel.

122

Leaning on his pole, the fisherman pointed to a house whose crooked aspect contrasted strongly with the line of about a dozen roughly cubic dwellings built on stilts. It was difficult to know what to think of this shack: were those weird angles, those irregular expanses covered in patches of wooden shingle blackened by the damp, the inexplicable ruptures and the sudden excrescences growing on its facade like tumours intended to divert the winds, the rains and the floods, or was it one of those more commonly seen "enhanced" cabins, the builders of which, having never before sawn a plank of wood, had thrown together as and when they were able to procure the materials? In most cases, these constructions were either overcome by a heavy fall of snow and ended up collapsing on their occupants, or else they were destroyed by fire.

"Go on, *otome*, seize the opportunity!"

THE INN OF THE Two Moons in the Water was so named because sometimes, whenever beads of mist hung over the water, an optical illusion produced two moons on the waters of the Yodogawa.

The house had a lopsided jetty that extended over the river. Several large vessels were moored at the stakes that supported it.

A heady stench of moss and damp flour arose from the Two Moons, due to the mushrooms that colonised the wooden walls. Mingled with it, from inside the establishment and from out of the cracks in the walls, wafted a fragrance of cloves, camomile and rice powder, producing a scent that was unusual for an inn.

Without needing to put her ear to the lintel, Miyuki caught the sound of female voices, young for the most part, in the midst of which there was the occasional shrill moan, like the sound of a frightened little dog.

When Miyuki entered, women in a state of undress were enviously watching a girl submerged up to her shoulders in a barrel out of which rose coils of steam. To stop it getting wet, the bather

124

had spread her long brown hair over the edge of the barrel, which made her perfectly round face look like the centre of a flower with dark petals.

Back in the darkest part of the room, an elderly woman, with a bloated face, a snub nose and a large wide mouth, moist like a toad's, whose body seemed to float within a smock squeezed into red trousers that were tied at the ankle, was intermittently throwing water over a prostitute bound by ropes and suspended from a roof beam.

As they dried, the bonds shrank and cut into the skin of the girl being punished. It was she who was yelping like a puppy as the ropes dug ever more deeply into her flesh.

Despite the gloomy light in the part of the room where the torturer stood, Miyuki could see that she had green lips. She deduced that this must be the elderly madam she should approach to ask her to do her the favour of initiating her and procuring for her generous customers who would make her rich enough to restock her load of carp.

Still spraying water over her victim, who moaned and rocked above her, the *obasan* listened to Miyuki's story. She puckered her green lips and exhaled like an angry cat.

"Tomorrow, before the hour of the Sheep* is over, you will have earned not only enough to fill your baskets, but also the wherewithal to buy Okano's boat, his poles, his nets, his fish tank, and even the two good-for-nothings who serve as his crew. But do not imagine that you owe any of this to your beauty, and still less to your caresses. For, to tell you the truth,

_____
* From one o'clock to three o'clock in the afternoon.

after a favourable first impression, one only has to look a little more closely to discover that you are not as pretty as you seem to think: the lower half of your face is considerably narrower than the top, your lips stick out as though you wanted to give a kiss – ah! never give anything, neither a kiss nor anything else: if I am foolish enough to give satisfaction to that wicked catfish Okano by taking you aboard my boat, you should know that you must not give anything to the men who accost us without my consent; if they come and rub the side of their boat against ours, it's a sign that they are ready to pay for the least of your favours, even your breath brushing their face, and at that point they have to go through the old *obasan*, because everything has to be discussed, everything weighed up, everything assessed, I am the one who fixes the price and, believe me, I can make gold out of the tiniest drop of your saliva that, like a bird, goes and perches on their noses – and now I seem to have lost the thread of what I was saying, can you remember where I was?"

"My lips, which you objected to, *obasan*."

"Open them, so that I can see your teeth."

Miyuki obeyed. The old woman let out a mocking laugh.

"The way you open your mouth! Won't people say that you are rolling up a blind that has been drying all summer, in which every strip has cracked? Has no-one ever told you that you should lick them first with your tongue to make them shine and to lubricate the mechanism? And those teeth," she added, hiding her face in her hands, "those teeth! A married woman lacquers her teeth with black."

"I'm no longer a married woman, I am a widow."

"Have you never noticed that animals don't carry out *ohaguro*?* White teeth put you on the level of animals."

Remembering the little oxen in Shimae, Miyuki said that she loved animals, that she enjoyed their company, and that she did not feel humiliated to have teeth that were the same colour as theirs.

"I warn you," the madam said, "I have a good reputation on the Yodogawa, I will not allow you to tarnish it or disappoint my loyal customers."

Despite these threats, and perhaps even because of them, Miyuki realised that she had won the verbal battle with the old woman. Just to make sure, she decided to press home her advantage.

At that moment, the punished prostitute started to bleed from the bite of the linen cords in those areas where her flesh was most tender. It began as a faint rash on her skin, then each tiny bubble of blood became a steadily growing rose.

"Untie her now. I beg you, *obasan*," Miyuki said.

Bowing very low, she held out the *kaiken* from the young man who had died on the banks of the Yodogawa – better to slash the bonds rather than struggling to untangle each twist and turn, especially since the madam, mindful of scratching her cheeks as she applied her make-up, had cut her nails very short, making them unsuitable for undoing knots quickly.

If Miyuki bowed so low that her forehead touched the old woman's feet, it was so that the punished prostitute should be relieved of her distress as soon as possible, for the fisherman's wife

---

* *Ohaguro* is the act of putting black lacquer on one's teeth.

127

could not stop herself thinking that Katsuro, who must have been greatly in need of relaxation after the long hours of strain making sure that the new carp for the Office of Gardens and Ponds were acclimatising themselves to their new environment, might perhaps have enjoyed the company of this girl. Miyuki did not feel at all jealous about this: those moments of pleasure that her husband had granted himself were merely clusters of sparks, like those left in the wake of the burning arrows fired to expel the demons during the rite of exorcism on the last night of the year.

But for some reason, the *obasan* demurred from using the blade herself. Miyuki took hold of it and, with a quick blow, sliced through the ball of knots in which the ends of the linen cords that held the prostitute in position were gathered.

The girl barely had time to reach out her hands to break her fall. She landed on the palms of her hands, her folded forearms crushed like springs beneath her undernourished weight, and for a moment she remained flat on the ground like a terrified spider. At last, she leaped to her feet and flung her arms around Miyuki as she blurted out incomprehensible words. Her voice was shrill, animated and high-pitched, and her hair, soaked by the watering the *obasan* had inflicted, gave off a sweet smell of alluvia. Katsuro had claimed that the river sirens chirped like swallows and smelled of the silt that they wriggled about in to extract the water, and so Miyuki decided to call her Nyngyo.*

The only *yūjo* permitted to spend the night inside the inn were those whom the madams had chosen to warm themselves

---

* Siren.

128

against by cuddling up to them or by slipping their feet under their dresses to place them on their warm bellies. Nowhere near plump enough to be included in this class of human warmth dispensers, all of whom were selected from among the chubbiest girls, Miyuki followed Nyngyo and ten or so other skinny creatures to the jetties and into the heavy black boats that the young prostitutes and the madams took to meet their customers.

"We work from the hour of the Rooster," Nyngyo said. "But the rituals of making-up and dressing begin much earlier. Whenever the madams decide to make their way to the river, we have to be ready. Any lateness is punished severely. You have seen what it cost me not to have finished plaiting my hair in time – what impertinence on my part, I admit, to wear it loose as though I were a woman of the nobility!"

"It's so lovely, so long," said Miyuki admiringly, whose own hair was gathered in a vague bun that she held together as best she could by pegging it with an ever-increasing number of combs and pins she improvised with small branches and stalks she found in the undergrowth.

Nyngyo's hair, on the other hand, hung freely down to her waist, a large black cascade of such brilliance that she had only to move her head for it to quiver with sparkles of light and give off the sugary scent of the oil the young *yūjo* used to make it sleek, as well as the fragrance of camellia balsam that was meant to sheathe it in a sort of varnish.

After sitting on the edge of the jetty for a while and having put to rights the world in general and the Two Moons in the Water in particular, the two women set off for the boats that had been assigned to them. They took shelter in the sort of snug hut protected by pale blinds made of reeds that, situated in the middle of the boat and strewn with mats and cushions, was used to shield the frolics of the *yūjo* and their customers.

Before slipping into her shelter, Miyuki secured her baskets so that they should not topple over even if the Yodogawa became rough, jolting the boats and making them bump into one another. Disturbed by the threatening storm and by the river that they could sense was very close, the two surviving carp circled inside their prison in the same feverish state as when they took on the currents of the Shuzenji falls to spawn in the quietest part of the Kusagawa. Streaming through the water of their circular baskets, the lightning made their scales shimmer like so many garnets, topazes and tourmalines.

Leaning over the gunwale of her boat so that she could see them better, Nyngyo could not stifle a little cry of admiration.

"Get back!" Miyuki exclaimed, brandishing her *kaiken* under the nose of the young prostitute. "You owe the fact that you were relieved of your punishment before the allotted time to this blade, but I would not hesitate to use it against you if you even thought of touching my carp."

Reluctantly, Nyngyo withdrew from the baskets. To placate Miyuki, whom she had also not yet thanked for her intervention, she offered some sustenance – strips of vegetables with pickled rice and sweet chestnuts – that the *obasan* had had distributed to each girl (except Miyuki, as the old woman with green lips was probably waiting to see what she was capable of before committing herself to any expenditure).

"You're allowed rice in the evening, even after being punished?" Miyuki said in surprise.

"The customers choose the boats that are lowest in the water, those that indicate that the courtesans aboard them are nice and fleshy. If you deny her food, how will a girl be so podgy as to almost capsize the boat?"

Miyuki admired the efficiency of these madams who thought of everything.

"Do you think that I am sufficiently plump to please the Yodogawa men?"

Her two brown eyes fluttering over Miyuki's body like a butterfly exploring a meadow of flowers, Nyngyo scrutinised her carefully.

"I fear not," she said at last. "Well, all you have to do is fill the front of your garment with padding. And don't forget to stuff the sleeves as well."

"But where am I going to find padding?"

"On the tip of your *kaiken*!" said Nyngyo, laughing. "Just pinch a kimono or two off the *kusobaba*.* She's as skinny as a branch in winter, so she pads all her clothes at the shoulders and the hips."

"And why does she put green make-up on her lips?"

Nyngyo gave a mocking laugh, reawakening the traces of bleeding that still marked her skin where the cords had pressed into her flesh. Then her laughter came to a sharp stop and turned into raucous little yaps as though she had strangled herself with her own mirth.

"But she doesn't put on any make-up! Her mouth is always like that, green and flabby, and anyone who goes near her notices

---

* Old shrew.

131

her smell of decay, of rotting fish and animal dung. If you ask me, she's dead, that old creature. But the fact that she's dead doesn't prevent her being alive."

"How do you explain that?" said Miyuki, puzzled.

Katsuro had never appeared to her since his death. Whatever Natsume and the women of Shimae had said to encourage her to set out for Heian Kyō, she did not believe that the coils of mist with the vaguely human forms that she had seen on the steep paths of the Kii mountains had been disembodied manifestations of Katsuro: he was not the sort of man to haunt Miyuki like an inconveniently placed insect bite whose itching becomes more irritating the longer you vainly try to reach it.

"I can't explain it. But it's true. That woman has something of the monster about her, at least that's what I reckon. She released me, but apparently three other girls who were strung up like me are now dead. I don't know whether that's true, but it's quite possible."

Miyuki was still asleep when the madam with the green lips climbed aboard the boat. Muttering some incomprehensible words, she laid out the ointments and the accessories for the beautification of her *yūjo*: the balms for the hair, the blend of wax and oil for the face, the thick white make-up composed of rice powder and water, the bamboo brushes to spread it with, the absorbent lichens to remove the excess, the sticks of paulownia charcoal to draw false eyebrows, and the ingredients to make the lacquer for blacking the teeth, which she prepared from a powder extracted from the excrescence of a sumac tree.

With everything now arranged, she woke Miyuki and,

shoving brownish balls of woven material and strands of silk from burst cocoons under her nose, she ordered her to go and impregnate them with the morning dew that she would find on the lespedeza blossom and on the scarlet leaves of dogwood trees, so that the *yūjo* could polish their faces with them and retain the pallor of their complexions.

"Don't be long. I'm not going to wait for you to return before setting off. Business has been hard since the power struggles broke out. Many men have deserted Heian Kyō to go and defend their distant homelands, as though a civil war was threatening!"

"Don't you think it will happen?"

"I don't ask for your advice, so spare yourself the trouble of asking me for mine."

When she came back, the madam had planted her pole in the riverbed, and the heavy vessel was already moving away from the shore. She did not unclench her green lips to warn Miyuki to be careful and was happy merely to watch her take a run-up, almost fall into the water when she skidded on the slippery bank, and just about manage to jump aboard. With her hands clasping the balls of silk soaked in dew, she had nothing to hold on with and she fell flat on her face in the bottom of the boat. She picked herself up, covered with dirt, and the madam smacked her across her cheekbones with the back of her hand.

Now the wind had dropped and the sky had brightened, the river lapped softly against the sides of the boat, which the downstream current carried into the midst of a flotilla of other craft laden with long sheaves of oats, or weighed down with waste gathered from between the stilts of the houses, which elderly sailors were taking downstream, towards Naniwa Bay, where it would be thrown into the sea.

There were five girls on board, as well as the madam who was leaning on her pole.

Like the others, Miyuki found she had been given a landing net that she was supposed to hand to the customer – supposing she were ever to have one – so that he could put in it the scrapings of incense, the copper bands, the rice, the salt fish and the strips of silk that he wished to give her in gratitude for her services, and that would end up in the hands of the madam, who would only return a small part of them to her after deducting various fines that she had incurred and that she had not always been warned about.

Miyuki went back to Nyngyo and the other prostitutes. Leaning against the gunwale and beating on tambourines that they clutched to their shoulders like small monkeys, they were singing to attract the men:

> My great lord
> Gave a dread command:
> So I parted from my wife,
> Though filled with sadness;
> When I look at such a person
> And with a strong man's
> Heart steeled myself –
> That's what I showed –
> And when I left my gate,
> O'erflowing with love,
> My mother stroked my hair;

And, as young grass,
My wife held me close . . .
. . . while I am here,
The spring haze
Around the islands rises and
The calls of the cranes
Sound sadly;
When my distant
Home I recall,
My bow case
Rustling on my back,
How I do grieve. *

Multiplied by the occupants of the increasing number of boats that, since nightfall, had joined them in drifting along with the current the voices of the *yūjo* mingled with the calls of seabirds returning to their nests. Disturbed by this ill-assorted concert of whores and birds, certain shopkeepers with premises on the shore, or who sold goods from their boats, tried to chase away the "love boats" by loudly slapping the flats of their oars on the surface of the river.

If Nyngyo were to be believed, the most effective way of arousing men's desires was to use a scented powder especially produced by the madam with green lips. It was placed in small heaps on the gunwale and one blew on it, consigning it to the wind that carried it to the nostrils of potential customers.

◉ ◉ ◉

---

* By Ōtomo no Yakamochi (718–785), a member of the "Thirty-six immortal poets".

It was close to the end of the hour of the Dog when Miyuki noticed the glow of a lantern on the riverbank, which a figure was dangling from the end of a pole.

The madam immediately steered the boat towards the bank.

A man was standing on the shore. The glow of his lantern was not strong enough to reveal his features, but he nevertheless kept his head down and, like a child attempting to fend off a slap, hid his face behind the drooping sleeve of his coat. Even though the coat was not of a formal colour and the man wearing it had not displayed any stamp of dignity, it was obvious, merely from the manner in which he greeted the madam, that the man with the lantern must, in one way or another, be someone of standing at the Imperial Court.

The five girls came and pressed themselves against the railings, but the noise of shingle driven by the current prevented them from picking up the details of the conversation that the madam was having with their future customer.

"Just listen to the old hypocrite calling him Lord this, or Lord that, I reckon she's going to demand the highest price," Nyngyo said. "I bet she's asking him for a silk dress."

"Would she dare, do you really think so?"

"Embroidered with autumn flowers," Nyngyo said.

"That's at least twenty-five days' salary for a good worker!"

"Then he'll certainly be for Akazome," whispered one of the *yūjo*, pointing to her companion.

Miyuki turned her head a little to look at the girl they called Akazome. Very white skin stretched over a round and slightly chubby face, deep-set eyes beneath eyelids that allowed very little to pass unnoticed, long and naturally curved eyelashes, a mouth which, without being truly voluptuous, displayed well-shaped lips. How beautiful she is, Miyuki thought.

It was then that she saw the lantern tracing a long and graceful orbit through the night sky, and come to a halt so close to her that she thought she could feel the warmth of the candle stroking her face through the oiled paper shade. It was not an illusion: her forehead and her cheekbones had become flushed and burning, as though aglow from an inner fire.

Nyngyo, too, had followed the arc of the lantern.

"I was wrong," she murmured as she took the young woman's hand and pressed it to her lips. "It's you this man desires, Amakusa Miyuki. It will be yours, the silk dress embroidered all over with autumn flowers . . ."

As soon as he had stepped over the gunwale, the man kicked off from the bank with his heel, launching the boat towards the middle of the river, thus indicating that he was in charge of the vessel and its passengers.

Emitting little grunts of pleasure like a cat preparing the place where it is going to sleep, the client took his place on the cushions that the *yūjo* had strewn over the bottom of the boat. Sitting on his heels, he brought to his lips the bowl of sake that the madam had offered him. He was counting on the alcohol so that he would not fail to honour the courtesan he had chosen even before he had had time to scrutinise her – he had singled her out in the dusk, relying on her waist, her slender figure, the cut of her profile and the tone of her voice when she had whispered words of welcome to him, but he could not be sure that she would meet his secret desires.

137

This was the game, the risk, which he not only accepted, but sought.

Half the time – or else on two out of three occasions – he had misjudged his chosen *yūjo* and found himself in the company of a coarse girl whose hurried and clumsy caresses irritated his senses instead of satisfying them.

He submitted without protest, without even asking for a little more tenderness. His venal love affairs were a reflection of the world as he conceived it: the sweet and pretty prostitutes symbolising Heian Kyō, the Imperial City, so refined and so spotless, where everything was perfectly understated, and the common girls representing the other nations, the distant countries that did not even have names and maintained neither trade with Japan nor an embassy. For, even if no-one ever spoke about them, the man was sure that other territories, probably vast ones, must exist, beyond the five seas and the six thousand, eight hundred and fifty or so islands of the Japanese archipelago. By climbing aboard one of the love boats on the Yodogawa, he was not merely soothing his sexual urges: each *yūjo* being a foreign land, he was setting sail each time for one of the vast world's mysterious kingdoms.

He was not a demanding lover: the features, the voice, the scent of the courtesan were enough for him, he felt no need to make love to her, nor even to gaze at her nakedness – a naked body had limited attraction for him because he considered that this physical vessel was merely a fragment of an infinitely more complex creature, *true* possession of which he knew was impossible.

"Which trader do you obtain your sake from?"

"From a very discreet dealer, sir, one who intends to remain so," said the madam with green lips. "But you should know that the exquisite beverage that I served to you this evening is *bijinshu*, the sake of beauties."

"*Bijinshu*, really? I thought that ancient method had been discontinued a long time ago?"

"You are correct in saying so, sir. But I know a supplier where the miracle of the grain of rice becoming alcohol is still obtained by diligent mastication and the saliva of young virgins who are no more than seventeen years old."

As the client leaned backwards to drain the last drop of his sake, displaying his face to the moonlight, Miyuki was able to examine his features.

He was clearly an elderly man, but age had partly spared him: he was like those temples from bygone centuries in which one could gauge, from the scars that criss-crossed them, from the burns that blackened the tangles of their wooden frames, from the amputated bodies of dragons decorating their roofing, that they had endured fires and survived earthquakes, from which, if not unscathed, they had emerged strengthened, enhanced, and sometimes more remarkable than before the incidents.

The madam waited until the client had disappeared into the dark cabin where Miyuki had preceded him, then she planted herself in front of the entrance and placed an enormous paper umbrella stretched out over thin strips of bamboo to shield them from the curiosity of passers-by who might be walking along the banks.

The shelter was so narrow that the client had no choice but to lie down on top of Miyuki, who was already stretched out on the cushions scattered over the bottom of the boat.

Miyuki shuddered as she felt the old man weighing down on her.

"Please forgive me," the man said gently. "I did not want to hurt you."

"You have not hurt me, sir," she replied from behind the screen made by her fingers (she had put her hand over her mouth so as not to upset him by breathing on him), "but I am shivering because I am afraid of not satisfying you: I have only ever made love with one man, he was my husband, and when he died we were still astonished by one another, and we did not care how we made love. But you shall have everything you desire from me provided you remember that I am inexperienced, and probably rather foolish; you should also express your wishes clearly, guide my movements, and shape and position my body according to your preferences."

Despite the man's weight, which plunged her deep into the stuffing of the cushions, Miyuki managed to free her hands and, by wriggling, seize hold of her chemise so that she could pull up her gown.

Only the madam was witness to what went on behind the screen of the paper umbrella. She remained as unobtrusive as possible, still managing not to miss anything that was happening for, if a client should complain, it was vital that she knew exactly what the courtesan had done – or failed to do – to cause his displeasure.

At the same time, as she kept watch on the couple's lovemaking, the madam continued to push on the pole, propelling the boat with a smoothness that contrasted with the impetuousness of the sexual exchanges.

The other girls dozed, obliged by the narrowness of the boat to lie overlapping one another. Cast limply over the gunwale, the hand or foot that had been unable to find space for itself drew graceful trails through the insects on the surface of the water. As their cheeks rubbed against one another like bunches of *koshu** grapes, their white make-up began to disintegrate and the soft pinkness beneath began to show.

Astutely maintained in the flow of the current, the boat was not subjected to any jolts apart from when it encountered a barge heavily laden with bundles of oats which the boatmen were hauling upstream to the Yodogawa.

While her client struggled to free his penis from the jumble of folds, ties and flaps of material that hampered him, Miyuki reflected: what would she feel in surrendering the most intimate part of herself to a stranger?

Katsuro's penis had been the first and last to be received inside her. When her husband died, she had experienced a compelling urge that became tyrannical as the days passed, to make love with him one more time. She woke up several times during the night, convinced that she had heard someone walking about in the house, the footstep of a vigorous, determined man who, out of respect for her sleep, still set foot on the floor with a measure of restraint. It could only be Katsuro's step. He was dead, of course, she had seen the smoke from his funeral pyre rise up into the sky, but perhaps death was more permeable than one might think, perhaps it was like the cliff that overlooked the weir at Shuzenji – it

---

* A pink variety of grape, very common in Japan. Well known since the 8th century.

gave the impression of an impenetrable, solid wall, but when the Kusagawa burst its banks, faults opened up in this cliff and jets of water spurted in all directions. Miyuki was careful not to open her eyes, but she smiled in her semi-slumber and reached out her open palm so that Katsuro, when he came to lie down beside her, could lay his cheek in this hollow, on the warm, soft cushions of her fingers. Unfortunately, she always fell asleep before she could feel her husband's cheek against her hand. But when morning came, and she opened her eyes again, her first impulse was to sniff the palm of her hand, and she had no difficulty in persuading herself that it smelled of the river, of the damp clay of the carp baskets and the powdered, woody, violet scent of the irises on the riverbank.

No longer being able to appease her carnal urges in the present, she satisfied them from her memory. Just by lying down with her eyes closed and recalling her husband's face leaning over her, she could feel with startling intensity Katsuro's penis penetrating her, the caress of his shaft of flesh moving to and fro inside her vagina, the walls of which she managed to tighten around this ghostly organ.

As long as everything remained peaceful around her, as long as no nightjar started to chirp, as long as the rain did not pound the straw roof, she could make the illusion last until the overwhelming moment came when she was convulsed by an orgasm, quickly followed by a second, even a third.

But tonight, the elderly man who had singled her out from among the other *yūjo* would enforce the stamp of his own penis on her – if, that is, he managed to find it again among the great jumble of his clothing – and Miyuki was afraid that this penetration would feel more like a burglary.

142

She needed to be ready to control herself, to take charge, to convince herself that she was not betraying Katsuro's memory, that this customer was nothing and nobody, that to call him "sir" did not mean he really existed, and that she had only to imagine the figure of the Yodogawa fisherman, Okano Mitsutada, standing arms akimbo in the early dawn light, his shoulders bent under the weight of the carp he had caught for her, and the old man of the night would disappear like those powdery white geometrid moths that thudded against the paper lanterns, stunned themselves and dropped dead on the floor of the boat.

The old man finally succeeded in liberating his penis. Freed from the shackles of the fabrics and invigorated by an influx of blood, his organ had immediately shot up and, as though throwing back his head to bay at the moon, he had pulled back his foreskin and directed his penis skywards, a pointed, red penis that, Miyuki thought, looked like a wolf, a little Honshu wolf.

She lay down on her side, allowing the man the choice of rolling her over on her belly or on her back. He turned her over on her belly, then stretched himself out against her, the gnarled and bumpy parts of his frame seeking the soft hollows of her flesh.

She closed her eyes. There was nothing to see, in any case. Beyond the boat's reed blinds the banks streamed past, alternately covered with tangles of cryptomeria roots or clusters of ferns whose fronds fluttered like a rustling of fans flourished by groups of ladies impatient for a show to begin at last.

For his part, the old man did not seem to be in a hurry. Now that he had succeeded in freeing himself from his clothing and his penis had acquired a more than honourable stiffness, he was taking his time.

While he fondled Miyuki's buttocks, she wondered whether he would notice their peculiarity; the right buttock was roughly pear-shaped, and the left one round like a globe. Although the difference was not significant, Katsuro used to marvel at this dissymmetry: could it be a defect from birth, or else an accidental mutilation – perhaps the left buttock had originally been a bulbous pear like the right one, but for some reason, the tip of the pear had been trimmed and only the bulbous part remained?

Leaning over Miyuki (she could feel his tepid breath skimming over her from her coccyx to her neck), the client had apparently not noticed anything. After all, the difference between the two buttocks was perhaps not as evident as Katsuro had claimed, at least not in the eyes of a casual lover.

However, although he was breathing increasingly noisily, which could be taken as a sign of excitement, the old man had still not penetrated Miyuki, nor even given a hint that he was about to do so.

Having kneaded her back, he remained stretched out against her for a long while, perfectly still and thoughtful.

Then he raised himself up above her, on all fours, with his stomach contracted as if to avoid any contact between their two bodies.

And now he drew back, with that crisp slowness of an empty drawer that one had hoped might contain something precious and that one closes again with regret.

"Do I not please you, sir?"

He did not reply immediately, continuing to edge away

carefully, as though distancing himself from something unbearable.

Miyuki recalled the people of Shimae, one winter night, withdrawing in silence, walking away from a cluster of homes that had just been destroyed by fire and of which nothing remained apart from the ashes that fluttered in the air and the still-flickering embers of a few houses. She remembered the footsteps in the snow, the imprints of wooden sandals that came suddenly to a stop, followed by an area where the villagers had shuffled about as though uncertain about what behaviour they should adopt – should they go on further or turn back – and there were prints of some sandals that had stepped backwards, for although people had drawn away from the tragedy, no-one had dared to turn around completely, no-one had turned their backs on the stumps of smoking beams, on the walls dotted with black pustules, on the charred bodies that all wore the same grimace, the same enormous sockets where the eyes had melted; and Miyuki had observed that the returning footprints were deeper than those approaching, as though the villagers now bore the burden of something overwhelming.

"Would you like me to call another *yūjo*?" she suggested.

The old man shook his head.

"But you have not had what you wished for, sir."

"The fact is," he said, "I remain frustrated. Deeply frustrated. And above all, disappointed. As though I had gone into an inn with the intention of feasting on a dish of eel only to be told that there wasn't any today."

To be reduced to the level of a dish of eel, which incidentally Miyuki disliked, was of course humiliating, but it was nothing compared to the shame she would feel if the madam decided to tie her up and suspend her from the ceiling of the Two Moons in the Water to punish her for having displeased an important customer.

The latter was leaning against one of the ribs of the boat and contemplating his now-flaccid penis.

Miyuki crawled over to the old man, bent down and, with the aid of her tongue, applied herself to the awakening of the listless organ. But the client pushed her away.

"No, it's no good. You see, it comes from you . . ."

He stopped suddenly.

"Yes, sir?" she said, encouragingly, hoping that he would provide her with reasons for her failure, and that she would be able to repair the situation to the advantage of both of them – she felt sick at the possibility of spending several hours tied to the inn's ceiling, and, to a lesser degree, she was annoyed that, thanks to her, the old man should not have enjoyed the pleasure that he had no doubt been expecting.

Since he said nothing, she pressed on:

"What is it that comes from me? Have you seen something on my body that offends you? Something you find repulsive? An impurity, a stain, a speck of dirt, a slight blemish, a mark, a scar, how would I know?"

It was possible, after all. Not owning a mirror, she had never been able to examine her own back, or her shoulder blades. The only reflections she had at her disposal were those that appeared in the carp pool and whatever Katsuro had revealed to her about her appearance. And, apart from amused speculations concerning the imbalance of his wife's buttocks, Katsuro had said very

146

little about her physique. However, the idea that she was not attractive enough to merit such comments would never have occurred to him, on the contrary: he had thought her so beautiful that words capable of describing someone such as Miyuki had neither entered his head nor left his lips.

"Do you think I would have chosen you if there had been anything repulsive about you?" the old man said.

"But how could you have known, sir? How would you have been able to see anything through the eight dresses that I was made to put on, one over the other, so that the fusion of all this silk would produce the purplish plum shade of springtime at sunset, which is how our *obasan* insisted on attiring me this evening? Purplish plum of springtime at sunset," she repeated, pursing her lips. "Now, I ask you! How's that for a colour? It doesn't exist in nature, neither does it in spring, nor at any time of the day or night. Ever."

"It's not merely a matter of seeing!" said the old man, irritably. "You are not just an object to be looked at. Have you ever heard tell of an old man, much older than me, called Kichijiro Ueda?"

"Where might I have heard tell of Kichijiro-*san*?"

"In your own world: there was nothing he loved as much as courtesans. Where they were concerned, he was insatiable! Every night he had to have one, and she had to be different from all the previous ones. Was this consuming need that he had for women a desire to contemplate their beauty? No, no: believe it or not, Kichijiro Ueda was born without eyes, a sort of curtain of skin covered his sockets."

"But then if nothing about me displeases you . . ."

"The scent," he said.

She frowned. The false eyebrows that Nyngyo had painted on her forehead, a finger's width above the real ones that she had shaved off beforehand, creased.

"The . . . scent?"

She would have understood if the old man had mentioned smell, or perfume, but "scent" was one of those countless words whose meaning Miyuki did not know.

"The scent," he repeated, wrinkling his nostrils, "the scent you exude."

Then she guessed what he meant. And at that moment she felt so cold that it was as though the boat were suddenly filled with all the water of the Yodogawa, and as though this black and icy water had swallowed her up, leaving only her mouth protruding so that she was still able to utter a few despairing words.

"Do I smell?"

"Did I say that? No, I simply observed that you smell of . . . something. I don't know what it is, it's a smell that I have never yet breathed on the neck of any *yūjo*. But I do not find it particularly pleasant, that's all."

"Can I . . ."

"No," he said, "there's nothing more you can do."

His tone of voice had become distant, and his manner was as dry as the haggard, shrivelled skin of a dead lizard. He raised the door of strips of reed and slipped underneath it. Miyuki could hear him sighing with relief as he emerged into the fresh air. She imagined his nostrils, vertical and slender as almonds, dilating and filling with the cold night air.

❀ ❀ ❀

He led the madam aside while the *yūjo* took care of Miyuki and helped her to straighten her clothing.

"Are you vexed, sir?" the madam enquired anxiously, seeing a worried crease on the old man's brow.

"Where did you recruit this courtesan?"

"I didn't recruit her, strictly speaking. She arrived of her own accord at the Inn of the Two Moons in the Water. She asked me for one night's hospitality in exchange for another night when she would work for me, whatever this work might be. It was the evening when that storm went on and on, you remember, when it rained so heavily."

"Was this not yesterday?"

"Yes, indeed, yesterday. In any case, I couldn't leave her outside."

"Did you question her? And examine her?"

"No. The thing is, you see, I was busy punishing a *yūjo* who had misbehaved. A punishment that required my full attention: I've already lost girls by correcting them in this way, I did not want to have this one die because of a momentary lapse of concentration. So, I simply cast an eye over the new girl who had come to us from somewhere or other. It was dark, it seemed to me that she wasn't too ugly – isn't that your opinion, too?"

"It doesn't matter what she seemed to be! It's her aroma that alerted me. She has a fragrance – or else she stinks – I am still not sure which – of something wild, a whiff of the forest, of crumpled grass, of sodden earth, of a lair."

"Of . . . a lair?"

"Of a lair, yes. I have an idea that this creature could well be a *kiyūbi no kitsune*."

Like most people who watch the world go by, the madam with green lips had heard tell of *kiyûbi no kitsune*, those foxes that are able to take on a human appearance, and preferably that of a young and attractive woman.

But to have a chance of metamorphosing itself in this way, a fox would have to be at least fifty years old. If it reached a hundred, its transformation was assured, but the circumstances of life, that of the hunters as much as that of the foxes being hunted, meant that vulpine centurions, and therefore the ladies who derived from them, were few in number. And yet how could one doubt their reality when even emperors vouched for their existence by welcoming them to their court?

"You say it was dark when the girl came to you?"

"Except for when flashes of lightning ripped through the sky, the darkness was so deep that you would have thought that daylight would never be able to dispel it," the madam said, pouring a generous further shot of the sake of beauties into the client's bowl. This time, she knocked back a good swig herself, straight from the flask – she found it increasingly hard to tolerate any reference to the supernatural whatsoever, because it reminded her of the possibility, however slight, that a Beyond might exist where she would be asked to account for the most negligible of her actions.

"Do you not think that a young woman wandering alone on a night hardly conducive to walking could easily be a *kiyûbi no kitsune*?"

"Not this woman," the madam said, without hesitation. "Not Amakusa Miyuki."

"Amakusa Miyuki," the client said. "Is that her name?"

"Well, it's the one she gave me. Does it mean something to you?"

The old man shook his head: the name of Amakusa Miyuki did not remind him of anything, and yet he had a vague impression of having heard it mentioned before. However, in a city like Heian Kyō that was constantly buzzing with excitement, one paid no more attention to the names that flew around from all sides than one did to the flocks of birds that streaked through the sky.

From the depths of his coat, the man took out some copper rings that were pierced with a central hole and threaded onto a rush cord.

"How much?" he asked. "How many coins? Unless you prefer some silk, an embroidered dress, for example?"

"Neither silk nor coins," the madam said. "How ashamed I would feel were I to be paid! Through the reed blinds, I heard you upbraiding this *yūjo*. I should have been more vigilant, I should have examined her, sniffed her carefully before suggesting her to you."

"You didn't suggest anything to me, *obasan*. It was I who chose this girl. I had alternatives, did I not?"

She responded with a lengthy whistling sigh that caused tiny bubbles of saliva to form and burst between her green lips.

"Certainly, sir. Personally, I was convinced that you were going to ask for Akazome's favours."

"Akazome?"

"'Akazome with cheeks so round and so pale that the moon . . .'"

"'. . . is jealous of them,'" the old man rounded off the line.

"Yes, yes, it's a song we all know: it's what they always say about courtesans who are ill, or too childlike. But I only had eyes for the other one – what's her name again?"

"Amakusa Miyuki."

"Come now," he said, becoming impatient, reaching out his hand with the coins glittering in his palm. "Take what is owed to you. And give Amakusa Miyuki the portion that is owed to her."

"The portion that is owed to her," muttered the madam, "is death. For she has offended you, you whose reputation . . ."

He drew back sharply as if to escape the halos of light from the paper lanterns that swayed on the arch above the cabin. She held him, just as sharply, by the sleeve.

"No, no, you have nothing to fear, despite the honour your custom bestows on me, I am not going to disclose your name; but knowing it, and knowing your rank, your credentials, your nobility, I maintain that the *yūjo's* offence is all the greater. And so she shall die. We shall do it quickly and properly."

She leaned over the rail, letting her right hand draw level with the bank, and snatched some long acorus leaves.

"We knot these plants and we plait them, it's quite sturdy, and we complete the lacing with a sort of tourniquet, all one has to do is place it around the neck and tighten it. Do the verdict and the method have your approval, sir?"

The old man drained his bowl of *bijinshu*, more to win time than for the pleasure of drinking. This sake is strangely unstable and volatile, he thought, a reflection of the girls who had contributed to its preparation.

"No," said Watanabe Nagusa.

"But, sir . . ."

152

"Ask her only to tear off one of her fingernails and give it to me, as the *yūjo* do when they truly wish to prove the genuineness of their feelings to the most merciful and generous of their protectors."

Towards the middle of the hour of the Rabbit, when the last of the four wealthy customers who had followed the Director of the Office of Gardens and Ponds had disembarked, the madam reckoned that the night had been sufficiently rewarding.

She steered the boat towards some landing stages built on stilts where several dark, pot-bellied boats were already docked. Once they were moored alongside a large launch that gave off an irritating smell of onions (the gunwales and the framework had been lavishly impregnated with them to discourage predators, children and animals from going near the cargo of honey it was transporting from Mount Miwa for the doctors at the Imperial Court), the madam made the *yūjo* who had participated in the nocturnal navigation parade before her. They all received a bonus, which usually consisted of a silk scarf with frayed edges.

Miyuki was the only one to whom the madam handed some copper bands.

"Don't be too thrilled at being better paid than the other girls. By way of compensation, your benefactor asks that you make a gift to him of one of your fingernails. The middle fingernail has the greatest value. It's also the one that is most painful to pull out."

"A fingernail?" said Miyuki, instinctively placing her hands behind her back.

"Giving a fingernail is a tradition. And a great privilege."

"The pain must be excruciating," Miyuki said.

"It is. That's what makes the present you are going to give so valuable. The object itself, blackened and stained with dried blood, is not particularly attractive. And, over time, it starts to smell badly."

The madam pointed out that the bands of copper that the old man had given to Miyuki represented genuine wealth. With a quick mental calculation, she concluded that these bands would enable the young widow to buy at least fifty good-sized carp.

"But what's the point of acquiring more fish than I can carry, *obasan*?"

It was a pertinent question, but the madam did not answer. All she saw was one thing: once she had replenished her stock of carp, Miyuki would not stay long at the Two Moons in the Water where her offensive smell ran the risk of putting off other customers. True, it was a smell that had upset only Watanabe, for nothing particularly disagreeable had disturbed the madam's nostrils. It was also true that the Director of the Office of Gardens and Ponds had been endowed in his youth with a particularly sensitive sense of smell; his nose had become large, blotchy and ugly with age, but if its owner was to be believed, it had still retained more developed olfactory abilities than other noses in Heian Kyō.

"I would prefer to wait until daylight before we proceed with the removal of your fingernail," said the old woman with the green lips. "A clumsy movement can occur so quickly! I never carry out this little ritual without first taking all precautionary measures, the first of which is to see clearly what one is doing so one does not risk damaging the nail. You can't imagine how fragile it is, a woman's fingernail that has been detached from its supporting flesh. Go back to the inn and get a little sleep while you wait."

She was careful not to talk about the intense throbbing pain that Miyuki would experience when the blood accumulated beneath the fingernail before it had been completely severed from its roots. It was Nyngyo who raised the subject, as the *yūjo* walked along the path that linked the landing stage to the cluster of houses.

"Above all, she must not touch your fingernail. She is sure to pull it out very, very slowly, on the pretext of not damaging the nail. And all that time, you will be screaming with pain. But I know a way of leaving this old *kusobaba* dissatisfied."

Nyngyo bent down to pick up a flat, blue pebble, which she skilfully skimmed over the surface of the water.

"Your turn," she said, selecting another pebble for Miyuki.

"I don't know how to do that."

"Really?" said Nyngyo, in amazement. "And yet I thought you lived by a river?"

"Yes, the Kusagawa. But it's much too rough to bounce pebbles across. In any case, Katsuro would not have liked his wife to waste her time skimming stones: we never stopped working, you know."

Nyngyo agreed: she did not have time to waste either. She had stopped more to allow the other *yūjo* to walk past them than to demonstrate her skill at skimming stones. Having assured herself that the *yūjo* had continued along the fern-lined path and were not turning back, she grabbed Miyuki by her arm.

"Now that we're alone," she said, skimming one last flat stone across the river, "I'll explain to you how we're going to trick the *kusobaba*. Did she give you your bonus?"

"Yes, even though I didn't give the client what he was expecting from me."

"He'll obtain his pleasure in another way. He'll imagine what you are going to endure when the madam pulls out a fingernail. It's a stomach-churning pain, and he knows it. Of course, he won't see any of it, but it will be enough for him to think about it to experience a divine pleasure. Men are like that. Not all, but many of them. They call this particular thrill 'raindrops on red poppies'. The raindrops, they're your tears, and the panic-stricken dance of your injured fingers are the bleeding poppies. But this time, there will be neither a rainstorm nor red flowers. Tell me, since you now have enough to pay Okano Mitsutada and his companions, is there anything to prevent you taking possession of the carp they caught for you?"

"If they have caught them . . ."

"Of that you can be sure, Okano Mitsutada has no equal on the Yodogawa. So, this is what you do: you remove a scale from one of these fish. Take a scale that's fairly big and as rounded as possible. I shall transform it into a beautiful fingernail, newly plucked from . . . let's see, which finger?"

"The *obasan* mentioned the middle finger," said Miyuki, holding out her hand. "Which one is that?"

No-one had ever taught her the names of the fingers. What would she have gained from such knowledge in Shimae? It was better for her to know how to identify at first glance the insects that were harmful and the weeds in the rice fields.

"I'm also going to apply make-up to your finger," Nyngyo

said. "We shall need a little blood – not yours, don't worry – it will be enough for us to crush a few *mushi** and make a sort of bluish green pulp, I shall add a drop of ink to darken it, we'll smear the top of your finger with it, and that will be that."

For good measure, the *yūjo* rubbed Miyuki's finger with a tuft of hairs taken from a weasel's lair. The musk that impregnated the rotting prey and the nests of these rodents was enough to give Miyuki's middle finger the fetid smell that was a typical feature of digits that had had a nail removed.

Before the dawn glided over the still, night-filled waters of the Yodogawa, Miyuki presented the old *kusobaba* with her supposedly uprooted fingernail. Then, her cheeks bathed in perfectly imitated tears of suffering, thanks to a few streaks of sesame oil, she turned away, stumbling as she did so, supported by Nyngyo, who was doing her best not to giggle.

The Inn of the Two Moons in the Water was vibrating with the gentle snoring of the young *yūjo* as Nyngyo, laughing silently, forced open the drawers of the chest where the madam kept her most beautiful clothes. She gathered up an armful of outfits that the old woman would never wear again, and whose existence she had probably forgotten: she thereby laid claim to a dress coat that was the colour of red plums, to another that was the colour of blueberries, to a third that was the colour of a mauve aster, and, for the fourth, the one that would be worn closest to her body, she chose a wine-coloured silk garment.

She was about to close the chest of drawers when she noticed

---

* Old name for insects.

157

Miyuki staring at a long white kimono. It was lying at the bottom of the drawer, discarded rather than folded, but it had such gracefulness about it that one might have mistaken it for the warm, soft body of a girl who had died moments earlier.

"Not that one," Nyngyo whispered. "We can't steal that from her: it's what she will wear on the day of her funeral. She showed it to us, holding it by the collar, making it quiver and move limply as though it were a real person, a sort of former lover returned from the depths of her memory. We tried to find out more, but apparently she's incapable of remembering the name of this lover; no matter, she assigned another patronymic to him, and that's quite enough, I suppose, to be burned on a funeral pyre."

In order to carry all these clothes that Nyngyo had stolen for her more conveniently, Miyuki put them on, one over the other.

"That's what the noble ladies at Court do," the *yūjo* said approvingly. "They can pile on as many as fifteen. The colours are superimposed, they blend with each other until one single shade can be seen, a shade that the lady must be the only one to wear and that . . ."

Nyngyo suddenly stopped.

"How beautiful you are!" she exclaimed.

The *yūjo* was drowning in love for Miyuki. Miyuki, for her part, beneath all these layers of silk, was drowning in sweat. The two drowning women embraced one another and exchanged a long and heartfelt farewell kiss.

When she had set out from Shimae, Miyuki had resolved to keep a faithful record of her adventures. She had no doubt that Katsuro would listen with interest to her account of the journey, even if he mocked her gently for her slow pace. "Two full days to go from Hongu to Tsugizakura? No, I don't believe it! Did you meet a witch who transformed you into a snail, or something? When I did the same journey myself, and with the disadvantage of leaving before dawn and having to walk through driving rain, I set off at the hour of the Rabbit and I reached Tsugizakura at the hour of the Horse . . ."

But all of a sudden it became obvious to her that Katsuro was dead and that she would never hear his voice again.

She had by then lost all sense of time. She had given up counting her small footsteps and her long strides, stopped counting the stones that marked out the distances, ceased adding up the alternating days and nights. Not bothering anymore about time – oh! not at all – but solely concerning herself with the health of her carp, with their well-being and their brightness (the fish that Okano Mitsutada had provided were almost as fine as Katsuro's and visibly more alert, although it was true that they had not had to endure the confinement of the baskets, nor the putrefying stagnant waters for so long), she therefore arrived within sight of Rashōmon, the monumental gate at the southern entrance to the Imperial City, without the slightest idea of the time she had spent walking. In any case, judging by the filth that covered her and the slime that had spattered her, it must have been a long journey.

THE DIRECTOR OF THE Office of Gardens and Ponds left the Imperial Palace through the Kenshunmon, the gate allocated to ministers and senior officials.

The fact that this gate was reserved for dignitaries did not prevent a crowd of artisans, hawkers, tattered stallholders and puppeteers from using it, without a thought for the fact that their social rank did not allow them to associate with the authorities who had the privilege of passing beneath its gabled roof. It was of little consequence, in any case, since the penalty they incurred was limited to two or three blows with a stick on the shoulders, intended more to make the aforementioned shoulders give a symbolic flinch than to really thrash their owner.

The jostling, the noisy promiscuity and, above all, the indiscipline of ordinary people struck Watanabe Nagusa as one of the most loathsome aspects of the decadence that consumed the empire: the central administration had gradually allowed itself to be stripped of its most important privileges to the benefit of the large landowners, chief among them the Fujiwara clan who, by cleverly marrying their daughters, granddaughters or nieces to imperial princes, had succeeded in taking full control of the

160

reins of power. Depleted by a dynasty that took what it needed to ensure its own growth, the essence of the empire was draining away rather like a crab that sheds its shell, but then, having rid itself of its small carapace, realises that it has not produced a replacement exoskeleton and is thus condemned to such sluggishness that its days become numbered.

He had thought it miraculous, the number of girls, mostly pretty to be sure, that the Fujiwaras had, over the centuries, been able to offer as wives for the young emperors who had inherited the throne – so many unions that they were able to rule flawlessly over the empire without having to seize power themselves.

But now the spring seemed to have run dry. After the most constant, the most immutable of blooms, the cherry tree was bare: the Fujiwara clan had not a single young lady to offer to the next ruler.

After the storms that had raged over recent days, the sky had become clear and calm. Watanabe walked down the Avenue of the Red Bird in the direction of the Sixth Bridge.

He had put on his ceremonial *eboshi*,* powdered and made up his face, and he wore a voluptuous scent.

Some children were squatting on the ground and playing at applying willow leaves above their eyes to make them look like eyebrows. They were leaves that had recently fallen, probably blown off by gusts of wind, and their colours ranged from faded green to pale bronze by way of indeterminate gold – a gold that,

---

* A black headpiece made of lacquered gauze in the shape of a top hat.

depending on whether you turned it towards the sun or away, was either the yellow of ripe fruit or red like a plum. To stick on their false eyebrows, the children coated the thin oblong leaves with their saliva, made sticky by the sweetmeats they had been gorging on – for it was a feast day and the air smelled of sugar and warm rice.

Watanabe promised himself that one day he would paint his own eyebrows in green jade.

Green jade at his age? It would probably make him look ridiculous, but anything was better than this slow and irreversible fading that was the destiny of old men. He had seen too many prominent people reach a conclusion of their careers that did not coincide with the conclusion of their lives and had seen them sink beneath the Court's indifference as though they stood on shifting sands. One evening they were there, violet shadows behind a bamboo blind, silhouettes that the moon projected onto a screen, and the next day they had disappeared, the blind quivering blankly in the morning breeze, and the screen, its panels folded, lying on the ground against a wall. This was why Watanabe had vowed that he would grasp, even provoke, all possible opportunities to show himself off, to remind people who he was, and to make his existence known. Judging by the latest gossip that had unsettled the Imperial Palace, he reckoned that if he daubed himself with inexplicable and absurd green jade eyebrows, people would talk about him for at least one moon.

He paused in the middle of the half-moon bridge where he had arranged to meet Kusakabe Atsuhito, his assistant, who had the elegance of a dancer and who unsettled many of the employees of the Office of Gardens and Ponds (or rather, Watanabe was keen to convince himself that he was not the only one to be thus affected) with his way of puckering his lips to imitate the fleshy mouth of the carp.

Ever since he had taken on this young assistant, Watanabe Nagusa had scrutinised him for defects. Physical ones preferably. Not out of petty-mindedness or jealousy, but because he liked nothing so much as to expose the slight impurities that affected all kinds of beauty, be it the charm of a dawn morning or that of a young person. The imperfection, which he was often the only one to detect, left a kind of subtle, imperceptible veil, a fleeting mist, over the landscape or the young person, just as the faint chips in an earthenware bowl reveal the vulnerability of its glaze and make the beverage it contains all the more precious.

If Kusakabe Atsuhito was not just any assistant, the Rokujo, at the top of Sixth Avenue, was not just any bridge either: the banks of the narrow canal it spanned had once been the official location for carrying out the death penalty. For some two hundred years, however, the executioner's sword had not swung once, so to speak, unless it was to cleave sheaves of straw for training purposes. The influence of Buddhism was increasing, along with its teaching that putting a person to death was one of the sins of which it was hardest to purify oneself. Certain emperors had taken the respect for life so far as to prohibit the consumption of beef, horsemeat, poultry, dog or monkey between April and September. But one could always fall back on wild boar, and the peasants took full advantage of it: they simply renamed it *yamanokujira* ("mountain whale"), and the wild boar escaped imperial protection.

Neglected by the justice system and given over to knotweed burdock and sage, the area beneath the bridge had become the refectory and dormitory of the homeless, who were fond of this place and the shelter it provided from prevailing winds and from rain or snow showers.

To forget the irritation prompted by Kusakabe's slight lateness, the Director of the Office of Gardens and Ponds leaned over the red-painted parapet, keeping a hand on his *eboshi*, which had a tendency to slide over his oiled hair. He observed the poor, who bustled and shuffled about the narrow banks for no apparent reason. A swarm of mayflies, a cluster of scatterbrained midges, thought Watanabe, wondering whether he might not be inspired to compose some *tanka** or other as a way of passing the time as he waited for Kusakabe; the wretchedness of other people did not bother him in the slightest, he contented himself with affording them, from the top of the Rokujo bridge, the same degree of distracted attention he paid to the games the ducks played on the Kamogawa.

Inspired by the sound of the water running over the stones scattered on the bottom of the canal, Director Watanabe devised some clumsy verses in which the river, although confined by the rigidity of the banks, retained sufficient liberty to wriggle about lisping the words *yoroshiku onegaishimasu, yoroshiku onegaishimasu*, delighted to meet you, enchanted to make your acquaintance . . .

---

* Ancestors of haiku, in the Japan of the Heian period the poems known as *tanka* constituted one of the highest forms of literary expression, to the point where only members of the imperial court were allowed to write them; anyone of a lower rank caught composing a *tanka* was subject to the death penalty.

◎ ◎ ◎

Several days had passed since Watanabe had asked his assistant to look for a place where the Office of Gardens and Ponds could house the widow from Shimae, the latter being obliged to remain in the Imperial City until it was certain that her fish would acclimatise to the ornamental pools of the temples. Although the majority of the carp accepted their new conditions in the sacred ponds without any problem, some of them, after the fresh waters of the river where they had been caught, became disturbed by the stagnation and cloudiness of the temple ponds of Heian Kyō. You would see them rubbing themselves against the banks, patches of red or even lesions resembling spots of candle wax appearing on their sides or their bellies, after which their skin would flake off and they would eventually die. This had never happened with the carp supplied by the fisherman Katsuro, but who could foresee what would become of those that his widow would bring – if she ever managed to reach Heian Kyō?

This morning, at last, Kusakabe had announced that he had found a fairly suitable place to accommodate Amakusa Miyuki.

"To the west of the city, Watanabe-*sensei*, in the quarter that even the impoverished escape as soon as they can, exasperated as they are by the river flooding. Flooding that will not fail to occur again this year if the beginning of winter is as rainy as it has been in late autumn. But do you think, *sensei*, that the carp fisherman's widow would take offence at a little mud and water?"

Watanabe was careful not to reply. The last time he had chanced a prediction of a woman's behaviour – in this case, no less a woman than Nakatomi Shungetsu, one of the Empress's

165

ladies-in-waiting – he had failed pitifully. It had happened during the night of the Monkey, a night when it is advised that one should not succumb to sleep on any account lest worms slither into your sleeping body and steal your most shameful secrets. What the worms did with these secrets once they had them, how they benefited from them, no-one had the least idea; it was unpleasant enough to know that you had been robbed of thoughts you wished to keep buried.

Watanabe had wagered a carriage and a pair of white oxen that Nakatomi Shungetsu was sufficiently devoted to the Empress to remain awake at her mistress's feet, ready to crush ruthlessly the merest worm, caterpillar, larva, maggot, or even snake that showed any sign of wriggling its way in Her Majesty's direction. But, dashing Watanabe's hopes, Lady Nakatomi had fallen asleep, and had even allowed herself to snore gently. This proved contagious, and the Empress had fallen asleep herself. At dawn, two emissaries of the man who had bet against the Director of the Office of Gardens and Ponds had come in search of the latter to take possession of his richly decorated vehicle, with its four blinds, its interior curtains and the two white oxen.

"Take me to see this place where you plan to house the fisherman's widow. It's to the west, you say?"

"Yes, *sensei*, near the Dantenmon gate, on the hallowed domain of the Saiji."

Of the vast sanctuary where, up until the fire of 990 that had largely destroyed it, the Saiji – the Temple of the West – once stood, only a five-storey pagoda remained. The rest of the site was merely an array of charred and dilapidated buildings scattered over wasteland that was given over to ruderal plants, foxes and thieves. The ground appeared to have been ravaged, destroyed by an extremely violent fire that had left a sort of dark crust like the residue of a lava flow.

Their fences broken, their roofs collapsed, their walls colonised by mosses that had proliferated with the repeated flooding, the former shops and the monks' quarters exuded a stench of sodden undergrowth and cinders.

Kusakabe Atsuhito had located a former *kyōzō* there, a modest utility pavilion used for the storage of sutra and books relating to the history of the temple, which had emerged almost unscathed from the fire. Not a single scroll remained inside, obviously, but the shelves blackened by the flames were still in place. Some swallows had appropriated them for their nests.

Among the advantages that this house offered was its proximity to the Western market. The widow would always find something to pick up there. And as long as she knew how to coax them, the few monks who kept the sanctuary going would probably provide her with a little of the rice that the pilgrims left as an offering to Buddha.

"I therefore think that this woman's stay will cost the Office practically nothing, neither for her food nor her accommodation," Watanabe said. "Thank you, it's much appreciated."

The Director's satisfaction arose mainly from the fact that he could pay his assistant a justifiable compliment, one that displayed none of the fawning that, in Watanabe's opinion, poisoned the language of all those who flitted about behind the screens and partitions of the Imperial Palace. For, when praise was given with the sole aim of flattering, when it was always passed on with the same grandiloquence, when, in short, the praise was self-perpetuated, it became impoverished, it lost its capacity to surprise, to stimulate and to expand, it was no more than a background noise like that of the morning rain on the roofs.

AFTER SHE HAD PASSED through the recently whitewashed walls and vermilion pillars of Rashōmon, Miyuki turned into the Avenue of the Red Bird.

Although not very marked, the difference in level between the northern gate, where the Emperor's residence stood, and the southern gate, through which she had entered the city, gave an almost bird's eye view of the layout of the city. It resembled a huge draughtboard made up of even squares whose borders were indicated by clay walls, the yellow ochre colour of which was the third dominant colour of Heian Kyō, after white and red – or, more precisely, the various reds, which ranged from rosy incarnadine to the deepest of purples.

What first struck Miyuki was not so much the size of the Imperial City as the precise manner of its construction, so far removed from the chaotic way that the people of Shimae had built their village, the houses scattered about according to people's whims or their social position.

Miyuki thought to herself that she could have lived a long life in Heian Kyō without ever coming across the same person twice as she walked along these streets that cut across each other at right angles.

Interspersed here and there by roofs with curved edges, the perspective gave her the illusion of an endless city, and this city was the most beautiful thing that Miyuki had ever contemplated, with the exception, of course, of Katsuro's body on nights when, after tending his fish, he would clamber out from the carp pool, naked and gleaming, and shake himself, happily throwing up a spray of water droplets in the direction of the moon as though he were seeding the sky, after which, still naked, his penis shining with water and mucus, he would clasp his wife, squeeze her until she cried out, and make love to her standing up. That was truly the most beautiful thing Miyuki remembered having seen, but immediately after the nakedness of Katsuro as he was making love came the sight of Heian Kyō, spread out and glowing in the mellow light of the hour of the Monkey.[*]

Carefully protecting her yoke from the jostling of the crowd, Miyuki walked along the middle of the avenue, amid the sweet stench of dung and manure left by the cart-pulling cattle and the cavalry.

Thanks to the stories that Katsuro had told her about his trips, she knew how to find the Office of Gardens and Ponds, she had a fairly accurate idea of its location within the bounds of the Imperial Palace, and of what it looked like, and she knew the number of steps that she had to climb before she would be received by Director Watanabe and would at last be able to free herself of the baskets that cut into her shoulders.

Perhaps this senior official to whom Katsuro had shown so much deference (he had lowered his gaze and voice whenever

---

[*] From three o'clock to five o'clock in the afternoon.

he mentioned Watanabe Nagusa) would agree to take her to the sacred ponds before nightfall, so that she could dip her hand in and lick it to assess the sapidity of the water – a sweet, slightly alliaceous taste, with an after-note of celery and mushroom provided by certain herbs that settled in the silt at the bottom; at least, that was what the fisherman asserted, and he never failed to taste the water where he was going to release his fish to be sure that they would be happy there.

It was at that moment that a sort of tremor was felt on the Avenue of the Red Bird, which lay before Miyuki: the shadows of passers-by and ox carts that paraded along it became blurred and grew dim, and they then disappeared behind what appeared to be a curtain of mist that had descended without warning.

From behind this curtain, cries could be heard with hurried footsteps and creaking sounds.

What Miyuki had taken for mist was nothing of the sort: it was smoke which, in the absence of any wind, fanned out in extended trapeze-like shapes that resembled the branches of dogwood trees.

A fire had broken out in the dwelling of a *bugaku**** dancer, Mutobe Takeyoshi. The poor man was seen rushing outside, his face hidden behind his *karura*† mask, the terrifying bird-man, his burning clothes like immense, roaring, red plumes.

Even in his agony, he preserved the perfect grace that had made him one of the masters of *bugaku*. He convulsed in pain

---

* A traditional dance, slow, majestic, subtle and complex in the extreme, the prerogative of the elite of the imperial court.

† The divine bird of mythology.

171

with an instinctive sensuality, almost as if he were still dancing, and the explosions from the burning houses sustained his performance like percussion drums, the six-stringed *koto** or the mouth organ.

The smouldering sleeves of Mutobe Takeyoshi's kimono were like large half-charred trees swaying in the wind before they collapsed in a spray of sparks.

No-one came to his aid, but, in any case, it would have served no purpose for his movements were already slowing, his knees were buckling, and he could no longer stand.

He fell to the ground in a heap. Sated, the flames settled, wreathing his face in a last purple halo that was kept alight by his burning hair. He himself was totally blackened.

In the course of his frenzied dance, Mutobe had transmitted the flames that were devouring him to some of the houses, which, in turn, caught fire. Sixteen buildings were destroyed in this way, and how many lives! Most of the victims were asphyxiated by the smoke and the fumes, but it was recorded that others burned to death in the heart of the blaze.

When the roaring of the fire had ceased, a swarm of cicadas unleashed a deafening din.

With her hand over her nose and her mouth, Miyuki walked through the curtain of smoke.

When she reached the rectangular wall that surrounded the Emperor's residence and the principal government buildings, including what remained of the Office of Gardens and Ponds,

---

* A traditional instrument. A long cithara with plucked strings.

Miyuki was obliged to wait for a long time among the crowds of people who were hurrying to the Taikenmon, the Gate of the Welcome of the Wise Men, the only entry to be supervised by guards, and therefore an obligatory one for visitors who had never yet been granted admittance to the twists and turns of the Grand Palace – the riffraff, the crooks and the ghosts above all, who, it was said, swarmed into the Palace after sunset, clearly preferring to weave their way through entrances that were poorly and little supervised.

The fire that Miyuki had just witnessed was the subject of every conversation. One day soon, which according to the soothsayers was more likely to be a night, it would be the entire city that would go up in flames; and people were already discussing the possible places where, on the advice of the geomancers, the Emperor could establish his new capital.

Watanabe and his assistant Kusakabe had also been stopped between Fifth Avenue and Konoemikado Avenue by the blaze caused by the dancer on fire.

Overcome by the smoke, the Director of the Office of Gardens and Ponds felt very close to fainting, but, rather than collapsing, he chose to huddle against Kusakabe's sturdy chest instead. He would certainly have derived some pleasure from this had he not started coughing until he was breathless. Each new fit made him double up, forcing him away from the ideal refuge he had found in the arms of his assistant.

"But you're coughing blood, Watanabe-*sensei*!" Kusakabe exclaimed in alarm, as he caught sight of the red stain that was spreading over the sleeve of his tunic. "Let us postpone our visit until later. In any case, the widow from Shimae has not arrived. We know that she has set off, but, since then, none of our clerks responsible for overseeing travellers has mentioned that she has passed by."

"Really?" Watanabe said, as he did his best to control his cough and hide his sleeve behind his back. "Have they questioned the *omisan* from the Hut of Just Retribution – a certain Akiyoshi Sadako, I believe?"

Although Kusakabe Atsuhito knew that Director Watanabe was blessed with an exceptional memory, he was always amazed when Watanabe gave further evidence of it. It was as fascinating as watching an acrobat nonchalantly perform a balancing act that one would have thought impossible.

"I sent messengers to all the inns between Shimae and Heian Kyō, *sensei*. That was how I discovered that the Hut of Just Retribution was no more than a ruin after it was pillaged by pirates from the Inland Sea, and then set alight by the *bushi* sent to defend it."

"What is happening to us?" said Watanabe in a low voice.

"What do you mean, *sensei*?"

"Nothing," the Director said. "Nothing in particular. But all the same, don't you find the way things are nowadays make no sense? You're young, Atsuhito, so much younger than me, you don't remember the time when an incident such as the one you have just described would have been unthinkable: *bushi*, gentlemen warriors summoned to protect an inn, and who come and plunder it in a worse way than those who attacked it in the first place, now that's something that surpasses understanding."

"As for the other inns," Kusakabe interrupted, apparently

impervious to his director's distress, "they have received no-one who matches the description of the fisherman's widow."

Leaving Watanabe sitting on a boundary stone and soothing his cough with the help of the poppy seeds he always carried, Kusakabe set off to search for a vehicle that would enable his master to continue his journey more comfortably. But everything that passed was occupied as the inhabitants of Heian Kyō fled the fire they feared might spread, even though it was now under control. The city had experienced too many fires that were supposed to be out, only for a single puff of wind to revive them in all their fury.

Watanabe and Kusakabe eventually found room in an impressive sedan chair constructed of bamboo and borne along by eight barefooted men. This long oblong box was already occupied by two women who were hastily trying to conceal their faces behind the sleeves of their kimonos, wailing that they had committed an offence against standards of morality by allowing men to enter the sedan without knowledge of their identity and, more especially, their intentions.

"Peace be with you," Kusakabe said to them (having exhausted himself with the effort of hoisting Watanabe up and settling him in the chair, he had no desire to reverse the operation). "Your act of goodwill towards us will count in your favour later on, most certainly! The Buddha of the Pure Earth keeps a record of the least of our actions. Even what we believe to be our most secret thoughts, Amitabha unearths them, probes them, analyses and ponders them."

The propensity of certain women not to consider the consequences of their actions fascinated the official from the Office of Gardens and Ponds. With a light brush that barely skimmed the paper, he composed a number of *tanka* that condemned the casual attitude of such girls. Being a provident man himself, he knew that in due course he would recite these verses to young ladies he wished to seduce, and so the frivolous heroines of his poems were always depicted as butterflies, rather than women. Let those who could understand do so. In fact, most young people did not take long to decipher the metaphor; and to prove it, they would form their lips into a trumpet-like shape that they pressed all over Kusakabe's face, pretending to gather nectar from every orifice.

"It was I who ordered the bearers to stop, I who beckoned you to come closer, I who invited you to take a seat," the older of the two women said, nodding. "Whether it's a fire, a flood or an earth tremor, disasters always affect me in the same way: with every one of them, I have an irresistible desire to help my neighbour. Do you remember the last earthquake? I was at the Rokkaku temple and there, set down in the middle of the path, was a magnificently decorated palanquin that the bearers had leaned against the trees bordering the path. Three of them were asleep, the five others were massaging their legs. The palanquin being empty, I supposed that the occupant had got off to go and pray in the temple. It was then that the ground began to shake. And, in a flash, the lake that adjoined the temple rose up like the sea on a stormy day. The bearers of the palanquin took fright and fled – what a thoughtless attitude, don't you think? When the earth begins to tremble beneath your feet, you know that it will shake you no matter where you go. In any case, I did not move. I embraced the trunk of a large tree, a tree that was too solid to be uprooted, and I waited for everything to calm down. It was the right thing to do! After a few seconds, I saw a beautiful creature appear, a very young boy who was no more than ten or eleven years old. He wore extremely elegant clothing, made up of textures and especially colours that I had never seen before. I assumed that these were colours reserved for His Majesty, and that this remarkable child must therefore be our new Emperor. But even though his clothing indicated a rank of the highest order, the heart that beat in his chest was no more than a pitiful organ shrivelled by fear: the young prince was actually running towards the palanquin screaming in the way that only children and wounded horses can."

Watanabe noticed that the elderly woman paced her delivery to keep time with the beat of the naked feet of the bearers as they struck the ground. She did this so naturally he concluded that she must have been using this means of transport for a long time, and regularly too, for the hammering of the feet had become as familiar to her as her own heartbeat.

"It could not have been His Majesty," Kusakabe said. "The Emperor is young, certainly, but he's no longer a child."

He looked at the old lady. Her face was not very lined and the harmonious colours of her five layers of dresses – autumn leaf, plum, malachite, bronze and carmine – emphasised the elegant pallor of her complexion, although a sagging of the temples, cheekbones and jaws betrayed her advancing age. The earthquakes and the Emperor of whom she spoke might perhaps have dated from a former reign, he thought.

The old lady was on the point of responding, but Kusakabe had already turned towards Watanabe.

"What do you think, *sensei*? Since it concerns the Emperor himself, I would not wish to reply incorrectly."

But the Director was no longer listening. As he aged, he felt more and more indifferent towards subjects that did not directly concern him. Ideas that might have seemed of the utmost importance to him in his youth, so much so that he would have risked his life to defend them, now struck him as dull and not worthy of his support, even if it was just by a vague raising of his eyebrows.

What did it matter if the noble lady who had taken them onto her sedan chair, and thanks to whom they were now crossing the animated city as though on a feather, should confuse the Emperor with a frightened little boy? One would have to be Kusakabe Atsuhito and not yet seventeen years old to be alarmed by such confusion. He, Watanabe, would be dead before long, he felt as though his life would soon be blown away like a candle that flickers and is extinguished because, in the depths of the Palace, a servant wishing to gaze at the full moon has raised a blind and caused a stream of sharp and freezing air to ripple through the corridors, sweeping away the little flame.

But who would really care? What consequences would the death of Watanabe Nagusa have for Japan? Come now, none at all! All things considered, it would be the ideal pretext for closing down the Office of Gardens and Ponds altogether.

Watanabe yearned for just one thing: that the weather should be fine on the day of his death. For, unlike proud warlords who are unable to countenance leaving this world without taking their henchmen with them, it gave him pleasure to know that life would go on without him. After one last walk (and if his legs refused to carry him, he would have no difficulty, if he searched his memories, in remembering some ideal stroll), he would leave this life as you leave a garden, a temple or a library, without disrupting the quiet, normal course of things, so that scarcely anyone notices your disappearance, which should make no more noise than an insect falling from a blade of grass. He hoped that the Western market, which the carriage was passing at that moment, would continue to echo with the sound of the bamboo drums that the shopkeepers were now beating frantically to remind customers that the fire had dispersed like a flight of sparrows.

He prayed, therefore, that the day of his death should be a sunny one, with birds playing in the damp half-light of a coppice – birds do not play, of course, they don't have time, they have their survival to ensure, but Watanabe expected that he would still have sufficient imagination at the moment of his death to picture a flock of blue flycatchers chasing one another through the bamboo trees, with their slow and melancholy cry, a perfect cry to accompany the death of the last Director of the Office of Gardens and Ponds.

The eight bearers slowed their pace.

"I think you have arrived," the old lady said, as she pointed to the five-storey pagoda that overlooked the remains of Saiji.

Drawing up one of the side blinds, she tapped on the shoulders of one of her bearers several times. The man squatted down, the seven others did likewise, and the chair was lowered to the ground.

The Director and his assistant made their way into the *kyōzō*, disturbing some enormous crows that flew off towards a clump of camphor trees, issuing terrible cries as they went.

Before they had suffered several fires, the walls of the little building had been decorated with screens representing landscapes of gentle hills planted with round trees beneath gleaming sunshine. Damaged by the fire, and still more by the water that extinguished the flames, they had been put away and were leaning against a wall in the darkest part of the temple. Then, due to a phenomenon that had as much to do with the chemistry of the pigments as with the secret life of the works themselves, their colours had dimmed and darkened of their own accord to be replaced by a sort of brownish twilight shade that, rather like mildew, had eventually infected all the paintings.

The rest of the pavilion was scarcely more attractive: its dilapidated roof let the rain in and the rush blinds were mottled with large patches of mould.

In the midst of this debris stood Miyuki, motionless and very straight.

The uprightness of her position and the perfectly horizontal rod across her shoulders made her look like a crucified woman. Or a tree in winter, a spindly tree stretching out its branches in the pale sunshine. Or a seabird drying its wings that were still damp after a night of fishing.

She was the first to bow, deeply, and she remained in that position for a long time.

When she saw Watanabe enter, she had immediately recognised him as her client from the Yodogawa River, the elderly man who had informed her that she gave off an unusual smell – a simple remark, he had not really reprimanded her, it was just an observation, and he had paid her more generously than the other *yūjo*, had even affirmed his interest by asking her to make him a gift of her torn-out fingernail.

As Miyuki bowed as low as her burden would allow, her nose drew closer to her belly and, it seemed to her that an unusual scent did indeed rise from this lower part of her body. It was a warm, fruity smell, with a slight acidity that reminded her a little of the astringency of the flesh of the kaki.

As she waited to straighten up again, further emanations grafted themselves onto the original fragrance of persimmon. Miyuki would have loved to identify them, to remind herself where and in what circumstances these scents had clung to her in the manner of burdock moth, but their aromas blended too quickly with each other.

She tried to recall how Katsuro had smelled when he returned from Heian Kyō. The scent lurked in her memory, but, like everything else concerning her husband, it had become a hazy and fragile thing that she found hard to put a name to.

In actual fact, Katsuro's reappearances smelled of damp moss, sake, pine resin, straw and soya, clothes that reeked of sweat and urine, and something else that could only be described as an excessive smell, a crude smell, a vulgar smell, rather than by reference to material things.

After several days, these occasional whiffs disappeared, and Katsuro smelled, once more, of good Katsuro, that is to say of the river, of warm rice, flowers, wood, rope and clay.

"Who are you?" Kusakabe said.

"I am Amakusa Miyuki, from the village of Shimae. Katsuro,

the fisherman Katsuro, the most skilled carp fisherman in the province of Ise, was my husband. I am now taking his place. Not to fish for carp, but to choose from among those he had caught before his death, to comfort the fish, to load them into these baskets" – she nodded alternately to the one on the right and that on the left – "and then to walk for many days through the forests, the mountains and the cold rains, until I reach the Imperial City and deliver these carp to the Director of the Office of Gardens and Ponds. His name is Watanabe, Watanabe-*san*."

"Watanabe-*sensei*," Kusakabe corrected her.

"Watanabe-*sensei*," Miyuki said as she bent even lower. "I went to the Office that he oversees, but he was not there. So I was told to come here and wait. And that Watanabe-*sensei* would know how to find us, my carp and me."

Standing back slightly, Watanabe had not recognised her as the prostitute whose services he had engaged on the boat on the Yodogawa. It is true that, perturbed by the various aromas she had emitted that night, he had not examined her features. In any case, did not *yūjo* all have the same chalky white faces, the same gaze of endless black silk, the same narrow nose with pinched nostrils, and, above all, the same lips that were too scarlet, too dry and too hot, whereas Watanabe liked them pink, moist and cool?

"I can probably find you a *yūjo* with wet lips," the madam of the Two Moons in the Water had told him. "That type of mouth is fairly common among maidservants. But I urge you to consider the fact that, if their mouths are wet, it is because of an excess of saliva. I was worried that that might be repugnant to you."

Watanabe had not replied, pretending to follow the jerky flight of a moth, his hand raised, ready to crush it. The lack of understanding that certain traders had of their customers never failed to baffle him.

"You are Amakusa Miyuki, are you not? As for me," he went on, without waiting for the obvious reply (what other normally constituted young woman would stand erect as a T in this deserted room, with a heavy weight across her shoulders?), "I am Watanabe Nagusa, an official of the upper sixth rank major, Director of the former Office of Gardens and Ponds which is now under the authority of the Office of the Emperor's Table."

"The Emperor's Table!" Miyuki cried, recoiling so suddenly that she jolted her baskets; a little water escaped and fell like raindrops on the floorboards. "Oh, but I have not made this long journey to supply the Imperial Table! The carp that cost my dear Katsuro his life are for the temple ponds, for the deities, not for boiling and dismembering and serving at His Majesty's table."

Unlike the ladies of the Court, Miyuki did not paint false eyebrows higher up on her forehead, hers were in the place that Nature had ordained, and they were eyebrows made up of genuine black, gleaming hairs that, in her moment of upset, she raised in such a way that Watanabe had to conceal a laugh behind his hand.

"Although I have no need to justify myself before you," he said, "I only mentioned the Office of the Table in regard to my own Office. To clarify the level of hierarchy between the two. You would not understand, of course – does the word 'hierarchy' have any meaning for you?"

"Not really, sir," Miyuki said.

And yet she remembered having been happy with Katsuro

without ever having needed to know the meaning of the word "hierarchy".

Then, even though she was aware that she might be thought insolent, she looked the senior official straight in the eyes. There was no doubt, this was indeed the old man who had come aboard the boat belonging to the *kusobaba* with the green lips and who had criticised Miyuki for giving off a disturbing smell. But he did not appear to remember. Or else, he recalled only too well his disappointment at not having been able to make love with her, but, because he was a powerful man in the empire and she a peasant who was a nobody, a wisp of rice straw floating on the breeze, he was trying to show her how, in spite of everything, he knew how to be magnanimous.

Having allowed Miyuki to scrutinise him from head to foot, the Director of the Office of Gardens and Ponds stepped forward as many paces as she had moved back.

It was then, the second time that he approached her, that he breathed in her aroma. It was not a single, isolated smell, but a long series of scents, like a ribbon that floats and coils in on itself. And in his memory, the image returned to him of the boat drifting through the night on the Yodogawa, and of this woman who had given up her body to him, a body that he had not wanted.

He looked at her mouth, at Miyuki's lips, and, without his being aware of it, his left wrist began to slide beneath the sleeve of his plum-coloured *hō*.*

"Is this where the Office chose to accommodate you?"

"Sir, you should know better than me . . ."

---

* A long robe with very wide sleeves, closed at the neck and tightened at the waist with a belt.

"It's here, yes," Kusakabe said briskly. "This room is not very welcoming, I admit, but that is because the *kyōzō* has been deconsecrated due to the Kamogawa flooding. The doors have rotted and have not been replaced. As you can see, *sensei*, the animals from the nearby forest have made their home here. But there is another room upstairs, just as big and far more sanitary. The animals do not go up there."

Watanabe was not listening. His gaze slid from Kusakabe's mouth to Miyuki's. Bygone desire, recent desire, both unsatisfied, and both would probably remain in the realm of fantasy. But it was not unpleasant to dream of impossible things, these focused reveries being a useful replacement for the muddled ideas that one could not make head nor tail of.

"Up there," Kusakabe continued, pointing to the ceiling, "the walls are sound: the level of the river never rose as high as that, of course! Only the swallows, occasionally. They loved to build their nests on the shelves where the monks stored their papers. But I have had the floor swept and I have removed what remained of the nests. If you would like to see . . ."

"Let her show us her fish first," Watanabe said, in a voice that had become slightly hoarse.

With a wave of her hand, Miyuki encouraged him to come closer. He took one hesitant step forward, then a second, then he came to a complete stop.

"It's strange."

"What is strange, sir?"

"I'm not sure," muttered Watanabe.

Something invisible swathed the fisherman's widow, something followed the contours of her body, embraced both the well-rounded and the slender parts, cloaking her like a second layer of flesh, but invisible, inaudible, untouchable. This sort of aura, a perfect ethereal replica of Miyuki, a nuanced body replacing the actual body, only revealed itself to someone with as well-practised and keen a sense of smell as the Director of the Office of Gardens and Ponds.

And then Watanabe remembered the circumstances in which he had already encountered this young woman's scent.

He shook his head as if to free himself from the tangles of a spider's web.

"Can you smell it?" he whispered to his assistant.

Kusakabe looked around him. The walls bore traces of damp, patches of rot, with piles of feathers and small bones scattered here and there. The remains of a fox had decomposed at the foot of what had once been an impressive eight-sided rotating book-case where the monks had kept the sutras. It was obvious that none of this could give off a pleasant smell.

But was the smell that came from Miyuki a pleasant one?

"Do I smell what, *sensei*?"

"The egg. At least, that's what it seems to me."

"The yolk or the white?"

Kusakabe put the question as though Watanabe's reply could change the face of the earth. And Watanabe started to ponder as though he, too, attached extreme importance to his answer.

"The egg that you tap on the side of a bowl, the shell cracks, you separate the yolk from the white, normally you should not be able to smell either the one or the other, and yet you can, the white especially."

"What would you say this smell reminds you of, *sensei*?"

186

The question could seem pointless to many people, but Kusa-kabe Atsuhito never let an opportunity to educate himself pass by. The son of a simple shopkeeper, he had had the privilege, from a very young age, of being introduced to writing and arith-metic by a great-uncle who, having chosen to join a religious order, had withdrawn to a monastery in the mountains where he was in charge of an extensive collection of learned books. Kusa-kabe had spent almost his entire adolescence in this remote mon-astery, benefiting from the violent snow storms that isolated him from the rest of the world so that he was able to absorb invaluable works that were mainly used for the education of samurai.

"This smell," Watanabe said, "reminds me of overwashed, overheated, overcooked rice, and of a silk dress that a careless maidservant has left out in the rain, which is now permanently ruined, and, more than anything else, it reminds me of sickness, of tainted beauty, and also of dying birds – but all of these are rather similar, are they not?"

"Oh well, a dying bird is nothing much," said Kusakabe, who particularly enjoyed hunting and therefore made great sacrifices to maintain an aviary of falcons whose residents, poorly cared for and meagrely fed, died in quick succession.

"Do you think so, Atsuhito? Myself, I believe there is noth-ing that gives a better idea of disillusionment than a bird with cold, stiff wings."

Miyuki listened, but did not understand anything. How, from a simple observation about swallows and the small forest animals that came to make their nests and homes in the *kyōzō*, had these two considerable characters (she had inferred the importance of their ranks from the magnificence of their garments) managed to converse about starving birds and the whites of eggs that stank of wet silk, and ended up with death?

Her chats with Katsuro, lengthy night-time gossips interspersed with caresses, rubbing and silky licking, had never taken such a disjointed path as this discussion between the director and his assistant. These men, she thought, as she observed Watanabe and Kusakabe, had a rather disconcerting notion of conversation. What was more, with all their remarks about dying birds, they paid not the least attention to her. Miyuki could have left the room and they would not have noticed that she had disappeared.

She coughed, shuffled her sandals against each other (not daring to go so far as to stamp on the floor like an impatient horse), but there was nothing to be done: the two men had turned their backs on her and were continuing to converse in lively fashion.

As it pressed into the muscles at the top of Miyuki's back and shoulders, the bamboo pole that bore the baskets had eventually imprinted a long, bluish furrow in her flesh, stretching from one shoulder to the other. The slightest tilt of the pole now provoked a sharp pain that was all the more vivid because it was difficult to soothe the sensitive area by massaging it: to do this she had first to relieve herself of the weight of the pole, and therefore find a safe place to set down her baskets.

But, although it was in need of a good scrub – and in this respect, it was not very different from any of her other lodgings on her way to Heian Kyō – the floor of the *kyōzō* appeared to be quite stable. Suppressing her groans, Miyuki cautiously rolled the heavy bamboo pole down her spine until she could feel it becoming lighter, a sign that the baskets had touched the ground.

". . . to compensate for certain taxes from which His Majesty exempts it," Kusakabe was saying at this moment, "the province of Hida sends us each year a hundred carpenters who are renowned for their excellence." (There we go, thought Miyuki, these two have changed the subject yet again!) "They are appointed for one year at the Office of Repairs and there is no reason why they should not restore this wretched *kyōzō*. Unfortunately, they are kept very busy with the reconstruction of certain buildings in the Imperial Palace, which a recent fire reduced to ashes. But I don't imagine that you intend to stay long in Heian Kyō?" he concluded, turning at last to Miyuki.

"As long as necessary," she replied. "I shall not leave the city until I am completely sure that Katsuro's carp are adapting to the sacred ponds. While we are on the subject, I should like to see what they look like."

Director Watanabe gave a strange little laugh – it was as though he had his mouth full of pebbles and was swallowing them all at once, and you could hear them hurtling down his throat, tinkling against each other – while Kusakabe gazed at the young woman in astonishment.

"And what do you expect them to look like? A pond is a pond."

"But these ones are sacred."

"There is no visible difference between what is sacred and what is not," Watanabe said. "To our human eyes, at least. Well, let's have a peek at those fish," he added as he leaned over the nearer of the baskets.

Bent over to see better, the old man looked as though he were bowing respectfully before some noble dignitary. It was only an illusion, of course, but Miyuki told herself that her carp were incapable of telling the difference between a posture of deep respect and that of an elderly man obliged to come as close as possible to make up for his short-sightedness. With the tip of her sandal, she tapped gently on the side of one of the baskets to startle the fish and arouse them from their torpor. As though they had understood what was expected of them, the carp shook themselves, fluttered their tail-fins and rounded their lips as they rose up and sucked the air at the surface.

"They're not bad," Watanabe said.

"They are magnificent," Miyuki corrected him.

Watanabe pursed his lips as though he were about to smile.

"You are justified in boasting of your wares," he said. "But 'magnificent' strikes me as a little excessive. What is certain is that they look as though they have withstood the long confinement of their journey well enough. Better than you," he added, scrutinising Miyuki with his creased eyes.

"I was responsible for them on your behalf, sir. Apart from hunger, what could worry them? From the depths of their bowls, they could not see the storm clouds darkening, swelling and merging together. They did not have any idea that the path I trod was slippery. And that more than once I almost fell in the mud because I could not balance the pole as I held on to the branches. What would have happened if I had fallen, if the baskets had been turned upside down and had emptied, if the fish had had no more water?"

"They would have died," Kusakabe said, nonchalantly.

"And what about me?" Miyuki muttered.

Her eyes swam with tears. Like slowly rising water that is a prelude to flooding, and that nothing can prevent, Miyuki's tears gradually filled her entire being, her skin wept, her belly wept, the hollow of her loins, the palm of her hands.

Flickering in time with her breathing, a thin curtain of nasal fluid closed one of her nostrils, like the veil of mucus that seals the opening of a snail's shell.

MIYUKI LURCHED. WATANABE ONLY had time to reach out his arms to absorb her fall.

Later, that strangely invisible autumnal evening rain began to fall. You could feel its patches of heavy, cold dampness without seeing any drops emerge from the sky, nor hearing it rattling on the doors or the paper blinds, and yet the city still became humid and clammy, oily and glistening. Glossy droplets of rainwater glided along the gutters.

Having taken refuge in his house on the Avenue of the Red Bird, the Director of the Office of Gardens and Ponds was watching his servants as they prepared the ice bath he demanded. Plunging into it would be a far harsher test than usual, since he had rejected the cup of warm sake that he normally enjoyed before his bath. This evening, however, he was eager to immerse himself in the bitingly cold water that would purify him.

For when he was leaning over the baskets to observe the carp, he must have drawn close to Miyuki, he had brushed against her, had almost touched her, enough to smell the warmth that arose from her skin, the sweetish aroma of death given off by her clothes, and the acrid, salty scent of sweat and urine, and he had deduced at once that she was not the kind to show respect for conventions.

Watanabe had moved away from her immediately, but "immediately" no longer had the same meaning of haste now that he was an old man. Before he could put a convenient distance between himself and her, he had first had to straighten up, and this movement had been painful, and therefore slow, leaving him exposed long enough to be brushed against, dirtied and infected by the stains she had amassed on her journey.

He would only be able to rid himself of this dirt by subjecting his body to the icy lash of the waterfall that gushed down through the cedar forest on Mount Atago (always supposing that he was capable of climbing up there); but his gloomy cold bath this evening would at least be proof of his willingness, of his submission to the gods.

As a senior official, he was not obliged to remain secluded at home, he could continue to manage the office that was his responsibility. But the impurity that he had contracted did not allow him to participate in funerals, even though one of his duties was to provide aromatic wood for the cremations; he was forbidden to visit the sick, even though one of his nephews, Takamine, was prey to unexplained fevers; and, above all, since the prohibition for defilement prevented him from taking on the duties of a judge, he feared he would have to give up his role as president of the jury that appointed the winner of the *takimono awase*,* which the entire Court was eager to take part in. How could he justify his withdrawal to the Emperor when it was His

---

* A perfume competition.

Majesty who had personally granted Watanabe the honour of this precedence?

He felt so overwhelmed that he could not suppress a cry when the icy water, seeping through the spotless clothing with which he had tried to protect his genitals, gripped his penis with such a freezing grasp that it seemed to be burning him.

"Is everything all right, *sensei*?" enquired one of his servants.

"Everything is as bad as it could be," Watanabe said, with a calm smile that belied his words.

Far from intending to smile, he had attempted a grimace to convey his exhaustion; but, at his age, probably on account of a weakness in certain facial muscles, all his grimaces now took on the appearance of smiles.

He would have wished to be able to forget the fisherman's widow just as he succeeded, between two bouts of shivering, in disregarding the coldness of the water that was transforming his body into a sort of pale, trembling jelly. But even though she was a nothing-much sort of creature, one did not get rid of Amakusa Miyuki just like that. Once he was purified, the Director of the Office of Gardens and Ponds would have to try and keep her away from the Imperial Palace in general and from the rooms where the fragrance contests took place in particular; for this woman was not filled simply with blemishes: she also exhaled unseemly smells (how to explain that Kusakabe, so neat, so delicate, so refined, had not been upset by them?) that, floating among the exquisite aromas of agar powder, cloves, musk, white sandalwood and boswellia resin, could not but debase the *takimono awase.*

⊙ ⊙ ⊙

194

While Watanabe was sneezing in the purification bath where he would eventually catch a chill, Miyuki was lying on a scrawny mat that she had found upstairs in the *kyōzō*.

She laid out the baskets on top of a moonbeam. According to Katsuro, carp liked the moonlight, and it had been a long time since Miyuki's ones had bathed in this ash-blue light. In fact, the moonlight had barely shone on them before the fish, despite the constriction of their prison, began to tack about with a sort of sensual delight they had never displayed before, going so far as to swim on their backs and to nibble each other's lips – the same hungry kisses as Katsuro's.

Even though she was not happy, Miyuki felt satisfied at having carried out her task so well. Shall we say that she was proud of it? No, we shall not say so: pride was an unknown emotion for a widow who had no expectations other than to become a peasant woman again, stirring the urine and the dung of the Shimae cattle. But it is not unlikely that she would have asked Katsuro, wherever he was – assuming of course that he was somewhere – whether he was pleased with her, and that he would have replied that he was – yes, he must be satisfied.

Within the vast pond of life, Katsuro had laid out a small, protected kingdom for Miyuki. At the beginning of their liaison, this territory had been hardly any bigger than the open arms of the fisherman, and then it had expanded to the size of the house at Shimae, before enlarging itself to the firefly-filled trees on the banks of the Kusagawa, and now as far as the walls of the Imperial City. If Katsuro had not died, who knows how far Miyuki's kingdom would have reached . . .

◉ ◉ ◉

Miyuki fell asleep with the memory of Katsuro and had the following dream. After releasing her carp into one of the sacred ponds, she plunged in after them. As the last carp disappeared beneath the surface of the water, all that could be seen were Miyuki's little toes vanishing in the middle of the concentric circles that marked the place where she had dived in.

The pond was not very deep, but the density of organic matter hanging there meant that Miyuki was able to evade the gaze of the many spectators gathered at the water's edge to witness the release of the fish before any of them could make the slightest attempt to catch her.

Oscillating like a dead leaf, she sank into water that was as black as ink, one of those inks made from smoke with the gelatine from a stag's horn added to make them look glassy, as shiny as varnish.

As she let herself drift down to the bottom of the pond, Miyuki wondered which would be the best way to drown. Should she simply let herself go, allow the water to sweep over her as her own weight carried her down, to swamp her body and mind like a liquid sleep, or should she take an active part in her own drowning, unclench her lips, open her jaws to broaden the cavity of her mouth, hold her tongue back so the water could fill the space, and drink, swallow, ingest without breathing, drink, drink again, drink until she achieved the same end as Katsuro?

All of a sudden, she felt a sort of cold sparkle on her face: amid a wash of bubbles, her husband glided up to her, his kimono puffed out by an enormous pocket of air.

He observed Miyuki, alert to her attempts to drown herself quickly and properly – for if she was not intending to drown, why else would she have plunged beneath the surface?

When at last she touched the bottom of the pond, Miyuki lay down on the soft and sticky mud. Katsuro came to rest on top of her. He opened his kimono to free his penis. And at the same time, the pocket of air escaped, which, had it continued to cling to him, would have drawn him back to the surface and foiled his attempt to penetrate his wife's body.

His organ was transformed into a carp's snout with four lively barbels quivering; the small and fleshy ones on the top lip were tickling Miyuki's clitoris, while the two larger ones, situated at the corners of the nose, were stroking the walls of her vagina.

In her dream Miyuki had several orgasms during the night. Her body arched like the half-moon bridges she had walked over to cross the Kamogawa River. And, in fact, she was indeed a kind of bridge, because the intense pleasure she experienced from every dreamed caress of the carp's snout penis washed over her and ran dancing from her belly to her head.

She had a final orgasm at dawn, as the sun was rising. Her plait dripped with cyprinoid. Her moan of pleasure merged with the shouts of the stallholders who were flooding the Western market on its opening day.

At the hour of the Snake,* Kusakabe came to fetch Miyuki to take her to the sacred pond in the west of the city.

At the very last moment, Watanabe had let it be known that he would be unable to join them, the Emperor having summoned him to the Palace to ask his advice about a difficult choice

---

* Between nine o'clock and eleven o'clock in the morning.

he had to make. However, he had obtained agreement from the Palace that his assistant and the supplier of carp should be provided with a carriage yoked to an ox, borne on two enormous black-lacquered wheels and escorted by eight pages. Like the doublets worn by these young equerries, the hood of the carriage was tinged with the purple wisteria emblem of the powerful Fujiwara clan, which was supposed to encourage the rabble to stand aside as it passed.

"And your carp?" Kusakabe said in surprise, noticing that Miyuki's shoulders were not crushed by her heavy yoke. "Are you not bringing your carp?"

"If we release them before they are accustomed to the new water in which they are going to live, they may die. I must first prepare a small pool for them in a corner of the pond, a little place just for them, safe from other fish, birds and cats, where they will have all the time they need to learn the water."

"Learn the water?" Kusakabe repeated, raising his eyebrows. "What does that mean, learn the water?"

"I don't know, sir. They're Katsuro's words. His way of speaking. In any case," Miyuki continued, "we cannot release the carp before."

"Before what?"

"Before the Emperor has admired them."

"Your fish have nothing to do with the Emperor."

"And yet it was His Majesty who ordered us to supply them – us, the people of Shimae. The entire village gathered to greet his messengers."

"Did they say they came in the name of the Emperor?"

"Of course," Miyuki said. "Otherwise, Natsume would never

have offered them a banquet. The amount they devoured, it's all food that the poor people of Shimae did not eat."

"The Director, Watanabe-*sensei*, sent this mission," Kusakabe said. "And he did not inform the Emperor: negotiating the delivery of a few fish is hardly a state affair!"

"Yet if we had died on the way, my carp and I . . ."

"Who would have known? And supposing we had been told, do you think we would have bothered His Majesty with the death of a stranger? Think *onna*:* how many of the Emperor's subjects die every day without him ever knowing?"

"I'm not sure I know how to count that far," said Miyuki, meekly.

"That's just what I thought," Kusakabe said. "In any case, the Emperor is too taken up with the organisation of the *takimono awase*, the perfume competition. He is taking part personally for the first time this year. And, all of a sudden, all the prominent people, or those who think they are, have entered the contests. Apparently, residents are prepared to spend fortunes in exchange for a few fragrant grains and chips of agar- or sandalwood."

"How can they be so stupid?" Miyuki said in amazement.

She had barely completed her sentence before she received a short, sharp slap on her mouth that made her lips bleed.

"Who has given you permission to make judgments about people of such note?"

"I only meant to say that if the Emperor was taking part in the competition, who would dare prefer another candidate to him?"

---

* Woman.

"Oh, I imagine that he will not involve himself as a creator of perfume: he will merely preside over the judges' meeting. But no doubt his opinion will prevail: has the Emperor ever been wrong about anything?"

Emerging from a winding little lane near the Western market, the heavy carriage was preparing to join the Avenue of the Red Bird. The pages were screeching as best they could to request the stream of pedestrians to stand aside. The black wheels ran over mushy fruit, piles of dung, congealed cowpats, armfuls of aromatic leaves and entrails of fish and shellfish, and produced combinations of powerful smells, like perfume burners without flames.

"Even though he's only fifteen years old?" Miyuki persisted as she surreptitiously licked her punctured lip.

Kusakabe gave her a look full of contempt.

"What do you mean? Don't you understand that an emperor's fifteen years are in no way comparable to the fifteen years of a creature such as you?"

Miyuki did not answer. In actual fact, she had never been fifteen years old, she had only lived two years: a first period, very long, very pointless, up until her marriage, and a second one, dazzling but too short, that had come to an end when the villagers of Shimae had brought back the frozen, muddy body of her husband. One might have thought that a new year – the third, therefore – had begun with the death of Katsuro, but no, this supposed third year had never really existed, it unravelled and crumbled away as its moons went by, like those fleeting dreams that disperse the more desperately you try to retain them.

"What is the prize given to the winner?"

Kusakabe settled back into the nest of silk cushions that he had arranged for himself on the right side of the carriage. He thought for a moment.

"To start with, they will have the honour of receiving congratulations from the mouth of the Emperor himself."

"And after that?" Miyuki said.

Once again, the heavily ringed hand of the young official struck at her lips.

"Insolent girl! Does not His Majesty's satisfaction seem to you sufficient?"

"Indeed. But about satisfaction, I may as well warn you right now: Watanabe-*sensei*'s and your own gratification will not be enough to pay me for my carp. An agreement was passed between my village and your Office of Gardens and Ponds – will you respect it?"

"That depends on Watanabe-*sensei*, not me."

After a pause, Miyuki continued,

"Does one have to be a member of the nobility to take part in the competition?"

"Yes, of course," said Kusakabe curtly. "But you shouldn't have any regrets: even if you were an imperial princess, you would not have a chance of winning. Watanabe-*sensei* was quite right the first time he approached you: you stink. Your smell would spoil the scent of even the most exquisite incenses."

He quickly began to roll up the carriage blinds to help the air to circulate, signifying that there was an unbearable stench beneath the hood.

Miyuki did not react either to the humiliating words or to his actions. She was aware of being dirty, but that only affected her outer frame, it did not involve her real being.

At Shimae, when the low mists glided over the tall grasses and concealed the ground from her, she sometimes tripped on a hidden stone and fell, spilling the buckets of liquid manure for the crops all over herself. Well, she did not make much fuss about it, even when bad luck meant she had been splashed right up to her face. For sure, she then gave off such a powerful smell that the birds shot up into the sky to avoid her. She laughed – about the birds, about herself. All she could do was offer her apologies humbly for this waste of good fertiliser and climb up into the hills of Shimae as far as a series of natural basins where volcanic waters smoked. Up there, she could wash her clothes in one of the basins, scrub her body in another, wash her face in a third, and, to finish, immerse herself in the fourth and last basin, where the water was warmest.

"Have you ever taken part in a contest of this kind yourself, Kusakabe-*san*?"

"Yes, but I didn't win. I ranked among the last competitors. I probably wanted to do too well."

"Did your perfume smell too strongly?"

"It was not the inhalation that was in question, but the inspiration. During a trip to Lake Biwa, the Emperor had honoured us with a few poems that he had crafted for the occasion. One of them described the mating dance of blue dragonflies fluttering above the waters of the lake. It was this image I chose to illustrate, in homage to His Majesty. For the base I used agarwood, which the Buddha said was the smell of nirvana, and I mixed with it haisoko roots on account of their scent of mint and aniseed, to make a fragrance of green freshness that should have recalled the smell of the lake, as well as a very light distillation of saussurea, which I relied on to give an impression of flight, of impermanence and dust."

"Of dust?"

"I have always found that the dragonfly is a dusty insect. It's a very personal opinion, of course. But is there anything more subjective than the *takimono awase*?"

FROM TIME TO TIME, a gust of wind mixed with fine hail would vibrate the Southern Pavilion.

At the centre of the ceremonial hall, Nijō Tennō, the seventy-eighth Emperor of Japan, was crouched on a tall, red-lacquered chair. It was not a very comfortable position for a particularly active and lively adolescent, but His Majesty submitted to it because this posture was meant to signify that he was far-seeing. Similarly, the great six-sided canopy that shielded the young sovereign and his chair, unnecessary in a room unaffected by bad weather, had a symbolic function: that of representing the benevolence of the Emperor towards the world. At least, that was the official reason for it being there: in reality, it had been put up after a recital of sutra by forty monks – so protracted that it was still going on at the end of the hour of the Rat – which had been disrupted by a shower of grey butterflies dropping from the ceiling. While the majority of the insects died when they hit the ground, those that fell on the monks survived for longer, creeping beneath their clothing and making the holy men wriggle about in an absurd way. The courtesans did not dare imagine how the young Emperor's dignity would be affected if some of these insects wove their way into his undergarments and obliged him to relinquish his crouched pose and start fidgeting.

Along the walls there were four large chests with feet, three smaller chests and a great number of boxes made of paulownia wood, the contents of which the Emperor himself did not know. He did not attach great importance to this gap in his knowledge: he was an emperor who lacked curiosity, perhaps because the education he had received had prepared him to absorb, digest and adapt to a culture that had been imported from China for centuries – had not the city of Heian Kyō been conceived as a faithful replica of Chang'an, the Chinese capital of the Tang dynasty and the largest city of its time? The only difference between the two was that, in order to be worthy of its name, which meant Capital of Peace and Tranquillity, Heian Kyō had been built without walls to defend itself. As to the education that the young ruler had received, its aim had been to contribute to the command of skills useful to the role of emperor rather than to develop a need, or even a desire, to explore new fields of knowledge. One day, someone would open the boxes made of paulownia wood. Then the Emperor would discover what they contained. Or not – for whatever had been put inside them might have disappeared, as the law of impermanence, the law that determined the destiny of men and objects in this world, required.

While the clattering of the officials' *geta* or wooden sandals could be heard from every direction as they fled from the hailstorm that had just taken them by surprise, the Emperor told Watanabe that he had decided to take part personally in the next *takimono awase*, which meant that he must win the competition.

"Whatever the Emperor undertakes he cannot fail to achieve

victory," Watanabe said. "Has Your Majesty already chosen a theme for the contest?"

A rumour had been going around that, this year, the contests would be inspired by the odorous transformations created by the heavy June rains when they pour down on gardens; when, rather like an assistant making incense, they grind, pound and crush the soft flowers, shred, slash and lacerate the leaves and the stalks full of sap, batter, fragment, knead and hammer the earth, pulverise the empty snail shells, the chitins of abandoned carapaces, the rich strains of the humus sustaining the freshness of the floral emanations. At least, that was how the Director of the Office of Gardens and Ponds smelled such things.

"The girl in the mist," said Emperor Nijō.

Watanabe looked at the sovereign without comprehension. Where did this girl come from, and who was she?

"The girl in the mist?" he said, arching his eyebrows.

As he had promised himself, he had redrawn them and painted them in green jade; but to his great annoyance, no-one appeared to have noticed. Was there an age when other people, be they your emperor or your underling, look at you but do not see you – until the day comes when they do not see you at all?

"We are imagining a garden," the Emperor said, "a garden filled with the morning mist. Spanning a stream, a very steep half-moon bridge links the garden on the right-hand side to the garden on the left. Only the raised part of the structure emerges from the cloud. It is then that, rising out of the mist that has shrouded the right-hand garden, a girl walks onto the bridge. She is walking quickly. Having reached the top of the half-moon bridge, she stops for a moment. Then, resuming her path, she is hurrying down the bridge to reach the garden on the left. And just as suddenly as she appeared from the mist on the right, she disappears into the mist on the left. If I were to follow in her footsteps at the very top of the bridge, what would I find there?"

"Alas, Your Majesty would not find anything, I'm afraid. Unless, in the interval when she stopped at the very top of the bridge – to admire the ducks, I imagine? – the girl had dropped a comb, a jewel from her belt, perhaps a fan?"

"No."

"No, Your Majesty? In that case, I don't see what . . ."

"The smell," said the Emperor. "It is the girl's smell that would linger at the top of the bridge."

"But the wind . . ."

"If there is mist, then there is no wind. Therefore, a girl has passed from one layer of mist into another, and, in her wake, a trace of her perfume has remained at the top of the bridge. What is this perfume? This is the brief for the *takimono awase*. Now, plan and carry out a formula that will describe this image without there being any need of words."

Open-mouthed, Watanabe stared at the young emperor in amazement: he had never heard anyone express a more beautiful theme for a perfume competition, and nobody had ever given him such a huge challenge.

Memories of unique fragrances came back to him, which he began to blend together in his mind: kansho, saussurea, nardostachys jatamansi, rei-ryokoh, daioh, beechwood sap and pistil of wild lilies. He wondered what original ingredients could provide victory for His Majesty.

◉ ◉ ◉

In the afternoon, the lashing rain gave way to a gentle, hesitant fall of snowflakes: the season for light snowfalls was several weeks early. Seven centimetres of powdery snow had already covered the ground when Watanabe shut himself away at home and began to consider the mission that had been entrusted to him.

None of the balsamic ingredients (resins, powders, barks, herbs . . .) which made up the balls of incense that were stored in a special shop on Second Avenue corresponded with the Emperor's expectations. The whole art of the *takimono awase*, of course, lay in the way the ingredients were blended together. Ever since the monk Ganjin, who had come from China two centuries previously, and had introduced to Japan the art of mixing incenses together by blending them with substances such as honey, nectar of flowers, molasses or *makkō* powder, virtually all combinations had been exhausted. By adjusting the proportions, one could convert a range of a hundred or so scents into just over a thousand, each composition being registered in a book in the custody of the Director of the Office of Gardens and Ponds in his capacity as the person responsible for the cultivation of aromatic trees.

Watanabe therefore knew better than anyone that no fragrant expression of the image of a girl in the mist crossing a half-moon bridge had existed to this day – and furthermore the Emperor had specified neither the season nor the time of day or night of her crossing. He was going to have to innovate, but Watanabe Nagusa had lost the habit. He felt weariness overcome him at the mere thought.

Kusakabe had accompanied Miyuki as far as the pond of the temple dedicated to the Buddha Amitabha, the buddha of buddhas, he who rules over the Pure Land, an eternally happy world that knows no evil or suffering, and is as vast as sixty-one billion universes on its own.

A biting wind had arisen, the haunting song of the last cicadas of the season could be heard, colonies of small insects with embryonic wings fluttering on their hairy bodies were scratching at the ground to bury themselves. Pouring through the delicate crimson leaves of the maple trees, the light was tinged with a scarlet glow that spread over the snow that had fallen during the night, and although the sun had barely risen, the temple was already glinting with the colours of sunset.

Surrounded by a tangle of azaleas and camellias, the water was not immediately visible. To have sight of it, one had to follow spongy paths over which wafers of grey mist stagnated.

After a final screen of bushes, Miyuki had glimpsed the mirror of the pond. She had rushed to it. Without bothering to roll up her sleeves, she had plunged her hands among the lotuses, cupped her palms and brought up a handful of water. She had bathed her face in it, she had drunk a little of it, rolling it around her mouth as those who are fond of sake do to allow the delicate flavours of their drink to evolve.

The pond had a very sweet, faded taste, that of out-of-season, unripe fruit, with a slightly muddy aftertaste due no doubt to the presence of a number of decomposing organic elements that only a breeder of carp would recognise.

"It's good," Miyuki said. "Even though it's too cold, but that's because of the snow that makes it . . . how do you say? . . . a little sleepy, a little . . ."

". . . *ajikenai*, insipid," Kusakabe suggested.

209

Miyuki had never used the word insipid before. Not in this context, at least. Because even if it was the correct word, it could not be the right word from the carps' point of view; for them, no liquid was flat, bland or harmless.

Close to the bank, a row of roughly cut posts emerged from the water in a shape roughly resembling that of a half crown. The water had seeped into the wood, which had frayed into long scales of gangrene-laden bark. Miyuki guessed that these were the stakes that Katsuro had told her about: after covering the tops of the posts with pointed nails to deter the birds from settling on them to watch the fish swimming and swoop down on them more efficiently, all that was necessary was to thrust them into the silt and stretch a net from post to post to mark out an acclimatisation pool where the carp could swim safely.

After she had joined her hands together and bowed low to pay homage to the pond, Miyuki turned to Kusakabe.

"Do you think the monks would like to watch the release of the carp?"

"How would I know!"

"But Director Watanabe, he will not fail to honour us with his presence, will he?"

By "us" she meant all the people of Shimae for whom she was the envoy. And, because of this mission, it seemed to her inconceivable that the Director of the Office of Gardens and Ponds would not be on the shore of the lake when she returned the carp to their element.

"Yes, I imagine so. But he's an important man – here, we say 'a grandee'. The grandees are busy from morning till night. Sometimes, they even go through the whole night without sleeping."

"And His Majesty the Emperor?"

Kusakabe looked at her in amazement; did this woman *really* believe that the sovereign would bother to come and watch a few fish wriggling around when the only noteworthy thing about them was that they had survived a hazardous journey?

"The ceremonies that Tennō Heika* honours with his presence are planned and rehearsed a very long time in advance. How would we have been able to prepare His Majesty for a release of carp when we didn't know exactly when you would arrive – or even whether you really would arrive? And then, after all, you're not intending to put more than three or four carp in the water . . ."

"Eight," Miyuki said.

"Three, four or eight, what's the difference? There are more important things than your fish, are there not? What a pity that I cannot take you into the Palace, for then you would see with your own eyes what His Majesty's days and nights are like: not a moment of calm, not a glimmer, no respite, no rest!"

Were the days and nights that Miyuki had spent with Katsuro so different from those of the Emperor, even though the thatched hut at Shimae obviously had nothing in common with the *shishinden*, the vast, formal building in which all official ceremonies took place, presided over by the descendants of Amaterasu?† After all, the fisherman and his wife had not known any respite either, especially when Katsuro, foreseeing that his fame acquired from the Office of Gardens and Ponds might

---

* His Majesty the Emperor.
† Goddess of the Sun. According to legend, she sent her grandson, Prince Ninigi no Mikoto, to Earth to plant rice and govern the world. Ninigi had a great-grandson, Iwarebiko, who, in 660 BC, founded the empire of Japan.

result in orders from other Buddhist sanctuaries, had resolved to dig a proper pool in which he could breed fifty or so carp and thereby be in a position to fulfil hurried orders without worrying whether the river water would be appropriate or whether the fish would want to take the bait or not. Miyuki had agreed to this plan, but not wanting Katsuro to waste his fishing time, she had taken upon herself alone the exhausting job of digging the soil, and then of filling the baskets with the earth, which she hauled to the hillside to prop up the terraced embankments on the rice fields. Once the pool had been dug, it had to be fed, and Miyuki had become a porter once again, carrying the water up from the Shuzenji weir.

Between two trips, she divided her time between the muck-spreading of the fields and the maintenance of the fishing gear that Katsuro treated with equal measures of efficiency and casualness, especially since he knew he could rely on Miyuki to mend bailers and torn nets, and produce new hooks of dogwood.

". . . more than a hundred rites to respect every year," Kusakabe was saying, "and as many ceremonies; sometimes the Emperor may be giving a banquet of Drunkenness with strong sake, a big religious meal and dancing girls (for which, just so you know, he will have personally overseen the rehearsals), sometimes he presides over the Tasting of the Early Fruits to celebrate the new rice, and occasionally he has to officiate until the hour of the Tiger,* again he sometimes judges the poetry competitions and the perfume contests, or else he has to listen to the long report on the death sentences delivered during the year, a

---

* Three o'clock in the morning.

perfectly useless report since capital punishment has not been enforced for a hundred years and more – but traditions remain traditions, do they not?"

Miyuki did not reply. Tradition: there was another word she did not know, at least she had never used it. Her own language was made up mostly of silences. At Shimae, she could spend a whole day without uttering a single word. Once evening came, when Katsuro walked up from the Kusagawa, when she caught sight of him at last and hurried towards him, her mouth would be dry, her lips shrivelled, her tongue tied.

"Respect for tradition requires total concentration at all times. But the night does not encourage watchfulness. Fortunately, at moments of strain, sake awakens our judgment while at the same time bringing calm – I am talking about brown sake, which is brewed solely for the Emperor himself. I have had the privilege of tasting it on occasion. The Office of Gardens and Ponds having been merged with the Office of the Imperial Table, I am one of the officials authorised to control the temperature and flavour of the dishes served to His Majesty. Well, Tennō Heika's sake is something special, believe me! Would it please you to dip your lips into it? Although a woman of your standing is forbidden to touch the Emperor's food or drink, I could probably arrange it."

She made a gesture of indifference. Kusakabe let out a groan. He was disappointed, he had thought he had kindled in her the small flame of curiosity, the small flame he nevertheless knew how to make flutter so well and that, even in this world of extreme decorum at the Imperial Court, he managed to make glow with a brightness that was more intense than anything his colleagues could manage.

213

Imagine. Placed in charge of welcoming suppliers to the Office of Gardens and Ponds, these being mostly peasants offering the products of their region (white blossom cherry trees from Mount Yoshino, plum trees from Yushima Tenjin, weeping chrysanthemums from Ise), Kusakabe always began the interview by congratulating them for being there, in the heart of the most glamorous city in the world. It mattered little, he told them, whether they did business or not: just by glimpsing Heian Kyō, they would leave richer than they had arrived. The peasants, who until then had only known their hovels, their rice fields and their patches of poor earth, listened to him open-mouthed. He had mastered his subject so perfectly that he could talk about the city until the sky filled with shafts of violet, until the twilight spread like a bowl of upturned ink, and the one hundred and twenty-two guardians of the gates started to remove all those who had no reason to spend the night in the surroundings of the Palace.

Similarly unstoppable on the subject of everything that entered the mouth of the Emperor, hurried down his throat, passed through his stomach and came out again through his penis or his anus, Kusakabe had prepared a long eulogy about imperial sake.

And was it of no interest to this foul-smelling woman?

(For he was beginning to agree with Watanabe-*sensei*: yes, this young woman did indeed give off a smell that was indefinable and not at all pleasant.)

Piqued but not discouraged, he returned to Tennō Heika's sake: on the rare occasions when His Majesty circulated his own cup, he himself had had the great honour of tasting it. Brewed

214

from rice from Echigo* province, supposedly the best in Japan, this sake was incredibly sweet, smooth and fruity – and Kusa-kabe began to search for words to describe this taste whose mere mention delighted him to such a degree that, closing his eyes, he became almost drunk on his own imagination.

Miyuki, for her part, had kept her eyes open, and the gloomy expression with which she greeted his speech persuaded the young official to go no further. Instead he sighed.

"Are you so little eager to educate yourself, then, Amakusa Miyuki?"

This time, it was her turn to find that she lacked the words to reply – due to tiredness, probably.

Yet what she would have wished to say was simple: what you learn matters less than the person who teaches it to you, that was what she was thinking as the snow redoubled in intensity.

She owed any knowledge she had to Katsuro. It had been he who had introduced her to the murmuring, chilly world of the river, to the ways of catching carp without injuring them, to the methods of soothing them and taming them to the point where they could be taken on a long journey, exactly like a dog, a horse, a hooded falcon.

The fisherman did not just tell her to do this or do that; he took his wife's hand and helped her into the water, as far as her calves to begin with, then up to her knees, and then up to her belly, and finally up to her breasts, and then he tipped her over onto her back, holding her buttocks with one hand, her neck with the other, and told her to lie back without fear, to feel how

---

* Today the prefecture of Niigata.

the river is solid beneath your body, how it supports you, how it carries you.

Miyuki's long black hair spread out over the water, and when small ripples were produced by a passing fish or by a branch falling upstream, it rose up as though it was breathing.

Katsuro believed – a rumour among the fishermen – that the Kusagawa became wider the further it flowed, that it opened up like Miyuki's loving and trusting legs, and that at the end of its course, over there, a long way downstream from Shimae and the Shuzenji weir, it entered the Pacific.

He would have liked to see how a modest river managed to flow into an ocean that was supposed to be endless. Did it happen by intrusion at night, like his marriage to Miyuki? Did it resemble the way his penis, dilated between his wife's thighs like a river enlarged by the help of its tributaries, buried itself in Miyuki's open waters, in her gentle, warm and salty lapping waters?

Katsuro and his wife had promised themselves that they would follow the Kusagawa as far as its mouth, before they died; and there, sitting side by side, embracing perhaps, on the same stone warmed by the sun, they would watch how their river managed to lose itself in the ocean. Miyuki had chosen and picked a *kaji** leaf, which Katsuro, on one of his trips to Heian Kyō, had entrusted to a scholar so that he could write down their wish. To have a chance of being granted, the wish had to be inscribed in calligraphy on the *kaji* leaf on the very same night that the stars that loved one another, the Herdsman and the Weaver, appeared to be about to meet, and naturally the leaf had

---

* A plant from the mulberry family.

been inscribed in this way. But something had not been done as it should, since Katsuro had died before he could sit on the warm stone beside Miyuki.

At the thought of this, she felt tears moistening her cheeks.

"Let's go back," she said to Kusakabe. "The snow is too bright, it's burning my eyes. We shall come back and release the carp tomorrow morning."

The bronze bell of the temple began to chime, releasing a vibration so dense that it split the thin layer of ice that had begun to freeze on the sacred pond.

It continued to snow all day long. The snowflakes banked up on the sloping roofs, then, with the slight warmth given out by the walls and roofs of houses where coal fires had been lit, the layer of snow underneath softened and began to melt; once it lique- fied, the entire snowy mass slid and overflowed from the roofs, crashing down with a sound like cow dung dropping onto the hard earth of the road.

Once back at the *kyōzō*, Miyuki remained close to the baskets in which the carp floated lifelessly, as though they were sleeping. Only brief ripples from their fins proved they were still alive.

She refrained from feeding them: she wanted them to retain sufficient voracity that, when they were set free, and despite the coldness of the pond that would encourage them to swim to the bottom to hide in the silt, their appetite would prompt them to explore their new surroundings to find something to satisfy their greed.

She was hungry herself – her weariness from the journey combined with the relief of having arrived must be the reason.

While she was inspecting the pond, Kusakabe had gone to the temple to beg some sustenance from the monks. When they learned that their almsgiving was intended for the woman who had brought the carp for their sacred pond, the monks proved to be extremely generous. Squatting down beside her eight fish, Miyuki devoured their gift of sticky rice, Chinese cabbage and thin slices of radishes in vinegar so quickly that she was immediately sick. No matter, she felt hungry enough to continue to eat feverishly, using all ten fingers to prepare two mouthfuls at once and wolfing them down simultaneously. When her bowl was empty, she licked the inside, flecking the tip and wings of her nose with morsels of food. She wiped her lips on the sleeve of her kimono, leaving a damp patch on the material.

Coming from the north, sweeping between Mount Hiei and Mount Atogayama, a violent wind, the *kogarashi*, "the one that denudes the trees", surged over the city, making the snow fall horizontally and blowing away the last leaves. The pair of gyrfalcons that dwelled in a former jackdaw nest in the Saiji pagoda flew off uttering sad cries. And it was night.

WHILE MIYUKI LAY CURLED up in blankets on her mat, two of Watanabe Nagusa's servants ran over to Kusakabe's home to ask him to report to the Director of the Office of Gardens and Ponds without waiting for daybreak.

Why two emissaries for the delivery of such a simple message? Because if one of them slipped in the snow, fell, over-exerted himself or broke an ankle, the other would continue running to carry out the assignment. In this monomania that Watanabe had for always imagining the worst, one can also discern the explanation for his long and glittering career in a world where the only certainty was impermanence.

Kusakabe wasted no time in sending away the prostitute whose services he had hired to warm himself on this icy night, and he set off at once.

He was delayed inconveniently by the unexpected arrival of a caravan laden with hemp cloth. The Rashōmon gate was closed for the night, and the porters, realising that they were doomed to camp outside in the snowstorm, reacted violently to the lack of hospitality of a city to which they were bringing goods that would provide work for dyers and tailors. Hearing them yelling and threatening to set fire to their goods to keep warm, Kusakabe sent someone to arouse a captain of the guardians of the gates and waited until they had opened the Rashōmon before setting off again.

The cold night air facilitated the diffusion of sounds; he heard the gong of the Imperial Palace chiming, announcing that it was already halfway through the hour of the Rat, when he finally reached the corner of Tomi and Rakkaku streets where one of Watanabe's servants, torch in hand, was awaiting his arrival.

Kusakabe wondered whether the young prostitute from whose arms he had had to tear himself (what did she declare her name to be? Ah yes, Bimyō, that is to say, the Beautiful One) would be wandering through the sleeping streets once more. She had not really deserved her name, she had short, chubby legs, an anus like a small violet cabbage, and she had admitted straight away her inability, unlike most courtesans, to improvise songs whose carefully chosen words were meant to excite the sexual ardour of her customers; but Kusakabe Atsuhito liked these unsuccessful, dull or somewhat ugly women who helped him to relax, for one night, from the exhausting quest for perfection which his position among the leading courtiers living in Heian Kyō obliged him to pursue.

If Watanabe did not detain him for too long, perhaps he would be able to find the erroneously named Bimyō again and take her home with him.

But first he was going to have to undertake the ritual of welcome, and squat before the raised tray where some sake and a few accompanying dishes were laid out.

The Director of the Office of Gardens and Ponds looked at him in silence, assessing him as though he were seeing him for the first time, and appearing to ponder the ability of his assistant to fulfil a delicate mission.

After having poured the sake, Watanabe, with the lethargic slowness of a butterfly emerging from its chrysalis and unfurling its wings, decided to describe his visit to the Emperor and the decision the latter had made to take part as a contestant in the *takimono awase*, the theme of which he had outlined himself – a theme that was so difficult to translate into scents that Nijō Tennō risked finding himself the one and only competitor.

"It would be irreverent if no-one were to take up His Majesty's challenge," Kusakabe observed. "Come now, what theme did the Emperor suggest?"

Watanabe succinctly explained the theme: the half-moon bridge, the two mists, the girl.

"There was never any question of a theme in the previous competitions," Kusakabe said in surprise. "All that was asked for was the creation of a delicious scent."

"But the Emperor probably wants to mark his reign with an extraordinary innovation: to make the incense tell a story."

On either side of the tray, the two men remained silent as if they were trying to assess the significance of what had just been said. Incense had long ago acquired its letters patent of nobility, it was famed for providing energy as well as for calming or stimulating the mental faculties, curing certain illnesses, attacking anxiety and insomnia, not to mention its aphrodisiac qualities. But no-one had ever yet ventured to suggest that it could also express itself like a poet.

Watanabe stood up and bowed low, as though he were in the presence of the sovereign.

"If Nijō Tennō would accept such an unworthy and wretched a challenger as me, then I would put myself forward as his opponent."

Kusakabe gazed at him incredulously.

"With respect, Watanabe-*sensei*, I know all the incenses that are kept at the shop on Second Avenue. I can assure you that none of them, whether taken on its own or mixed with other aromas, could ever conjure up the path of a girl on a bridge."

"On a bridge *and* in the mist," Watanabe said. "The fact is that this is an olfactory impression that has never been created. And I haven't the slightest notion of what it could be like. I'm too old for fogs: when the mist rises, I go to bed; and it's a very long time since I have pursued a girl."

He let out one of those elderly men's laughs, of the kind where you don't know whether they are mocking or despairing – perhaps they are nothing more than a kind of trembling of the jaw.

"So, you don't stand any hope of winning it?" his assistant said.

"Oh, none at all."

"But the entire Court will have their eyes glued to you . . ."

"Their noses more likely," Watanabe said, tapping his nostrils with the tip of his finger.

"Yes."

"Yes," Watanabe echoed.

"Yes," said Kusakabe once more.

On this triple "yes", they fell silent. There were some sighs which, in Watanabe's case, were confined to clearings of the throat, to slightly husky interjections, noises like *hai*, *ee*, *iya*, *yossha*, the sound of pieces of silk being rubbed together, but mainly silence, a sealed silence that neither of them seemed to want to disturb.

After a long pause, Kusakabe finally cleared his throat and said,

"In fact, it is more likely that the Court will bend its ears to you, since it appears that incense can be heard better than it can be breathed. Something comes back to me in this regard: is there not a sutra that says that the teaching of the Buddha is transmitted through smells and that there is no need for words to describe it?"

"The sutra of Vimalakirti, one of the closest disciples of Buddha Amitabha," Watanabe said in a voice full of respect.

"Did his teaching move you too, *sensei*?"

The Director of the Office of Gardens and Ponds smiled.

"Not his teaching, but the paper on which this sutra had been translated from Sanskrit, transcribed in calligraphy and preserved at Todaji, the temple where the widow from Shimae is to release her carp tomorrow morning. A paper of exceptional whiteness and purity. I had the privilege of admiring it, I was even allowed to stroke it, and I can still feel its indescribable softness on my fingertips. In this sutra, Vimalakirti speaks of being reborn in a pure land which he describes as 'sweetly perfumed by all the fragrances', and where the palaces, the houses, the streets, the gardens themselves, and even the food, are made not of clay, nor wood, nor stone, but of the sweetest smells."

"Do you believe such a thing is possible, *sensei*?"

"I'm not saying that I believe it, Atsuhito, I'm careful not to do so! But supposing that there should be another world after the present one, I prefer to imagine it delicately perfumed rather than stinking of rot and decay."

Watanabe's lower jaw trembled again. It was not due to old age this time, but to the coldness of the snow that was sweeping into the room. Of the three coal fires, two were already covered with white ash, only one continued to glow.

"Watanabe Nagusa and Kusakabe Atsuhito challenging Nijō Tennō in the first days of winter!" he exclaimed suddenly. "I assume that the competition will take place in the Pavilion of Purity and Freshness. No-one will ever have taken part in such extraordinary contests. I wonder whether the Emperor already knows what response he plans to bring to the wording that he himself has devised. Ah! Atsuhito, what a poignant situation: I am like that man who is given an anthology of poems written in a language that he doesn't know, while being ordered to translate them into another language that he cannot decipher either."

Kusakabe downed a fourth cup of sake. His eyes gleaming, he rose to his feet.

"I suggest we go there now. Straight away."

"Go where, Atsuhito? It's dark, it's snowing and . . ."

"The shop on Second Avenue. Let's secure the best incenses for ourselves before others can get hold of them."

Kusakabe knew what he was talking about: as soon as the opening of a perfume competition was announced, the likely participants, who comprised virtually all the aristocrats and officials from the higher third rank upwards, would send their servants to scour the shop on Second Avenue, with the purpose of bringing back, whatever the price, the greatest quantity of resins and roots or the sweetest-smelling seeds. No time could be

224

spent quibbling: the vital thing was not to obtain a bargain but to procure the maximum amount of substances, which one hurried to hide away in rooms with lowered blinds so that no-one could disturb the subtle palette of fragrances that were to be put together in the greatest secrecy.

Although a night visit required official authorisation even for a person of such elevated rank as the Director of the Office of Gardens and Ponds, Watanabe had no trouble persuading the guards in charge of security at the shop to open the door for him. The guards simply made sure that neither he nor his assistant had anything on them that could pollute or set fire to the precious goods stored there.

This restriction meant doing without any kind of lantern or torch, or even a simple candle. Without lighting, the shop was plunged into such darkness that it was scarcely possible to make out the characters painted on the countless little drawers indicating which aromatic substance each of them contained. The reflection of the moon on the snow would probably have provided enough light for them to find their way, but they would have needed to open the wooden blinds fully, and this the guards forbade absolutely.

"Come along now," Kusakabe said in resignation, "our sense of smell will compensate for what our eyes cannot see."

Watanabe liked this phrase. The two men disappeared into the darkness, faces pointed forwards rather like cats entering an unknown territory.

The guards had explained to them the criteria according to which the substances had been arranged: classified firstly by

225

families (resins and gums, roots and rhizomes, seeds and fruits), they were next subdivided into varieties (sweet, acidic, hot, salty and bitter) which were then distributed into finely shaded distinctions according to whether they were woody, animal, spicy, balsamic, earthy, resinous, heady, peppery, camphorated, herbaceous . . .

"Above all, don't touch anything," the guards had said, "satisfy yourselves with sniffing and memorising whatever interests you. You can come back to obtain whatever you have spotted tonight, but only once the Palace has announced the opening and the theme of the contest."

Watanabe had given the guards such an offended look that they had bowed very low as they reeled off streams of excuses, stringing them together in a frantic manner so as to be sure to have time to enumerate all those they knew.

"How could anyone suspect His Excellency the Director of the Office of Gardens and Ponds of thinking of spiriting away even the tiniest splinter of Chinese star anise?" Kusakabe said in an offended tone, adding very quietly in Watanabe's ear: "Actually, *sensei*, are we not going to take advantage of the dark to help ourselves without waiting?"

"What is taken can no longer be removed," Watanabe had replied, also under his breath. "I suggest we start with the chevrotain musk. It's the basis for everything. I couldn't consider anything without it."

Their sense of smell guided them unerringly to the drawer where an array of small, very thin leather pouches were laid out, covered in faint hairs and containing dark brown seeds, soft to the touch, which gave off a powerful scent. Watanabe and

Kusakabe each took a pouch which they concealed in the depths of their vast sleeves.

Then Watanabe set his heart on the gum-yielding ferula. He thought he could depend on its green and spicy aroma to symbolise the fog. Unless he were to decide ultimately to rely on the aromatic costus of which he removed a generous amount – could not the famous bridge crossed by the evanescent girl that the Emperor had dreamed about span a bed of violets and carnations, small flowers reminiscent of the smell of the costus?

For his part, and still using his sleeves as sacks of unfathomable depths, Kusakabe took a supply of storax resin.

Although quite tired, they did not want to part before they had primed their booty: after soaking it all in vinegar, they crushed as finely as they could the shells of twenty or so snails from the China Sea – *kaikō*, to set the perfumes.

Then Watanabe spread out two mats on the ground. Without saying a word, he stretched himself out on one of them and tapped on the other one with his hand as though he were summoning a cat to come and curl up. It was Kusakabe, of course, who lay down there, with a grateful expression on his face, for the north wind had strengthened, snatching and driving back the snowflakes as if constantly plucking the feathers from a white bird; the cold contorted the screens and the blinds which let in the insects' screeching sounds; and to finally dissuade Kusakabe from returning home in the icy wind and darkness, the long cry of a murder victim could be heard coming from a nearby lane.

MIYUKI WOKE EARLY. IN spite of the still unsettled weather and the persistent darkness that prevented her from making out the contents of the basins clearly, her first instinct was to make sure that her carp were alive. She greeted them with a gaze as searching as the one she gave Katsuro whenever she was the first to wake up, examining him to reassure herself that he had spent the night without mishap and that he was breathing peacefully; then she would touch him gently and pinch him to make sure his flesh was warm and supple.

She had been five years old when her parents had fallen victim to *wanzugasa*.* As soon as the first symptoms of the disease appeared, the villagers had made a monkey dance in the main square, because some of them claimed that the animal's capers would limit the extent of the epidemic. They also turned for help to an elderly flute player whose trilling was supposed to be unbearable to the ears of the *hōsōgami*, the demons of smallpox. The third precaution was to confine Miyuki to her parents' cottage to stop her spreading the plague to other families.

_____

* Literally an "eruption of peas", a reference to the pustules that covered the body and face of those suffering from the pox.

228

This was how the little girl came to spend several days at the bedside of her father and mother, who lay dying in silence as the pustules that covered their mouths and throats prevented them from speaking. It was by their stiffness that Miyuki, who never stopped stroking, feeling and kneading their bodies, realised they were dead.

She could be heard weeping, so they set her free. Rather than risk transmitting the disease by taking their remains to the pyre, the village chief, who was not yet Natsume but Norimasa, his father's father, decided to cremate Miyuki's parents in the place where they had given up the ghost, and torches were thrown onto the thatched roof, which caught fire immediately.

It was this same stiffness that had signified her parents' deaths that Miyuki dreaded noticing every morning with Katsuro – and her fear was generalised, it spread to all the living creatures that she expected to find in the morning after having left them the previous evening.

Now, during the night, she had heard rustling and creeping noises that sounded like something scratching the floor. Although the room was upstairs, and despite what Kusakabe said, it had not stopped animals, mainly birds from getting inside. Miyuki congratulated herself on having thought, before going to sleep, of urinating all around the area where her straw matting and her carp were placed. A magic circle of sorts, which the birds had apparently not dared to cross – the imprints of their little claws remained beyond the moist frontier which Miyuki had marked out by moving around and squatting, releasing her urine in long, jerky bursts.

Reassured as to the state of her carp, she walked over to

one of the windows. She had been restless during her sleep; her nightwear had shifted and it now only covered her partially. She readjusted the blind, which, though it had become a little threadbare through exposure to the elements, ought to have been enough to prevent an outside observer from seeing her naked while still allowing Miyuki to gaze over the city that gently made its way up to the walls of the Imperial Palace.

The snow, which had fallen through the night without interruption, had joined the roofs together in one long, fleecy line of white spines. Intermittently, blocks of the snowy mass would separate and slide down over the glazed tiles, picking up sufficient speed to slip over the protruding part of the roof and fly off into the sky. For a few fractions of a second, they would remain as though suspended in space, then they would crash down with a feeble thud.

Kusakabe's almost silent intrusion hardly took Miyuki by surprise. He was wearing the ceremonial dress of civil servants, the black lacquer paper *eboshi* on his head, the pale violet coat, a tunic of pinkish brown with a long train that trailed on the ground, and wide trousers puffed out by a cord strapped to his ankles.

Miyuki bowed three times.

"I am ready, sir."

"Are you sure?"

He looked at her in genuine astonishment.

"Are you going to keep on those clothes you are wearing? Or rather that are wearing you," he corrected himself, "because they are stiff with dried mud, filth and . . ."

"I haven't any others," she said.

"You made this journey without anything to change into?"

Katsuro had often told her that the people of Heian Kyō knew nothing of the lives of those from Shimae, and that they were not interested in them and did not seek to learn more about them, so Miyuki spared Kusakabe any comment on her wardrobe, which amounted to nothing more than the clothes she was wearing, together with a few rags that she used for working in, but which she had not wanted to encumber herself with when she left.

"In any case," Kusakabe said, "there will be no-one to take any notice of you. If there had been some sunshine, maybe, but with all this snow, there won't be anyone at the side of the pond. As for Watanabe-*sensei*, he won't be offended by what you are wearing. He's an ageing man now, his sight has diminished a great deal, his vision is blurred, and he confuses colours. And anyway," he added, concealing a smile behind his hand, "I am sure he won't attempt to come near you. Indeed, even if the word 'satisfaction' should still have any meaning for an old man, he would be all the more satisfied that he could keep his distance from you – eh! You can guess why, can't you?"

And he wrinkled his nostrils in a comical way, as though he were trying to make a child laugh. But Miyuki did not laugh.

"Can you guess?" he repeated.

"No."

"Let's be off," he said, without pressing the matter.

Instead of the ox cart, which was likely to become bogged down in the mud at any moment, Kusakabe had preferred the palanquin, which its bearers could make fly like a butterfly over the most uneven ground.

There had been a hard frost during the night. Beneath the ice, the pond water had become black; and the snow seemed to have engulfed the posts to which, according to Miyuki's instructions, the net marking the sector devoted to the acclimatisation of the carp had been tied.

Kusakabe reassured her: he had taken precautions, plotted a survey of the site himself, and the ice was thick enough to allow someone as slight as Miyuki to venture as far as the edge of the first posts without any risk.

All along the shoreline, monks formed a symbolic guard opposite the pond. The oldest ones, their waxy skin stretched over emaciated faces, floated in monastic clothing that was unlikely to protect them from the cold. But they remained stoical. The younger ones, some of whom still looked like children, were hopping from one foot to the other. Beneath their cheeks, their round, thick tongues could be seen probing their gums to dislodge morsels of rice, the bland taste of which they enjoyed, over and over again, rather like ruminants.

"Are you crying?" Kusakabe said as he saw tears suddenly well up in Miyuki's eyes. "Why are you crying? You have no reason to be sad: you are reaching the end of your journey, your duty accomplished."

"The cold," she stammered.

It was not the real reason. She was distraught at the thought that the moment was coming when she would have to part from the black carp, the only two that came from the Kusagawa. What they represented for Miyuki was not so much the memory of their native river as that of the fisherman who had caught them.

In the nervous quivering of their bodies and bristling scales, in the excited thrashing of their tails – one way or another they must have been aware of the proximity of the pond, perhaps they had a premonition that they were soon to be set free – Miyuki rediscovered Katsuro's elation, his outbursts of joy, his delight when he had the good luck to catch an exceptional fish. Thereupon he became a wonderful lover, as though the glory of his catch were reflected in the size and stiffness of his penis, in the suppleness and agility of his caresses, and his fingers, still permeated with mucus, unerringly found the most sensitive areas of Miyuki's body, gauging their pressure with the same delicacy as when he grasped a carp newly out of the water with both hands, squeezing it firmly enough to prevent it slipping through his fingers but nevertheless allowing it enough ease of movement so that it felt more protected than captive.

As she made her way, Miyuki had the sense that Katsuro was walking beside her: after all, they were *his* carp, which, at either end of the pole, had cut into her neck and bruised her shoulders, and it was right that he should accompany them, watching over them, and over Miyuki, in spirit.

But when the carp started to wriggle and dive to the bottom of the pond, Katsuro's ghost would disappear with them. With a final peal of laughter, the laughter of a child telling his young wife that he will never grow old, the fisherman would return to his death, to his eternity, and Miyuki would howl alone to herself.

The palanquin came to a halt.

The Director of the Office of Gardens and Ponds had come to watch the release of the carp.

233

What had spurred Watanabe to this course of action was not so much the ceremony itself as the pleasure he had promised himself of being able to enjoy Kusakabe dressed in his formal wear, standing out against the whiteness of the snow and going from person to person to give his instructions concerning the protocol, for even though it was certain that the Emperor would not honour the celebration with his presence, everything should still take place with the same solemnity as if His Majesty were presiding over the ceremony.

Before the arrival of the palanquin, the monks had opened a large hole in the frozen pond. Armed with poles, the youngest ones continued to beat the water to prevent it freezing over again.

Miyuki walked towards the ice, stepping in time to the rhythm of the sutra of Pure Land which the monks were reciting slowly; and this was just as well, for she dreaded above all tripping on some obstacle hidden beneath the snow and spilling her baskets as she fell.

. . . *everywhere in this kingdom of great bliss, this pure land of the Buddha, seven marvellous lakes filled with treasures can be found and they are filled with waters that possess the eight virtues. What are the virtues of these waters? They are their clarity, their light, their mirror-like aspect, their sweetness and their beauty, their lightness, their brilliance, their peacefulness.*

When she reached the very edge of the pond, she saw her image reflected in the dark water that the monks' sticks had struck, and she was almost astonished not to see Katsuro's silhouette close beside her. She smiled as she imagined that he would have been very hairy, very dirty and very smelly by now – he had always told her that it was during the outward journey that he accumulated most of the grubbiness, stains and injuries he brought back from his trips to Heian Kyō.

"No!" she cried all of a sudden.

An elderly monk had made his way up to her and, taking advantage of a tilt of the shoulder yoke, had succeeded in unhooking the basket containing the black carp.

"No," she said again. "Leave them with me for a little while yet."

But the monk, paying no heed to her supplications, walked away with his prey, swaying rather like monkeys do, the lines on his face indicating what his worn-out joints were forcing him to endure.

Miyuki could hear the splashes of heavy objects being slid into the pond.

"Katsuro!" she shouted.

She was shaking. Then Watanabe Nagusa came up to her. Curling his fingers like a claw, he grabbed her arm. She did not know whether it was to reassure her or to constrain her. Without relaxing his grip, he led her away from the shore. Miyuki turned her head, trying to look behind her, over her shoulder, in the hope of glimpsing for one last time Katsuro's carp swimming to freedom.

On the shore of the pond, the monks had begun their intoning again:

. . . and the bottom of the lakes of treasures is covered in golden sand. On each of their four sides, surrounding them completely, there are four descending staircases. These four ornate objects are very fine and beautiful. All around them are trees with marvellous jewels, and in between them sweet-smelling paths.*

---

* Translation by the Amitabha Pure Earth team.

Watanabe was standing so close to Miyuki that he could sense the warmth of her body and feel the beating of her heart.

He asked her why she appeared so emotional when everything was going so much better than they could have hoped, considering that the north wind might have chilled the monks to the marrow and paralysed their vocal chords; prayers chanted in a loud voice had a different sound, nevertheless, from those that were whispered between one's teeth and tumbled out by the cold.

Her only response was to lower her gaze and place her hands together; the fingers that were exposed to the freezing air gave her the paradoxical impression of having been dipped in boiling water. She bowed.

"When do you leave for Shimae?"

It was then that from Miyuki's mouth, before she could reply, a tiny pearl of saliva flew out. At the same moment, the sun burst out from behind a cloud, and its rays struck the droplet, which, for a fraction of a second, on its way from Miyuki's lips to Watanabe's face, sparkled like a miniature sun.

Now Watanabe cherished a secret passion for this opaline fluid – so sweet, so unappreciated, so uninteresting to the majority of people – that is women's saliva.

After many patient supplications, he had persuaded his wife Sahoko to leave a drop on the polished surface of a Chinese bronze mirror – an object from the Warring States period, one of the first presents he had given Sahoko. She had waited for a night when there was an eclipse of the moon to grant him this favour, and he had been able to admire the rebirth of the star in the iridescent bubbles that constituted what he called "Sahoko's gift". Then the sparkling little dome had evaporated, leaving a dry, dull smear on the mirror.

He had regretted not having gathered a little of the creamy dampness of Sahoko's gift on the tip of his forefinger, on the pad, so that he could moisten his top lip.

For the Director of the Office of Gardens and Ponds was extremely sensitive to the smell of saliva when it dried on the skin. It produced a scent that was reminiscent of honey, vinegar and the mauve pistil of certain flowers. But it was so unforeseen, so slight, that it could not withstand the coils of incense that burned night and day, summer as well as winter, in the rooms and corridors of the Imperial Palace, nor, moreover, the stench that stagnated in various parts of the city, notably near the markets.

There was nothing erotic about Watanabe's addiction. This singular olfactory pleasure, which he readily agreed other people might find off-putting, did not arouse any kind of sexual excitement in him, but when the scent faded, when its capricious fragrance was no more than a memory, he knew that within the space of a second, he had been a happy man.

After having demonstrated her generosity – "generosity" was Watanabe's word; his wife preferred to speak of "indulgence" – Sahoko had suddenly refused to satisfy her husband's "whim" (another of her words). He had then turned to the young ladies of the Court. But to obtain from them even a hint of the fluid that provided him with such intense joy was not so simple. For all that he had done his best to compile a list of credible excuses that he thought he could cite in order to obtain a little of this saliva that was so commonplace that the Empress's attendants

237

swallowed theirs without even thinking about it (he had calculated that they repeated this action about one thousand, five hundred times a day), he usually provoked their astonishment and obtained a flat refusal.

Nevertheless, he sometimes succeeded in getting what he wanted – oh, not more than two or three times a year, generally on the occasion of the ceremony of the Alleviation of Souls or the celebration of the First Fruits, for these festivals were accompanied by performances involving dozens of young dancers. Those he dared appeal to listened to him with their heads tilted to one side, but there was no contempt or disgust in their reaction, it was simply that they did not understand what he planned to do with what they were to give him if they should ever agree to his request; and then they would hold up a hand to their mouths to conceal a little laugh, and when their hands fell back, their eyes were full of compassion, and they murmured,

"I'll do so, willingly, *sensei*. I see no harm in it. Just tell me how you would like us to proceed."

Watanabe had discovered that the delicate fragrance mellowed best on the wrist, in the warm intimacy of silk sleeves.

Then he drew back one sleeve to expose his left wrist – for it is associated with the *yang*, and is therefore warm, shiny, strong and masculine – and positioned it to offer it to the parted lips.

As soon as he heard the faint sound of the mouth releasing the drop of saliva he so yearned for, and became aware of the warmth on his skin, he brought his wrist back into the opening of his sleeve. He bowed very low in front of the donor, even though she was of a lower rank to him, then he escaped posthaste, taking his treasure with him.

Once he had found a quiet corridor, he huddled in a corner, drew his left wrist out of the sleeve of his kimono again and hurried to plant his nostrils over the moist patch, which, already, was evaporating.

Despite long practice, Watanabe was incapable of anticipating the properties of the gift that the dancing girls granted him. He had noticed, however, that the young women who, in between performances, ate persimmons that were so ripe that their flesh had lost all their sharpness and had become almost runny, translucent and intensely sugary, produced a saliva that was slower to dry. Yet the aroma of the fruits obscured the *sui generis* fragrance of the offering. Now, in his aromatic celebrations, the Director of the Office of Gardens and Ponds was searching for the pure scent of the breath, the one that accompanies the word and the sigh, and makes a stranger – for most of the time, he did not know, and would never know, the name of his donor – become someone unforgettable.

Some of his memories dated back to the distant period when he was only a child, but they were imprinted so deeply within him that he could still, from memory, draw the lips, with all their lines and winter chapping, of his first benefactresses.

Miyuki's bead of saliva was already evaporating. Watanabe Nagusa quickly slipped his forefinger beneath his upper lip and curled it upwards to put it in contact with his nostrils. He closed his eyes and deeply inhaled an aroma that was unknown and perplexing, one that he would rather escape from or be buried in, he could not say.

"I'm the person responsible for paying you – you knew that?"

239

"No, *sensei*, I didn't know."

"So we shall have the opportunity to see each other one last time. Come at night, I'll be less busy. And perhaps you'll reveal your secret to me?"

"What secret, Watanabe-*sensei*? I'm a simple woman, I have no secrets."

The Director of the Office of Gardens and Ponds looked around him to make sure that no-one could overhear their conversation.

Kusakabe was standing some distance away, his tall, slim body swaying gracefully over the pond – he bent down, straightened up again, bent down once more like a reed shaken by the wind – as he tried to follow the movements of the carp. As for the monks, they continued their chanting imperturbably.

"Of course you do," whispered Watanabe, "you have one: the secret of what it is that emanates from you."

He realised he was still keeping his upper lip rolled up and tucked beneath his nose, exposing his upper layer of teeth where the black lacquer, which he had not renewed, was beginning to chip.

The following morning it was still snowing. In certain places, the thickness of the snow reached the height of an ox's withers. Whether on foot, in a palanquin or a carriage, it had become difficult to get around town. This did not prevent the Director of the Office of Gardens and Ponds from summoning his assistant to help him search for the blend of fragrances to make up the incense that would respond to the challenge of reproducing the exhalations of a young lady who, emerging from the mist shrouding a garden, walks over a half-moon bridge to reach another garden just as shrouded in mist as the first one.

The theme of the competition having been officially announced the previous evening, all the devotees of the *takimono awase*, both official champions as well as keen amateurs competing for the first time, had just one obsession: to identify, test and combine the fragrant substances in such a way that would best reflect the outline proposed by the Emperor Nijō, all being in agreement that the hardest challenge, the virtually insurmountable difficulty, not to say impossibility, was going to lie in the production of aromas suggestive of the moving body, of the long, free-flowing hair, of the face hollowed by the journey, and the quick breathing of the girl from between two mists.

This was the justification for the participants having to immediately abandon their other occupations to get their hands on whatever was on the shelves of the shop in Second Avenue. The most inspired must have already acquired all their components and proceeded to their first concoctions. All that remained for them to do was to feed their mixtures with a blend of honey and the flesh of plums which, as well as providing them with a little moisture, would help to enhance the aromas. Before dusk, servants would disappear into the snowstorm to go and secretly bury in the dark and loamy banks of the Yodogawa the paulownia boxes containing the concoctions prepared by their masters – the closeness of the river was thought to aid the preservation of incenses, and its banks were worn away by countless burrows which avoided the necessity of having to dig in ground hardened by the cold.

Watanabe and Kusakabe had not progressed this far. It is

true that they had allowed themselves to be delayed by the little widow and her wretched fish. How much time lost for a few carp! How could their listless swimming in a temple pond further the meditation of pilgrims who had come to pray to the Buddha?

"Let's stop worrying ourselves about this woman, *sensei*. Let us give her the agreed price – even though it strikes me as a bit exorbitant for eight miserable fish that any fisherman from the Yodogawa could have supplied – and send her home. Now, should you wish to punish her for her delay in delivering the creatures which, all things considered, have nothing exceptional about them (except perhaps for the two or three carp with black scales, the only ones that seem to me to be worthy of the carp the fisherman from Shimae brought us in the past), you have only to send her back without paying her, which would be a punishment in several ways. First of all, she would feel greatly humiliated at having to leave Heian Kyō without any payment; and secondly, she would tremble with fear all along the way home thinking of the punishment her people would have in store for her for coming back empty-handed. And the fact is that they would not spare her: I would go so far as to say that these peasants never have much pity for each other, that they are even quite cruel. Consider this, one day when she was sewing for the Empress, the Noble Lady of the Wardrobe service pricked her finger, blood flowed, and it drew a red snake coiled on her arm from her wrist to her elbow, which reminded us of that dreadful story of . . ."

But Watanabe was no longer listening. He was thinking of Amakusa Miyuki's face, her half-opened mouth that revealed teeth of such common whiteness, and from that mouth he remembered having seen spurt towards him a sparkling little bubble that had burst on his upper lip.

Then he faltered on his feet, not like an old man whose legs have given way, but like a young man discovering the overpowering and delightful poison of intoxication.

"Atsuhito," he said suddenly, "I entrust you with the two mists, and the half-moon bridge in the middle, and what it spans. Or what it contravenes. You have everything you need for that, don't you? Make lavish use of all those fragrances that we brought back from Second Avenue, concoct your perfumes in coarse grains, wrap them in a square of silk which you will tie with a ribbon trimmed with the branch of a plum tree, and if you think the incense should be enhanced by gold, to set it ablaze in the presence of the Emperor, then do not hesitate: grate, file down, scrape off as much gold as you need, you need only go through my jewels."

"But gold doesn't burn, *sensei* . . ."

"I know, Atsuhito, I know, it's not because I've grown old that my mind is as thick as a silly goose's. But even if it doesn't burn, gold melts at an intense temperature, it flows, it streams, it sketches lacework, estuaries, forests, so who is to say that it wouldn't also have a scent? What deep knowledge do we really have of smells? We say that something smells good or that it stinks, and we go no further. But we know scarcely any more about sweetness and foul smells than we know about Good and Evil. We pass through our lives flitting from one area of ignorance to another. We are toads, Atsuhito, we are toads. And now, listen: when you have created the incense of the half-moon bridge and the two mists (above all, take care to differentiate between those

243

two mists, His Majesty did not have the same inflexion in his voice when he described both of them), you will run and warn the carp woman that I am waiting for her. It will get colder and colder as the night progresses, the snow will turn to ice, so you must take this woman by the arm, Atsuhito, to hold her if she slips, and you will take her to my home, it doesn't matter what time it is, there will always be four lanterns lit."

IN A ROOM WITH drawn blinds, made more intimate by a series of screens that divided up the floor, Watanabe was dozing on a mat draped with a green material patterned with blue and black diamond shapes. It was no longer snowing, and the sky had cleared. The dawn light projected the pale shadow of a tree on the window screens. On a low table some sake was growing cold. The young servant girl who had brought and served it was also asleep, but on the floor.

Kusakabe was confused: he loathed delving into his master's privacy. The older he got, the less Watanabe, once so prudish, attended to his modesty. It was not exhibitionism, but rather a sort of negation of self. He was retreating gradually from the world of the living while continuing to inhabit it and derive certain pleasures from it as the presence of the sleeping servant girl testified. He was imitating the "retired" emperors who, no sooner had they been invested, had nothing more urgent to do than abdicate in favour of their sons, and to shut themselves away in a monastery where, protected from the troublemakers, the conspirators and the ambitious, they could continue to exert their influence with impunity and put their mark on their age.

245

Kusakabe shook the weary servant girl.

"Come on, get up! And light the coal fires, this house is freezing. If Watanabe-*sensei* falls ill, I'll hold you responsible."

Frightened, the servant girl leaped to her feet at once. Bowing all the while, she hurriedly tied the folds of her kimono and backed out of the room.

"What a commotion! Is our purveyor of carp there?" Watanabe said as he raised himself up on one elbow.

Kusakabe applied pressure to Miyuki's shoulder as she moved towards the mat. As soon as he was sure she was present, the Director of the Office of Gardens and Ponds lost interest in Miyuki and began to wriggle about, trying to achieve a standing position, which, these days, necessitated a painful exertion.

"Well, Atsuhito," he said. "Have you created the incense of mists?"

"Here it is, *sensei*," the assistant said as he held up two silk sachets. "It's still moist, but it will have time to dry between now and the opening contests. It will produce two scents in succession. The first – warm, fruity and sweetened, but with a dry, almost powdery base – will evoke the light cloud from which the lady suddenly materialised: rather than a mist, it will make one think of earth evaporating beneath the sun, a heavy earth with large, heady flowers – I imagine them being red . . ."

"Flowers that come from China, then, do you mean?" Watanabe interrupted, puckering his lips; like most of the population of Heian Kyō at that time, he had stopped believing that everything Chinese was superior to what was produced in the Imperial City.

"Further than China, *sensei*."

"Come now, what can be further than China?"

"I don't know the names of distant countries, and probably they are countless, but it is certain that there is something else on the other side of the sea."

"Some may indeed say so, but they have never been there. Do you think our imaginary lady could come from there?"

Kusakabe shrugged. He had no idea – that was for the Emperor to decide, for it was he, Nijō Tennō, who had created the image of this young woman between two clouds.

Watanabe soothed the forearm on which he was leaning, which was beginning to go numb.

"You spoke of two scents?"

"The second one will be as moist and fresh and rainy as the first will have been sunny. I ground up the scrapings, dust and resins, galbanum mainly, the most evocative of crushed ivy leaves and some undergrowth after it had rained."

"And for the bridge?"

Kusakabe puffed himself up with pride: he had devoted his night to the fragrant allegory of the bridge his Emperor had dreamed of.

"A wooden bridge, no nails but ropes, which gives it a certain elasticity – I'd lay a wager that it will expand and then bulge like a springboard when someone makes a dash for it. I have portrayed it with aromas of fir resin, burnt wood, hemp and also dung, for I suspect numerous and powerful troops of cavalry, banners flying, will have passed over this bridge."

Watanabe approved his assistant's visions: the Emperor would recognise his own in them.

As for himself, he had, as agreed, concentrated on the girl.

She should be someone youthful, a fresh but plucky young creature, someone ragged, yet graceful and shabby at the same time, slovenly but pleasant to look at, and pretty enough to have caught the imagination of Nijō (emperors or not, boys of fifteen years old rarely show bad taste where pretty faces are concerned), yet smeared with a sort of filth, which, from her hair to her toes, should reek somewhat.

He had thought initially that no incense could ever convey such a delicate fragrance, one which should be simultaneously ephemeral and alive. For while the ribbons of grey-blue smoke that rose in spirals from the perfume burners were accompaniments to life, embellishing it, making it more breathable literally and figuratively, they were not life itself.

It was then that he remembered the smooth, sugary scent, chiefly that of white clay and honey, that he had just had time to notice when a particle of Miyuki's saliva had landed on his lip.

"*Onna*," he said now, turning towards her, "the agreement reached between your village and the Office of Gardens and Ponds specifies the remuneration due to your community by way of compensation for the expenses on your journey, both coming and going, for the catching, porterage and delivery of twenty carp intended for the sacred ponds of the Imperial City . . ."

". . . remuneration," Kusakabe immediately filled in, "that amounts to a hundred rolls of silk taffeta. But the fact that you have only been able to provide eight fish, six of which do not really seem to match the quality to which your village had accustomed us . . ."

"Not my village," Miyuki interrupted. "My husband. It was

he, Katsuro, and he alone, who caught, selected and delivered the fish intended for your temples."

"In any event, your contract is only partially fulfilled. And so my master, His Excellency Watanabe Nagusa, has reckoned that it would be fair for the Office of Gardens and Ponds to pay you in proportion to what you have supplied us. Namely a bill of exchange relating to twenty rolls of silk taffeta, and not a hundred as was anticipated. Twenty rolls, it's still generous payment for the service provided."

Kusakabe stopped speaking. He kept his gaze fixed on Miyuki, ready to control her in case of an improper reaction on her part.

Watanabe was also watching Miyuki, but for another reason: he doubted that she would protest, but he thought she might be about to cry. She was still so young, even though she had reached an age when her death would not have upset anyone, so obviously exhausted, and so cut off from her own people, from her homeland.

It would probably be the last time in his long life that he would see – that he would *make*? – a woman cry, but it was not in order to savour her helplessness that he gazed at her so insistently: the room was actually so cold that he wondered whether, if she were to cry, Amakusa Miyuki's tears might not freeze on her cheeks.

If Mutobe Takeyoshi, the Deputy Managing Director of the Rites, were to be believed, this was a truly unforgettable spectacle. He recalled having seen it happen just once. Clasping a little monkey that she had wrapped in linen as though it were her own child, a woman, a certain Muroka, was walking along one of the Yodogawa canals. It was a winter evening and it was

249

extremely cold; the bricks that lined the canal were encased in ice, an ice that was so limpid, so transparent that it could not be seen, all that could be perceived through it was the rubble that covered the path; Muroka was not careful enough, and she had slipped, letting go of her monkey which had fallen into the river and been carried away, so that all that remained of it was the linen hood which, while protecting it, had become its shroud. After trying in vain to rescue her little creature, Muroka had been overcome with terrible despair, and it was on this occasion that the Deputy Managing Director of the Rites claimed to have seen this woman's tears turn into fragments of crystal as they streamed and froze on her face.

Watanabe doubted that such a thing were possible, for tears are warm when they spurt from the eyes, and he thought it very unlikely that they would have had time to grow cold before they had finished running down her cheeks.

After a short while, he became certain that Miyuki would not cry, and that he would not therefore witness the phenomenon that had fascinated the Deputy Managing Director of the Rites.

Then, drawing closer to her (he took advantage of the chance to breathe in the exhalations that arose from her small body – the success of what he had planned would depend on these fragrant wafts), he spoke to her gently.

"If you agree to help me in an undertaking that has assumed considerable importance for me, I shall cancel the reduction of eighty rolls of silk that has been imposed on you. Better still: you will not only have the one hundred rolls that were agreed had the Office of Gardens and Ponds been totally satisfied with you, but you will also receive one hundred more."

"What?" Kusakabe almost choked. "You're going to give her two hundred rolls?"

"And what must I do for that?" said Miyuki.

"Be."

"Be?"

"Be yourself, yes, in a place where you would never have believed you could be admitted, but I will introduce you and – oh, you will be dazzled, to be sure!"

She wondered what Watanabe meant by "be", and all her womanly suspicion, all her impoverished rusticity returned. Was not "being" the most natural thing there was, something that all living creatures share, and, in a certain way, inert things too? Since when was this worth two hundred rolls of silk taffeta?

"So," Watanabe said, "so you will *be*, you will *be* fully, you will *be* absolutely, but you will *be* simply – do you understand?"

"No, not very well, Excellency."

The old man let out a long groan and nodded gently. Miyuki could not help thinking that he looked just like one of those black bears that were sometimes seen high above Shimae, emerging from their winter hibernation.

"In any case, be careful not to let your *geta* clatter, for that would be very inappropriate. I would have advised you to go barefoot, but this snow that keeps falling makes me worry that the ground may be too cold. It would be best if you wore straw sandals. They would enable you to walk silently, almost surreptitiously, and they would not be seen beneath the hem of your *jûnihitoe*."

"Of my . . . forgive me, Excellency, of my what?"

"*Jûnihitoe*. The ceremonial dress that women who are

admitted to the Court wear: twelve layers of silk, the choice of their colours and the artistry with which they are arranged reflect the social rank and the good taste of the noble ladies. All this, Kusakabe-*san* will explain to you when he comes to collect you to take you to where I will be waiting for you. It won't be tomorrow, but the day after. And it would be wise for you to devote the hours ahead to thinking about this notable day. It doesn't matter if you tremble, or if your cheeks are on fire and your eyes are burning you, as long as you do not stop being yourself."

"What is it that will burn my eyes, Excellency?"

"The smoke that is going to spread all around you, with which you will fill, saturate and intoxicate your lungs. But be careful, Amakusa Miyuki: just your lungs! Do not give your body over to the pleasures of the incense. Yes, indeed, and don't look at me with those great, startled eyes. For that, you must know, is how the ladies of the Court ensure that they leave a pleasant aroma in their wake: they light the incense burner and cover it with a bamboo basket on which they lay out their clothing which then becomes impregnated with exquisite smells. And that's not all: these ladies sleep with their long hair stretched out over white porcelain boxes in which the captive incense crackles, not to mention the most risqué women, the most shameless ones, the most cunning ones, too who, in order to make their thighs, their bushes and their sexual parts more fragrant, stand with legs apart, vulvas open, over an incense burner. But you, no, oh no, do not yield to the voluptuousness of the fumes, do not use make-up, do not cover up the smell that rises from your flesh, even if you fear – and perhaps you are right to fear, you

252

are even certain to be right – that it distresses certain nostrils."

Miyuki could not understand: why would the Director of the Office of Gardens and Ponds not want her to smell nice? It was all the more disconcerting that Watanabe himself, on several occasions, had turned away from her, accusing her of giving off an unpleasant smell. And what is more, she agreed with him. With her own hands, she had handled heads that had been cut off, she had squelched about in pus and blood, she had sprawled in the mud; she knew she was filthy, that her skin was spattered with stains, and that most of the folds and recesses of her body were rotting. She sighed, her gaze lowered, her expression obstinate.

"I stink, Excellency, is that it?"

"Yes," he said. "There are not thirty-six thousand ways of saying it, my poor girl."

For the first time, he looked at her with a kindly expression.

"But the attractive or fetid smell that is given off never reflects the reality of a person," he continued. "It is only the way that this person appears to us."

"In this case, the least unpleasant one," Kusakabe observed.

"Why do you say that? Take a look at this woman."

Kusakabe squinted as he would if he were watching an insect crawl from one side of a lotus leaf to the other.

"I am looking at her, *sensei*. Well, tell me, what am I supposed to deduce from my contemplation?"

"Can you not see that she is beautiful?"

Kusakabe shifted from one foot to the other. When he was balanced on his right foot, he was tempted to take his master at his word, but when he leaned on the left foot, then it seemed to him that the *sensei* was making fun of him.

253

"Beautiful? Could Amakusa Miyuki be called beautiful?" he said, echoing his own words.

Even when pronounced in a dubious tone, the repetition of this incongruous term made the young woman to whom it referred laugh, so much so that she forgot to fan out her hand in front of her mouth, inflicting on the Director and his assistant the alarming spectacle of her horribly white teeth.

"Without a shadow of doubt," said the old man. "And if Amakusa Miyuki is beautiful, then beautiful too, that is to say good, are the aromas that belong to her, just as the peel is to the fruit, that thin layer that we remove because it is dirty in our eyes, dirty from having rolled beneath the tree, from having been lashed by the rain and gnawed by the moonlight, from having rotted in the dampness of barges, been mottled at the bottom of baskets, from having been fingered, smelled and weighed in the hand, from having endured the pressure of the fingers of lovers of persimmons in the markets of the East and the West. Do you know, Atsuhito, what Amakusa Miyuki smells of? Think! All you have to do, with minimal effort, is to substitute the good smell with the true smell. Have you got it? Have you understood at last why the Office of Gardens and Ponds is going to give her — I know it seems foolish to you, but I am still the Director — two hundred rolls of silk taffeta, and even three hundred if I can lay my old hands on them? The answer, Atsuhito, is that Amakusa Miyuki smells of life, that she exhales life from all the orifices of her body. Nine orifices if we are to believe the holy monk Nagarjuna, who is supposed to have lived for six hundred years and to have counted the openings of a woman's body, and, in six hundred years, he had time not just to count them

254

but also to verify his calculations. She secretes this life, she oozes it, and beads of it come from all the pores of her body. Therefore, Atsuhito, it could be quite possible – justify it as you will – that Amakusa Miyuki, who came from far away, from the very little known (by me, in any case) village of Shimae, may be precisely the girl between two clouds that His Majesty has dreamed about."

Kusakabe looked at the young woman then with different eyes.

DESPITE ITS DIMENSIONS OF thirty metres in length by twenty-five metres in width, which made it one of the largest rooms in the Palace, the Throne Room, the *shishinden*, was only opened for ceremonies of great solemnity, such as a coronation or a funeral tribute, and would never have been able to accommodate all the inhabitants of the Imperial City.

Furthermore, even if it meant displeasing the crowds, the Emperor had decided that the *takimono awase* should be held within the more modest proportions of the ceremonial room of the Pavilion of Purity and Freshness, which was adjacent to his sleeping quarters and encompassed the oratory where he worshipped.

The choice of this room provided two advantages: Emperor Nijō, who had not yet rid himself of his youthful shyness, would feel perfectly at home, and the relatively restricted size of the room would enable the scents to be constrained, and appreciated for longer, instead of being dispersed in a wide open room such as the *shishinden*.

For this reason, only a limited number of the public would gather for the first *takimono awase* of Emperor Nijō's reign; but the craze for perfume contests, which now aroused as much passion as archery tournaments or poetry competitions, was such that the most enthusiastic among the one hundred and thirty thousand or so inhabitants of Heian Kyō enlisted messengers who, after exposing their kimonos to the competing fumes of incense, rushed to position themselves at the main gates of the Palace, where, while updating their recruiters on how the contest was going, they shook their sleeves under the noses of the gamblers who could thereby gain an idea of the high level of the challenges and place bets on the victory of such or such a blend.

The contests began at the middle of the hour of the Sheep. They were supposed to finish when the daylight dimmed to the point where it would become necessary to light candles, the fumes of which might then distort the purity of the fumes rising from the scent-burners.

The participants, among them the Princess Yoshiko, who it was said would soon be elevated to the rank and title of Empress, were seated on low stools forming a semi-circle around a bronze perfume-burner the height of a man, the embossed decorations of which depicted scenes from the legend of Watanabe no Tsuna killing a demon at the Rashōmon gate.

Facing south, a pedestal made of Hinoki cypress supported the throne, a simple black lacquer armchair and a canopy attached to three anchorage points above it, also covered in black lacquer and framed by a vermilion frieze encrusted with mirrors and precious stones.

Still sealed, the perfume-caskets (the Emperor's casket, made of gold lacquer enriched with delicate pearl engravings, had cost several thousand rolls of silk) lay on low tables adjacent to the competitors' seats.

Blown in through the window openings, piles of snow were crushed against the partitions, the sliding doors and the screens illuminated by the two artists from the Office of Painting and Interior Decoration. For a long time, this department had consisted of ten or more artists, but its subsidies had been drastically reduced to the benefit of the Office of Military Affairs.

Following Watanabe's instructions, Kusakabe had positioned Miyuki close to one of the windows. But in spite of the gusts of cold air, Miyuki was suffocating beneath the twenty kilos and more of her *jûnihitoe* for which the Director of the Office of Gardens and Ponds had chosen one by the name of Lightning Red Maple. The first layer, being of white silk, served as an undergarment, and then ten other dresses were worn on top of it, which, as they became brighter, displayed virtually all the shades of red existing in nature, from the carmine of maple trees in autumn to the pale pink blossom of the plum tree, by way of the crimson tan of certain leaves and the violet of the lespedeza that deer feast upon.

To begin with, Miyuki had gazed ecstatically at this palette of hues that were so beautiful to contemplate, these silks that were so soft to stroke and that she scarcely dared to touch for fear of her skin being too rough for these extraordinarily smooth materials.

"*Onna*," Kusakabe had said, "as a rule two women are needed to help a noble lady put on the *jûnihitoe*. But here there is just you and me, and so I am going to help you."

And he handed her the first kimono, the white tunic.

"Come on now, let's get rid of that old rag, and put this on."

Her hands pressed to her breast, she hesitated.

"But why, Kusakabe-*san*, why? Who am I to deserve to wear such finery?"

"Who you are, *onna*, is of no importance. And what is more, let me tell you that the less people know about you, the better you will carry out the mission that Watanabe-*sensei* has entrusted you with . . ."

Once more, she wanted to know what this mission involved, but the tunic, as it slipped enveloped her, covered her mouth. She still went on mumbling beneath the white silk, but her words were inaudible.

Watanabe's assistant was already handing her the next kimono.

". . . and by way of additional recompense, you will be able to take with you everything you have worn this evening and carry it all back with you on the road to Shimae."

In the absence of a mirror in the *kyōzō*, Miyuki had to rely on Kusakabe's piercing gaze to have an idea of how the *jûnihitoe* had transformed her into a new person.

A hairstyle consisting of a long plait extending from the base of the neck down to her heels, balanced by a chignon at the top of her head, a powdered white face with narrow openings for the mouth, with black lacquered teeth (at last!), lips smeared in safflower oil, and a fan made of thin strips of cypress depicting bamboo trees and rocks beside a raging torrent completed the metamorphosis.

"*Onna*," Kusakabe said with a bow, "you will do honour, great honour, to Watanabe-*sensei*."

Miyuki did not reply. She wondered whether Katsuro would have approved of what they had made of her. She doubted he would. But the strange transformation they had imposed on her was not going to last, still less recur: she would soon leave Heian Kyō, and she could not imagine taking the twelve tunics that made up her *jûnihitoe* back to Shimae; she would have a hard enough time with the rolls of silk that Watanabe had promised her, as well as the agreed remuneration she would earn in the form of bills of exchange and copper bars.

The costume was so heavy that Kusakabe had to support her as far as the cart that he had ordered, which, amid snow piled almost as high as the wheel hubs, was waiting at the foot of the Saiji pagoda.

Miyuki had no idea where Watanabe's assistant was taking her, nor did she know what the Director of the Office of Gardens and Ponds was expecting of her once she got there, but she had decided to behave in an exemplary fashion.

For were he not dead, Katsuro would have taken enough potter's clay from the banks of the Kusagawa to sculpt a peony in full bloom, which he would have exposed to the moonbeams (they dry more effectively than do sunbeams) until its petals became hard and firm, and then he would have placed it in a box on a bed of ferns, and, on one of his trips to deliver carp to the Imperial City, he would have given it to Watanabe to thank him for the good care the Office of Gardens and Ponds had taken of his wife.

But Katsuro had left this world for the Pure Land of the Buddha Amitabha; he would never come back to make peonies out of red clay, so it was up to Miyuki to think of a way to thank Watanabe-*sensei* and his young assistant, and she had decided to offer them perfect obedience.

Most of the fourteen gates giving access to the Imperial Palace incorporated a hump-back bridge that prevented vehicles from gaining access. But Kusakabe's cart was able to pass safely through the Gate of the Will of Heaven, which was opened freely to the carriages of high-ranking people.

As soon as they had passed through the threshold, however, the cart had to stop to be unyoked: draught animals were not allowed on the inner paths of the Palace for fear that the Emperor might see their excrement, which would have resulted in several days of self-purification for him; the impending *takimono awase* meant that Nijō Tennō had better things to do than to remain shut away in his apartments.

Once the oxen had been unyoked, servants took hold of the shafts and tethered themselves to the heavy vehicle in order to pull it, using only their arms, to the Pavilion of Purity and Freshness.

The monastic simplicity of the building contrasted with the deployment of an impressive guard of honour, whose *nobori*, those narrow vertical banners attached to a pole, rustled in the wind.

From the majesty of this militia, from the shy gaze of soldiers who stared at her through the openings of their helmets, from the festoons of ice which, barely formed, melted on their breastplates, proof that living bodies inhabited these shells that

261

looked like demons, Miyuki realised at last why Kusakabe had attired her in this way: he was leading her into the presence of the Emperor.

She was frightened, her eyes filled with tears.

"Don't cry, *onna*, I don't have a cloth to wipe your face with; and nor can I put my fingers on your cheeks to stop your tears: I would risk spoiling your make-up, and you must be perfect to appear before His Majesty."

But she was not perfect, oh no, and she had always known it despite the compliments that Katsuro showered upon her. She was no fool: he had married her not for her virtues, but because he had dreamed of nets that were soft and smooth enough to catch his carp without wounding them, and because he had noticed Miyuki's hands, and her nimble fingers that could weave and knot the sprigs of willow. Later, these fingers that were so delicate and skilful proved, moreover, to be accomplished at love-making, fingers that were conducive to fondling, fingers that were succulent to taste – Katsuro loved nothing so much as to catch Miyuki stroking herself, whereupon he would swoop down on her like a bear on a honeycomb, and lick her, suck her and try to envelop her fingers that were moist with her pleasure, and so slender that he could squeeze them into a little pink bunch and pretend to swallow them as far as her wrist.

And she was still less perfect because there was this scent that came from her that she was not aware of, or was no longer aware of, but which had repelled the Director of the Office of Gardens and Ponds when, taking her for a *yūjo*, he had embraced her aboard the pleasure boat on the Yodogawa, and, more recently still, he had inhaled her again, finding words to describe her this

262

time, comparing her smell to that of overcooked rice, to a silk outfit left out in the rain, to the carcass of a bird.

And although she was far from perfection (in addition to what has just been mentioned, it should also be noted that the journey to Heian Kyō had caused her feet to crack, that the yoke had deformed her hands and etched two purple furrows across her shoulders, that beads of sweat tinged with blood sometimes formed on her skin when it was exposed to the elements, that her lips were chapped), Watanabe-*sensei* and Kusakabe-*san* had had the very humiliating notion of forcing her to appear before somebody who, unlike her, was considered by an entire nation as the perfect being *par excellence*.

Kusakabe pushed her forward as the sliding doors of the Pavilion of Purity and Freshness were drawn apart.

The Upstairs Room, where only the privileged, the nobility or the personal guests of the Emperor were permitted to enter, was filled with women who, like Miyuki, were overwhelmed by the layers of dresses that were as sumptuous as they were stifling, and who were squatting on the floor where they resembled a colony of enormous multi-coloured butterflies.

Set back from the throne, some musicians were perched on a platform, performing a slow and twanging piece; two percussionists were taking it in turns to beat out the rhythm on a large drum decorated with dragons.

Miyuki's sobs redoubled. She smothered them with the sleeves of her *júnihitoe*. Swept along by the inertial force of her twelve dresses, she made her way among the butterflies slumped on the floor, until Kusakabe held her back by a fold of her train and pushed her against a partition, equidistant from a brazier

263

and an open window which let in occasional flurries of snow.

"*Onna*," he whispered, "stay here and don't let anyone notice you. I will tell you when the time comes to mingle with the others."

To publicly demonstrate his concern for Princess Yoshiko, the Emperor requested that she should be the first to express her perfumed version of the allegory of the girl on the wooden bridge – a most significant favour, since the young girl's incense would thereby be burned in an atmosphere as yet unsullied by any other emanations.

The casket that Yoshiko had prepared contained small pots of a porcelain so fine it was almost translucent. They were filled with aloes, cloves, valerian, boswellia from the Arabic peninsula, cinnamon and agastache, the slightly mentholated scent of which was supposed to accentuate the youthful grace of the princess.

Unfortunately for her, although her concoction smelled pleasant – even if the perfumes chosen had not been especially original – the three referees considered that it needed a great deal of imagination to interpret from the princely fumaroles a vision of a girl, her mists and her half-moon bridge.

But because of the particular attention with which the Emperor honoured her, Yoshiko nevertheless was rewarded with success she did not deserve.

It was then the sovereign's turn to submit his own composition for the assessment of the gathering. Even though he had defined the subject proposed for the competition, Nijō Tennō recognised that he had only partially succeeded in conveying all the features of his brief.

He was reasonably satisfied with the effluences associated with the two clouds of mist (he had blended one of them with the smoke of plum blossom, well known for its resemblance to the mists of the Hereafter), and he was counting a great deal on a certain woody fragrance that was meant to evoke the half-moon, or moon-shaped, bridge, a scent that he had cleverly "chilled" thanks to the undertones of seaweed that suggested both the coldness of the moon and the idea of water flowing under the bridge.

But he had failed to represent the moving outline of the girl whose *geta* caused the deck of the bridge to echo like a giant drum. In fact, he had given up depicting it altogether in the end, making do with an incense that was conducive to sleep, inducing a kind of drowsiness that encouraged the sudden emergence of waking dreams in which the semi-slumbering dreamer, his oneiric perception sustained by an appropriate poem, might perhaps succeed in visualising the girl on the bridge – while the Emperor, whose voice had not quite broken, chanted through the coils of incense:

> *From the Katashinagawa*
> *Above the great bridge*
> *Wearing a dress printed in*
> *Red crimson*
> *And indigo from the mountains*
> *All on her own*
> *Would the beautiful child passing by*
> *Have a husband*
> *Or would she sleep alone?*
> *I should like to ask her . . .*

The spell, in any case, had a bewitching effect on Miyuki. From the first exhalations, she surrendered to these fumes that were so complex, so exhilarating, and so much more delicious (certain coils of incense appeared substantial enough to be bitten into and rolled around her mouth) than the vapours of medicinal stench that stagnated under temple roofs; and she experienced what felt like a flush of warmth each time she set eyes on the young emperor, for the body, and especially the face, of Nijō Tennō was still at that touching phase when man and boy are merging, like cherry blossom that, from the moment it leaves the tree, appears to be flying invincibly into the light even as it drops to the ground, where, within a flash, it will become yellow, withered and trampled upon.

But the more she admired the almost perfect beauty of the Emperor, the more Miyuki felt painfully affected by the death of Katsuro, who had been a man of no particular allure, who had even been ugly in some ways. Because his tireless expeditions to the riverbed had required him to keep his legs wide apart to resist the current, his limbs had grown crooked and bowed like those of cavaliers. His body had gradually become weather-beaten from the dual impact of the sun's reflection when the weather was fine and the biting cold of the icy water in winter; his face had been furrowed with fresh lines; he had experienced pain in his lower back and in one shoulder; and he had walked with a limp, slightly bent forward, not lifting his knees, though his dark eyes had remained alert, lively and anxious as those of birds, very different from those of warriors and samurai who had a strangely staring gaze – so much so, Katsuro used to say, that you could never immediately tell, when

266

you encountered one dozing in the saddle, whether he was alive or dead.

"Why do your eyes look anxious?" Miyuki had asked him.

"Anxious for you, of course. Always the fear of not finding you there when I come up from the river. Or finding you wounded or ill, I don't know. Everything that can happen between morning and evening to someone you love."

Now, Katsuro no longer had the eyes of a bird for her anymore, eyes that were on the alert; the sockets of Katsuro's eyes were now empty.

After the Emperor, it was the turn of the Pacificator General of the Barbarians, the *Seiitai shōgun*, to offer his attempt at the imperial sketch.

His versions of mist were moderately applauded. They were unquestionably striking – so much so that they made some women cough – but they did not have sufficient depth; and it was considered that his allegory of the bridge relied on fragrances that were too sugary to portray something so crude and masculine as a wooden bridge built with beams and assembled with hemp ropes and crude dowels. As for his girl in the mist, she had to be particularly evanescent, for if she walked across the bridge as the shogun encouraged his audience to believe by quivering his nostrils and rolling his eyes as though he were accompanying her on her way, she left no fragrant scent in her wake.

Once the shogun's fumes had been dispersed, with much fluttering of fans, a certain Kinnobu, *tokimori no hakase*,* crouched

---

* A doctor specialising in water clocks.

267

before the perfume-burner and offered his own scented translation of the imperial fable to the gathering.

But if his effluvia were among the most convincing, the physical behaviour of his incense turned out to be off-putting, to say the least: instead of creating arabesques, spirals, loops and knots, his coils of smoke rose up and took on the rather unattractive form of a slender, greyish snake balancing on its tail, whose mouth had to be sniffed from close quarters in order to breathe in the aromas.

After Kinnobu, the Inspector of the Northern Provinces, Tadanobu, and the Head of the Private Chancery both came forward. Their attempts were honourable, but nothing more.

In actual fact, the block on which all the competitors stumbled was the perfumed embodiment of the girl. Only the Emperor had come close with his recital of a poem over the emission of incense, but this was an expedient that contravened the rules of *takimono awase*. Since it was the Emperor, this departure from the norm might perhaps be tolerated, although the rather austere expressions on the faces of the referees did not augur well.

But their verdict would come later. For the time being, the three judges bowed towards the Director of the Office of Gardens and Ponds to signify that, if he was ready, it was his turn to present his interpretation.

Watanabe proceeded warily, as though every movement of his joints was a painful ordeal – which, indeed, it was. He gathered together the little silk bags that contained the different aromatic pebbles he was going to blend, and untied the threads, each of which was attached to a vegetal sample pertaining to the specific perfume that the incense in the sachet would diffuse.

268

Then, using small sticks, he placed in the perfume-burner a few pieces of an odourless charcoal, which had been stirred in a separate receptacle until it took on an ash-grey hue.

While Watanabe was preparing his performance, with movements as precise as they were slow, Kusakabe rejoined Miyuki beside the brazier.

"*Onna*," he murmured, "the moment has arrived. Please watch Watanabe-*sensei* closely. Do not take your eyes off him. And when his gaze meets yours, then you must go towards him. What he expects of you is this: go to meet him, go without any hurry, slipping slowly among all these lounging ladies who are going to breathe in (and with what eagerness), the incense kindled by His Excellency. Hindered by their clothing, numb from not moving for so long, you must not expect them all to stand up and let you pass. Don't let it upset you, do not stop, do not try to push your way through, simply glide on without worrying about a thing. The *jûnihitoe* prevent you from seeing exactly what is going on, but you can trust me: they are kneeling down, sitting on their heels, some of them appear to be lying down, perhaps they are asleep, life at Court is more exhausting than you might think, but don't worry about them, step over them, skip over them, and let the folds of your twelve dresses brush against them, caress them, polish them, soothe them like so many silken brush strokes. Except that, instead of dabbing them with a touch of colour, it is a scented impression that you will transmit to these ladies: the scent of the girl between two clouds of mist."

At this point in his advice, he looked at Miyuki with an expression of sudden anxiety,

"You will do what I've just told you, *onna*?"

"Yes, of course."

She looked at him in turn. She did not understand his insistence. What was he frightened of? It was not so difficult to walk across a room, even when it was crowded with women whose rich costumes all but prevented them from moving.

Being nobody, knowing nobody, Miyuki would slip through this gathering without being noticed, and the company of languorous ladies would reconvene in her wake like the river after a boat has sliced through it.

And Miyuki stepped away from the partition she was leaning against.

She had scarcely taken a few steps before Kusakabe noticed that the silk wings of her *jûnihitoe* seemed to flow and float more on the right side of her body, which had been exposed to the heat of the brazier, whereas they fell with a marked stiffness on the left, where the twelve layers of material had been subjected to the cold draught that blew in from the open window.

So now, he thought, the subtle aromas emanating from her must be more apparent on the side of her body where the air, made more volatile by the heat of the brazier, circulated freely between the silk layers of her clothes.

Since the throne upon which the Emperor sat was on Miyuki's left-hand side, the colder part of her body, Kusakabe immediately applied pressure to her shoulders to correct her path. Obeying his instruction, she advanced with small, gliding steps towards the blue fumes that rose from the perfume-burner, onto whose embers Watanabe had sprinkled the particles of incense that he had mixed together by crushing them in his hands.

Trying not to let her *geta* clatter across the floor, Miyuki moved so unobtrusively that by the time the noble ladies noticed her she was already on top of them, a term that should be understood in its true sense, because, in order to step over them without deviating from her course, she was obliged to cover them with her silks, allowing their twelve layers to run over them and, with a slow and careful sliding step, enfold each contour, each curve, each twist and turn of their bodies and their faces.

After having experienced the fragrant, casual caress of the *jûnihitoe* tunics, the butterfly ladies could only marvel at the unsettling aromas they had just breathed in. It did not occur to them that they could have come from Miyuki: immersed in the account Nijō Tennō had given of his dream and accustomed never to question anything that issued from the mouth of the Emperor, they believed that they had inhaled from the incense provided by the Director of the Office of Gardens and Ponds the trail of the imaginary girl running from one cloud of mist to another.

As for the physical reality of having their faces skimmed by Miyuki's dresses, which they might have considered humiliating, the blame, if there were any blame, lay with the excessive number of invitations that had been sent out without taking into account the limited space provided by the Upper Room of the Pavilion of Purity and Freshness.

In any case, they were careful not to criticise Miyuki, for it was very likely that this person, newly arrived in Heian Kyō, whom nobody had yet come across in the Tea Garden, at the Hall of Female Dancing, the Office of Dressmaking or the Shrine of the God of the Stove, might be one of those modest, versatile creatures whom the Korean or Chinese ambassadors offered the Emperor of Japan when he was tired of being given fighting fish, cormorants or thrushes capable of imitating the human voice; and it would certainly have been unseemly to disparage a gift intended for Nijō Tennō.

"How many unexpected fragrances there were in the wake of the girl in the story that His Majesty told us!" remarked one of the first butterflies that Miyuki had brushed against. "Her shadow passed by so quickly that I may have been mistaken, but I think I could identify the aromas of the undergrowth, of a forest path, and the moss after the rain."

"And damp manure, whose smell is liable to make one's eyes sting," said a second butterfly, this one dressed mainly in orange colours.

"Is it not rather the dry dung stirred up by the wind that stings the eyes?" wondered an elderly butterfly whose layers of silk encompassed every shade of blue.

"What is certain is that the ghost of the girl smelled more of moist eel than of sheep. It leads me to think that the cloud of mist from which she emerged before crossing the half-moon bridge is not Chinese but Korean. I have already observed that anything Chinese often has a stench of sweat, it comes from the rams, their country is swarming with them, you cannot move there without coming across a ram."

"As for me," whispered a butterfly with glints of emerald green and turquoise, who gave off a stench of bile, "yes, I thought I detected a whiff of vomit, and that is a smell I can easily distinguish because I find it so unbearable. It reminded me of mud, but sodden mud, the kind that lies at the very bottom of the water.

And, consequently, I wonder whether His Majesty, believing he was dreaming of a girl, might really have been dreaming of a *kappa*?"

"His Majesty could never have imagined a creature as hideous as those river monsters!"

"Creatures sometimes escape from their creator," said a lemon-yellow butterfly lady. "Now that I have smelled it, I confess that I am not sure whether this girl could have had this delicacy, this purity that the Emperor's dream attributed to her. For I thought I recognised . . . well, so it seemed to me . . . a vague, *vague* stench of urine – no?"

"In any case, these are the first fumes of incense which are so close to the reality of life."

"And of death, such as those foul smells people bring with them when they come back from Toribeno."

This reference to the former burial site on the hillside, where corpses were discarded and ended up being devoured by dogs, put an end to the chatter, and all that could be heard were Miyuki's *geta* echoing on the wooden floor, as well as the gentle sputtering of the incense.

Unmoved by the comments that she had inspired, but which she too thought applied to the ghost in the imperial dream, Miyuki continued her progress across the room, stepping over the still-kneeling ladies and mumbling *shitsurei shimasu, shitsurei shimasu*, the apology that Kusakabe had taught her to say if ever she felt she was about to be impolite.

As he crumbled up his incense, Watanabe never took his eyes off her.

When he saw her drawing closer to the pedestal supporting the throne, he motioned to her not to shy away whatever she did, and to draw as close to the Emperor as decency allowed.

But just as she was about to step under the canopy, where the fumes from the incense-burner drifted, driven by the flapping of an *uchiwa*, a large, rigid fan which the Director of the Office of Gardens and Ponds had vigorously activated, the foot of one of the chamberlains slipped beneath the *jûnihitoe*, caught one of Miyuki's ankles, and she fell suddenly at the feet of the Emperor.

Bewildered and confused, she tried to get to her feet at once, but, hampered by the weight and sheer volume of her dresses, she had no choice but to remain wriggling about on her back like a tortoise flipped over by young rascals.

Realising that she would not be able to get up, Watanabe hastily crumbled his last blend of incense over the embers.

"She has crossed over the bridge," he announced. "Here is the other cloud of mist, the second cloud, into which the girl rushes . . ."

The new haze he created was so fresh that the audience felt, as they inhaled it, that they were walking through drizzle, or beside a waterfall.

"Yes, yes," exclaimed one of the three judges, jiggling up and down on his bench. "That is it exactly, a complete success! A human smell, a human smell!"

"The autumn wind rolls around, fresh and scented, in the wake of an invisible, elusive girl – it smells of over-ripe persimmon, nashi pears with honey, and something else, something indefinable. I shall never forget this wind!" added the second judge, going one better, and nodding his head feverishly as he sought the approval of his two colleagues. "You are the winner, Director Watanabe, oh, you are the winner for sure!"

"For this *takimono awase*, the first of the Hogen era, we declare Watanabe Nagusa the winner," declared the third judge solemnly.

The astonishment of the Director of the Office of Gardens and Ponds was such that everyone could see, as he covered his face to conceal his emotions, that his sleeves were wet with tears.

He bowed low until his forehead touched the tips of the Emperor's slippers.

"I refuse to accept this victory, I forgo it entirely! The judges should kindly revise their first impression and grant success to the only one who deserves it: Nijō Tennō."

"No," said the Emperor. "The victory is yours, Director Watanabe. For my part, given the choice of the crown of success and the thrill of having been able, thanks to you, to believe for a moment in the reality of my dream, I choose the thrill."

He beckoned to his chamberlain, the very one who had caused Miyuki's fall, to wave his fan to draw the last fumes of smoke towards the throne. To which Watanabe responded with a few flaps of his *uchiwa*, discreet but forceful enough to eclipse the timid puff of air created by the chamberlain's flimsy folding fan, and to wrap Miyuki in the exquisitely scented mist.

Realising that Watanabe now wanted to protect her from the gaze – and no doubt the questions – of the Emperor, Miyuki withdrew into herself, curling up on the floor, as though spirited away into a perfect stillness and silence.

"So how did you manage to do that, Director Watanabe?" the Emperor asked. "Your clouds of mist are so seductive! Especially the second one, that final haze into which the girl has just disappeared, for, I know from having tried myself, it defies all logic to suggest the drizzle and the moisture of the mist through the dry and burning heat of blazing coals. Your evocation of the half-moon bridge was also very successful, too – did we not hear this bridge echoing to the clatter of the girl's *geta* even though she was only a dream? Did we not breathe in the miasmas of foul water and withered plants stagnating beneath the vault of the footboards? But the most astonishing thing of all, Director Watanabe, was the trajectory of the young girl. (I was about to say: her path among us, because to tell the truth, at a certain moment, I thought she was there, so close that I could follow her with my eyes – even touch her perhaps.) Tell me, what substances have you blended and burned in order to achieve this miracle? I find it hard to believe that you found them amid the clutter of Second Avenue. Might you have been provided with them by the private Chancellery where they keep the special incense used for Buddhist celebrations?"

"I must be honest and admit that one of the perfumed ingredients that I used, the most complex of all, came neither from Second Avenue nor from the private Chancellery."

"Could you have brought it from a foreign land?" the Emperor said, frowning. "And yet you know that we no longer appoint embassies, and nor do we receive any: Japan is all we need."

"The ingredient I speak of comes from the empire over which Your Majesty rules. But from a distant province of that empire; or rather a little-known one. I have never been there myself, but I have sent emissaries. That is where this constituent of the perfume that Your Majesty has thought fit to say corresponds closely to the damsel of his dream comes from. It is from there too – but this is a detail – that the carp which inhabit our sacred ponds come."

"It must be a beautiful region," said the Emperor reflectively.

"It is the village of Shimae, on the Kusagawa river. And here is its representative," said the Director of the Office of Gardens and Ponds as he pointed to Miyuki who was emerging from clouds of incense, her face buried in the folds of her *jûnihitoe*, still wreathed in smoke.

"I noticed her just now among the other women. She seemed to be looking for her place, a place she could not find. Would it be she who supplied you with the memorable perfume?"

"Amakusa Miyuki provided me with it, yes, Your Majesty. Most of it, at least. I confess that the first time I smelled it, I had no idea what I would do with it. No, I had not the slightest idea. It is so unexpected. There are aromas of very ripe persimmons and nashi pears in honey. In some ways, there is even something sickly about it. Persimmon, nashi pears in honey, probably, but not just these things. To tell the truth, I found it hard to endure the smell."

"I think she still has a few shreds of this substance in the folds of her *jûnihitoe*," said Princess Yoshiko, holding her nose in comical fashion. In fact, she twisted it as though she were softening it before pulling it off.

As soon as the Emperor had retired to his apartments, the Upper Room emptied. Servants came to extinguish the torches and the perfume-burners, sweeping up the hot ashes and soot, which presented a threat of serious fire.

Watanabe, Kusakabe and Miyuki were the last to leave the Pavilion of Purity and Freshness. It was no longer snowing, but a thick white carpet covered the pathways and buildings. The Palace, which, owing to the tracery of rammed clay walls usually gave the appearance of a biscuit, seemed to be coated with a thick cream this evening. Somewhere behind the maze of walls, a woman was crying out in the pangs of childbirth, and shadowy figures clasping wickerwork baskets full of moist, very hot linens, which steamed in the night air, were hurrying towards her bedroom. These matrons were probably wearing attractively coloured kimonos, but the snow was gleaming so brightly that, in contrast, they looked like columns of frenzied black ants.

In front of the porchway, some *daijō*, officials from the upper minor seventh rank, were exercising three splendidly harnessed white horses, their tails and their manes adorned with paper scrolls on which poems were inscribed.

The *daijō* from the Office of Horses explained to Watanabe that these animals came from the fresh, dry pastures of Shinano where the horses intended for the Emperor had been bred. The latter had issued orders that three of these mounts should be given to the Director of the Office of Gardens and Ponds to celebrate his victory this evening at the *takimono awase*.

Watanabe took the three tethers, and placed them in his right hand, laying them out in such a way that strands of equal length emerged from his finger joints when he clenched his fist.

"There is a *shinano* for you, Atsuhito. You have certainly deserved it. Choose," he said, offering the hand with the protruding tethers to his assistant.

Kusakabe pulled on one of them until he had unrolled the

full length of the rein, at the end of which one of the white horses reared up, standing on its hind legs, flicking its tail, its ears flat against its neck.

"Good, Atsuhito," Watanabe said. "Very good, of the three mares, fate has allocated the finest to you. The most demonstrative, in any case."

Seeing the gentle, firm way that Kusakabe hastened to stroke the horse's neck to calm it, Watanabe thought to himself that, when he was falling asleep in a short while, he would try to dream that he too was a restless horse of sorts, and that Kusakabe's warm hand was running over his body.

"Your turn, *onna*," he added with a smile.

It was the first time for ages – forty years, perhaps even fifty – that the Director of the Office of Gardens and Ponds had allowed himself to smile. Prior to this evening of fragrances and snow, Watanabe no Nagusa had contented himself with no more than a slight twitch – if that – of the corners of his mouth.

"Pull, *onna*, try your luck, pull on the tether that inspires you," Watanabe said. "At the end of it, there is a horse to take you back home, a horse to carry you and the treasure I shall give you as promised."

"No," Miyuki said. "I don't want a horse. I don't know how to ride it."

Watanabe looked at her in disappointment, regretting his smile. What was the good of waiting several decades before deciding to smile, if this grimace – for a smile was only ever a sort of grimace – merely produced a sullen and sulky refusal in return?

Miyuki shrugged.

279

"We only ever see those creatures beneath the bottoms of your emissaries when you send them to order us to fish for carp, the finest ones in our river, and deliver them to you."

Watanabe stepped towards her, but she moved away, her arms held out in front of her.

"Not so close, *sensei*," she said. "Don't forget that you loathe my smell. I know very well that you were appalled by it. I didn't realise myself, but it may be true after all that I smell badly – at least, compared to these scents that are everywhere here, on people, on curtains, and even in the latrines. I prefer you to stay away. It would not please Katsuro that you should be inconvenienced because of me. He would say that your embarrassment is more humiliating for me than it is for you. And he would not like me to be humiliated. In any way. He was always proud of me, even if he had no real reason to be. Between him and me, it all started with those nets that I sewed for him – but they were no credit to me, anyone could have plaited them together, those nets, it was just that he must have found it easier to ask me rather than some other woman."

She left. Despite the height of her *geta*, the snow clung to her ankles in rings of ice so painful she had a burning sensation. For her journey back to Shimae, she would wear her straw sandals instead, her *waraji*; they would be more reliable crossing the Kii range where, given the early arrival of winter, she should expect to endure intense cold and encounter slabs of ice on which she risked slipping and tumbling into a chasm. Should she have accepted the horse that Watanabe had offered her? She would never have ventured to ride it, but, by leading it by the reins and walking on one side or other of it depending on the wind, she would have been able to create a sort of living shield against the flurries of snow. Quite apart from the fact that the horse would be warm, and that by snuggling up to it she would have been able to share some of its warmth. And then – and this was no small thing – she could have talked to it about Katsuro in a loud voice and told it that she thought she heard her husband's footsteps behind her, following her across the cold earth.

"Listen, horse," she would have said to it – no, not "listen, horse", she would have given it a name, she would have called it Yukimichi;* nothing could have suited it better.

---

* *Yukimichi* means a snowy path.

THE FOLLOWING DAY, AT the turning point between the hour of the Rabbit and that of the Dragon,* when it was barely light, Kusakabe came to collect Miyuki at her lodging.

She was already waiting to leave, she had divested herself of the twelve silk layers of her *jûnihitoe* (– what would she have done with them in Shimae?), she had hung them on the posts of the mouldering screens in a corner of the *kyōzō*, then she had rolled up her mat and sat down on it as she would on a doorstep.

Kusakabe was carrying an impressive-looking package on his back, a sack covered with a red sheet bearing the arms of the Emperor.

"Here you are," he said hastily, "I am bringing you what you are owed. Or more precisely what my master, without asking anyone else's opinion, has decided to give you. Much gold and silk, *onna*, much more than they had led you to expect. But you can go through everything later, can't you, when you are far away from Heian Kyō. For here, you are apparently in danger of death. At

---

* Seven o'clock in the morning.

282

least, that is what the *sensei* fears. I am not sure he is right – at that age, you know, he suffers bouts of anxiety, the old fellow, anxiety that is most of the time baseless. Nevertheless, he has asked me to escort you to the Rashōmon gate. It is true," he added, when he had transferred his burden from his own shoulders to Miyuki's, "that this wealth that has come to you could tempt certain people. It is not so long ago that the very idea that criminals should enter our city would have made us scoff. Not that we think our doors are impassable once night has fallen, but we simply cannot imagine that the men swarming about on the other side of the walls could have evil intentions."

"The other side of the walls? Which walls?"

"What do you mean 'which walls'?" He looked at her in surprise.

"It's just that I didn't see any walls around the city."

Kusakabe turned away briskly, as if upset and preferring to put an end to their discussion.

She was about to ask his forgiveness, when he turned towards her again – she looked so wretched and so dirty that, despite this large red bundle on her back, there was little chance that she would arouse the greed of a highwayman.

"Very well, you are right, *onna*: there are no walls. But ever since Emperor Kammu made Heian Kyō the new imperial capital more than three centuries ago, its inhabitants have always had ramparts on their minds, they have always lived as though they were sheltering behind a parapet. But if – much as I doubt it – the *sensei* was right about threats hanging over you, an imaginary wall is not going to protect you."

◉ ◉ ◉

283

The previous day, at the hour of the Rat, Minamoto Toshikata, the Second Supernumerary Controller, Left-Hand Section, had arrived at Watanabe's home.

He was bearing the following *senji*:*

The Chief Supernumerary Counsellor, Fujiwara Akimitsu, declares he has received a command from the Emperor according to which Watanabe Nagusa, Director of the Office of Gardens and Ponds, was ordered to obtain one or more substances suitable for creating a new incense illustrating, according to the way the perfumes are used, the fleeting passage of a girl over a half-moon bridge in between two clouds of mist, this subject having been revealed to His Majesty in the course of a dream. It is acknowledged that Watanabe Nagusa has fully satisfied this obligation, but, in order that this fragrance should remain exclusively and forever symbolic of Nijō Tennō, Watanabe Nagusa is required to destroy everything that may remain of this incense, as well as everything that has contributed to its formation. Let this command be received and implemented.

The Director of the Office of Gardens and Ponds poured a cup of sake for the Supernumerary Controller and gave him by way of a gratuity eight sheets of an exceptionally soft leather that he had bought with the idea of cutting some bridles for Hatsuharu, his favourite horse. But no longer having sufficient strength or confidence to ride him – "old age is sweeping over me like corruption," Watanabe would say – he had recently made

---

* An urgent command from the Emperor, exempted from going through all administrative processes.

up his mind to part with everything connected to Hatsuharu. As for the horse itself, he planned to make a gift of it to Kusakabe. Watanabe had so identified with Hatsuharu that he had sometimes dreamed that, with Kusakabe perched on his shoulders, with Kusakabe clenching him between his sinewy thighs, with Kusakabe laughing like a child and pulling at his ears as though they were reins, he, Watanabe, was galloping alongside boggy fields, whinnying with joy as he clambered up green hills that were almost black, and leaped over the sparkling curtains of the waterfalls.

After Minamoto Toshikata had left, Watanabe reread the imperial command stipulating that he must destroy the victorious incense of the *takimono awase*.

No doubt Nijō Tennō, in the dazzling pride of his youth, had initially had his heart set on this perfume competition, the first of his reign, becoming legendary, and that, afterwards, generations of emperors and regents, shoguns, counsellors and directors of this and that would try to re-create the perfume that, accompanying the parade of a young girl over a bridge between two tissue-like curtains, had so aroused the passions of the Court; and the Emperor had imagined leaving a few clues to enable his successors to repeat the miracle. But he had quickly changed his mind: what an error, what a mistake he might have made! Quite the contrary, he should take every precaution to prevent anyone discovering the formula, so that the search of those copyists, those plagiarists, would never end. The glory of Nijō Tennō would be in proportion to their failure.

Even supposing that the keen interest shown in the *takimono awase* dwindled to the point that it no longer featured among the rituals and traditions practised at Court, folk memory would still recall this night of snow over Heian Kyō, this night when a senior official, to please his Emperor, had succeeded in re-creating the infinitely complex, infinitely moving, infinitely dynamic aroma of a young woman, of a young woman, every one of whose four limbs, bodily apertures and twelve dresses had released and intermingled her odours.

Watanabe willingly admitted that even the most beautiful things may come to an end. Had this not been so, would he have been as moved as he was by the fragility of plum or cherry blossom, and would he, above all, have savoured these final extracts from his own existence until he experienced a sensation close to intoxication?

"Not a particle remains of last night's incense," Kusakabe had assured him. "It smelled so good that it was allowed to burn itself out."

The problem that Watanabe now faced was that the imperial command stipulated the elimination not just of the incense but also of everything that had enabled its creation. No-one had foreseen that in order to create a perfect representation of the Emperor's dream, Watanabe Nagusa would have to mingle Amakusa Miyuki's natural odour with the delights of the incense.

His important role as Director of the Office of Gardens and Ponds had meant that Watanabe received an impressive number of gardening tools as gifts. Most of these were supplied with blades, flanges, picks or cogs, which he entrusted without any qualms to inexperienced gardeners who, after so many years of supervising them, he knew would put out their eyes, or maim or mutilate themselves with these tools. The inventory of severed fingers, slashed ears, and even gouged-out eyes already took up two rolls of mulberry paper.

But it was one thing to allow beginners to amputate a finger or two, and quite another to condemn a poor and defenceless young woman to death just because the Emperor had given an order without taking all the consequences into account – an order that was now entrusted to Watanabe and that he would have to pass on to Kusakabe, he himself not having the necessary physical strength to strike at anyone and cause an immediate death.

The murder, far from making his assistant the loving partner of the old man's dreams, would reduce Kusakabe to the level of a brutal accomplice of a despicable crime that he, Watanabe, would have instigated – a role equally vile and so much more cowardly than that of the killer. What awaited them both was not some soft matting directly beneath a translucent window carefully framed by a weeping willow – that gentle rustling that had always reminded him of the pleasure of caresses – but Jigoku, the Buddhist hell, beginning with the Chamber of Wind and Thunder, the gaol where murderers are punished. Then would come the Crushing Chamber where, between two enormous stones, those who have committed premeditated murder are crushed until they are no more than a bleeding pulp, and, to finish, they would experience, over a period of a few thousand years, the delights of the Heart Chamber where claw-like fingers continually rip out the hearts of men who have lacked compassion (it goes without saying that, having been removed by those bare hands, the punished hearts put themselves back together again so that they may be tortured anew).

Giving himself the excuse that the weather was extremely cold, Watanabe drank the remains of the flask of sake that he had begun with the Supernumerary Controller, which he had left to cool in the ashes of a brazier.

He looked down on the Avenue of the Red Bird below him. On top of the fresh snow, traces of two pairs of parallel footsteps could be seen setting off towards the Rashōmon gate. Shortly before they reached the building, one of the pairs had turned around and proceeded in the direction from which they had come. They must be Kusakabe's, thought Watanabe. The other footsteps, probably left by Miyuki, ascended the five steps of the staircase and continued on beneath the double ridge of glazed tiles.

Ever since political unrest, increasingly accompanied by violent uprisings, had begun to affect the Heian Kyō nobles' enjoyment of life, the vault of the Rashōmon was used as a night shelter for all the reprobates the city did not want: peasants fleeing the razzias led by the *rōnin*,* certain of these *rōnin* themselves, and the usual crowd of beggars, disabled and young children abandoned by families unable to feed them. These people ate what the city threw out. The peelings, the scraps and the rejected food had already been cooked, fried or boiled, but for it to be worth consideration as food in its own right it had to be heated again. This was why, from a vast number of earthbound hearths, great stinking spirals of smoke rose up and stagnated under the roof and beams already blackened by soot.

Coupled with an early, foggy twilight, these fumes prevented

---

* Samurai who had lost the leader to whom they had dedicated themselves body and soul, and who were reduced to living by their wits.

Watanabe from seeing beyond the eight vermilion pillars. Vexed, he sent one of his servants to tell his assistant that he needed to speak to him. Since he had accompanied her as far as the city gate, Kusakabe would know whether or not the widow had passed through the Rashōmon. If she had, it would not be necessary to concern himself with getting rid of her – the wintry nights and the perils of the journey would take care of that.

While he waited, Watanabe stripped naked and gave himself over to the care of three of his servants to be epilated, washed and then massaged with strongly aromatic oils that would make Kusakabe forget the disturbing scents of the little widow from Shimae.

AS THE LIGHT IN the forest was gradually brightening, Miyuki guessed that she was close to Shimae.

Even after their leaves had fallen, the trees had continued to form dark vaults and sombre, unfinished tunnels. Now that the dampness left by the autumn mists had blackened their trunks and principal branches, and the lichen had turned from beige to brown, this shadowy world gave the impression of being compressed and confined. The daylight had become tenuous, as if it had been absorbed by the murky glaze that seemed to seep from the trees. The forest appeared to be not only nocturnal, but also disorderly, tangled and impenetrable.

Yet for a couple of hours, the brightness returned.

Despite the difficulty of making her way over unstable ground consisting of a jumble of roots, scree and dead leaves, all held together by mudslides of claggy soil, Miyuki would soon make her way out. It was not that the light had improved, as if the sun had just broken through a layer of cloud: it was because there were fewer trees and all the threads in the tapestry of plant life had loosened. Inextricable until then, the scrubland of bushes and undergrowth had noticeably receded.

Miyuki ought to have found it comforting to be almost back in the village that she had never left before setting off on the journey to Heian Kyō. But, on the contrary, with every step she took, she experienced an irrational anxiety, a sense of oppression that gripped her throat as though a pool of sorrow had begun to well up inside her. Katsuro's death had been the source of this pool and had never stopped feeding it; but although it had sometimes risen to a critical level, the pool had never yet burst its banks. It was on the point of doing so now.

Even though the surroundings Miyuki was travelling through must have seemed identical to those she had left, certain aspects had changed: she did not recall having crossed such craggy escarpments bristling with sharp stones that tore the straw of her sandals, nor the trees, especially the pines, being twisted as though a powerful force had seized them to try to weave them together; she did not understand where they had come from, these claw-like, threatening branches that blocked the path the peasants from Shimae were always careful to keep free and unobstructed – but she was obliged to go around each obstacle, holding on to the roots to hoist herself up the verges that a mix-ture of snow, ice and mud had made slippery.

Was her memory playing tricks on her, or had this silent for-est, so composed in appearance, undergone an upheaval, which, without ruining it, had profoundly altered it?

Miyuki sat down on a tree stump, not so much to revive her energy as to try to rediscover her serenity before the final push that would lead her to the rice fields surrounding her village.

Raising her head, she realised that she could see the light

falling vertically from the sky, whereas usually the sun's rays, obstructed by the thick foliage, had to navigate the persistent sieve of thick branches. This different way of receiving daylight stemmed from a new configuration of the trees, each of them appearing to have acquired more living space after a long struggle, as borne out by the way they bent, curved and vaulted. Strangely, it was not the sickliest trees that had fared worst: their branches had become entangled as though they had been performing the dance of the Five Articulations, *gosechi no mai*, which consisted of raising your sleeves above your head five times, whipping the air with them and then letting them fall back over your face; these trees, however, had remained upright, while many of the old trees had fallen on their sides, exposing their enormous root system and revealing wounds that flowed with a dough-like mixture of sap and rotten wood.

The most puzzling thing was the silence of the birds. Normally, they were at their noisiest the closer one got to the edge of the woods, beyond which the activity of the village began, giving the birds their main source of fodder. Today, their silence was such that one would have thought the birds had deserted the forest.

Apart from one blackbird with slate-grey feathers, streaked with blue.

It was perched in a tree a short distance away from Miyuki, looking like a nail that had been only half hammered in. It must have flown into the tree trunk at very high speed for its beak to have been driven deep into the wood like an arrowhead. Although the shock would have killed it, it had clearly had a post-mortem reflex to try to free itself by beating its wings, for

292

they had stiffened into an open position, with the remiges fully spread.

Miyuki wondered what could possibly have provoked such desperate panic in this blackbird for it to lose control of its flight and smash into an object as prominent as this tree – a camphor of about a hundred years old, no less, which it would have inevitably been able to see, and which it would normally have had no difficulty in avoiding, even if it was being pursued by a predator.

Leaving her tree stump, she walked over to the bird. Even before she bent over it, and despite the slight whiff of camphor that came from the tree, she caught the stench of decomposing flesh. The blackbird had been dead for several days, but its plumage had performed a shabby cover-up, concealing colonies of flies and ants that swarmed about the blood-streaked pulp among masses of whitish eggs and maggots.

Miyuki recoiled. She had always had a horror of insects, especially those that buzzed around her face, and which, having been swatted away, returned persistently to gather at the corners of her lips and her eyes.

But this time the flies that had formed a quivering cluster around the bird's body flew away before Miyuki lifted even a finger, and the blackbird stuck in the camphor tree suddenly began to quiver, its tail feathers fluttering in the air. It was not new life coursing through it, however, but a long, sustained vibration of unknown origin that, having made the tree tremble, communicated itself to the bird after the insects had been driven away in a panic.

The whistling of the wind grew shriller, the bare branches clashed together to the tune of a *danse macabre*, while a rough,

293

hollow, grumbling sound rumbled beneath the surface of the ground as though it were being scraped from below by a gigantic file.

The mosses that carpeted the ground seemed to be breathing, rising up in patches and then collapsing back once more before reaching up again like a thick, soft blanket over the chest of someone sleeping. Where there was no moss, where the earth was bare, the ground cracked, creating fissures drawn like flashes of lightning in the shape of dry arborescences.

The entire forest had started to gently sway.

Miyuki clung to the camphor tree to steady herself, but the tree lurched as though it was being shaken to send its fruit to the ground.

Then she let go of the tree and fled with a cry.

When Miyuki emerged from the forest, there was nothing but a muddy stretch of earth in the place where she had always known there to be the espaliers of the rice fields. Levelled by an irresistible force, the ridges surrounding the fields had all been destroyed; they now covered the plots they were meant to protect, crushing the rice plants and driving the pools of water into the lower espaliers, where the same process began again, and so on until the former hill dotted with rice fields had been wiped away to form a barely mottled surface.

Miyuki did not need to consult one of those scholarly people who proliferated in Heian Kyō, specialists in rainbows, eclipses, haunted tombs and earthquakes, to realise that her village had suffered an upheaval that had buried the buildings and barns, turned over the fields and removed not just every trace of present-day life, but the very memories that a landscape could retain.

There, where pastures and food crops had once flourished, nothing could be seen apart from patches of stony brown earth that emitted a smell of flint.

A stream of mud and a variety of debris appeared to have obstructed the carp pool – *appeared to*, for, with all reference points removed, Miyuki was unable to situate with any certainty the place where her house had once stood, and, *a fortiori*, the location of the pool.

One vestige alone had remained, but without any landmark left now that the entire village had been wiped out, it was of no help to her in finding her bearings; it was nothing very much in any case, just a squat roof, beneath which the building that it once covered had disintegrated and been scattered to dust. But thanks to its frame of green wood, the roof had benefited from a certain elasticity and, having become detached from the walls that it had secured, it had caved under its own weight. It now resembled a crushed beetle.

A little boy, virtually naked, was squatting over it like a hunter on the back of his prey. Despite the blood and sores that spattered his face, Miyuki recognised Hakuba, the potter's son.

She walked towards the crouching child, with the same discretion she would adopt if she were approaching a small, frightened animal – which, she thought, must be Hakuba, whose black hair had grown straight up on his head before freezing in that position.

"Are you alright, Hakuba?"

The silence over Shimae was so thick, with only a few

subterranean rumbles breaking out intermittently, that she had no need to raise her voice.

"All the others, do you know where they are?"

No, Hakuba knew nothing. Or he preferred to say nothing. Or the shock he had suffered had left him dumb.

"And your parents?"

The child pointed to the ground, where a snaking ridge resembled a scar. At this point, the earth must have opened, swallowing up Hakuba's father and mother before the fault had closed again.

"I imagine that your house used to be here, beneath this roof. But you're not going to stay squatting over it waiting for it to grow again, are you?"

The boy shook his head. While not very clever, he was not stupid either, at least not to the extent of thinking that houses could grow. It was adults who believed in that kind of wondrous thing, who created legends that they solemnly brushed onto elegant paper, paper in colours so rare that some of them did not even have names yet – a yellow that recalled the newly grown capitula of certain half-opened chrysanthemums, or another shade of yellow, more intense, obtained through the fermentation of cows' urine with mangosteen leaves, or a colour conjuring up the panicles of pink lilac in a dawn sky.

"Tell me, Hakuba . . ."

"Don't call me Hakuba anymore, I am Gareki now."*

"Gareki," she repeated softly. "Let it be Gareki."

"This name is because of the earth that shakes, which has destroyed everything."

---

* *Hakuba*: white horse. *Gareki*: ruins, rubble, debris.

Confirmation of an earthquake, Miyuki thought, wondering at that same moment what had become of her imitation Tang salt pot with its peony decorations, the pot that had passed through the generations without a crack, and up until then the only tangible object that she could have kept from her happy years with Katsuro. She had often thought, and it had reassured her, that if something happened to the salt pot, she could count on Hakuba's father to repair it. But the potter had not survived the tremor, and all that was likely to remain of the salt pot would be earthenware dust in which specks of its former glaze would glitter, like the sparkles of mica on sandy beaches. She knew this from Katsuro, who had actually seen the sea.

She was not very sure, but it seemed to her that it was over there, into the waters of the Inland Sea, that the Kusagawa flowed.

On several occasions, Katsuro had spoken of learning the trade of a cormorant fisherman, should he have no further customers for his carp. And it was on the gently sloping shores of the Inland Sea that he wished to settle, for the cormorant prefers sheltered and shallow stretches of water. Katsuro saw a double advantage in this: a simple boat would be all he needed, and Miyuki would be less worried about him venturing too far from the shore. As for the training and harnessing of cormorants (he planned to use eight or ten of them, attached to the ends of long leads made from cedar fibres), he looked forward to it: he would not only have the most efficient birds, but above all those that were most familiar with the whole bay, and soon, like the Chinese fisherman, he would be able to let his cormorants fly around unfettered.

"You're not intending to stay here, are you, Hakuba?"

"Gareki," he said, in a sullen voice.

"Gareki, yes," she said. "Well, Gareki, my boy, there's nothing left here: not a thing, nobody, so it would be best for us to leave. Because what happened is going to begin again, you see – can't you feel how the earth continues to quake?"

Miyuki had never witnessed an earthquake, but among the inhabitants of Shimae, among the oldest of them, some remembered seeing the earth cracking practically beneath their feet and fleeing until they were out of breath from those hissing crevices that pursued them, spitting out spirals of stinking steam.

"It's down there," the child agreed. "But it's far away."

Miyuki became more insistent.

"It's coming up, it's searching for us, and it will find us. What shall we do if it catches us? We have only ourselves to take with us, so let's get out of here without waiting any longer."

"To go where?"

"I suggest the sea, at the very end of the river."

He stared at her, puzzled: he did not know what the sea was. Miyuki tried to suggest an image to him, but how should she begin to describe it? The salty taste, the rolling waves, the murky colour, the huge roar, the depth, the vastness?

Since dusk was falling and the first stars were twinkling in a clear sky, she used the canopy of night as an example that might give a child an idea of the infinity of the sea. It was easier to describe the waves: the ground was endlessly riven by long undulations that gave the impression that the plain of Shimae was built on a moving layer of water.

The little boy listened carefully. He had good memories of this slim woman, who was both gentle and lively, who never forgot, when he dragged himself, naked and shivering, out of the carp pool, with pearls of water dripping from his newly emerging facial hair, to hand him a piece of cloth to rub himself down. So, when she started to walk away with a decisive step, he followed her without hesitation.

The Kusagawa was unrecognisable. The earthquake must have generated a subterranean wave which, as it hurled the river from its bed, had also ejected the silt, the sands, the aquatic plants and the fish.

Some carp, carried away by the foaming mass that flowed along both banks of the river, had been swept far into the plain; whereupon, the water having withdrawn without regaining the riverbed, they had died of asphyxia.

Added to the number of dilemmas that confronted Miyuki, there was the fate of the inhabitants of Shimae. From what remained of the village, it could be assumed that the earthquake had killed most of them, and that those who had survived the first tremors had fled as far as possible. The seismic wave having spread from west to east, and with the north being filled with thick forests where one made slow progress, they had probably headed southwards – that is to say, in the direction that Miyuki and the child took.

But this did not explain why there was no trace of the survivors passing through. What had they done with their dead? Miyuki had not seen a funeral pyre anywhere, nor a burial place, however hastily thrown together. As far as the eye could see, there was nothing but a monotonous plain, scattered with patches of snow that roamed like whitish clouds against a grey sky.

She looked at the little boy. Tears flowed from his eyes that had the consistency and yellow colour of cream – which must be pus, she thought – and they formed swirls as they dried on his cheeks. His pupils were strongly dilated, which could be due to the night falling. On the other hand, the red colour of his conjunctiva signified a visual fatigue that Miyuki, without knowing anything about diseases of the eye, put down to the fact that the child must have spent long hours, day and night, on top of his crushed roof scanning the plain in the hope of spotting his parents, or anyone likely to come to his aid.

She also noticed that, besides the bruises and the coagulated blood, Gareki's much too scrawny body was covered in filth; and when she looked intently at the child, she saw him as a mirror of herself: she, too, was dirty, her cheeks were streaked with rain and dust, her skin mottled with purplish patches, her lips cracked, her long black hair tangled and filthy, her kimono tattered and soaked.

If, having left the epicentre of the earthquake behind them, especially the deadly danger of aftershocks, they were able to reach the fishermen's villages that followed on one from another along the length of the shores of the Inland Sea, they could begin a new life – either together or separately, they would decide once they were there. But one thing that Miyuki was already certain of was the curiosity they would be subjected to as survivors of an earthquake: the tremors must have been felt as far away as the Isle of Shikoku.

Although she had not bothered much about her appearance when she had mingled with the crowd jostling to get through the Rashōmon gate – down there, it was Katsuro's carp that were making their entrance into the Imperial City, and Miyuki with her black, mud-covered nails was merely their servant – she was still anxious to make a good impression on the people of Kobe, Ube, Okayama, Fukuoka, Yashima and the small estuary of Hiwasa, if she and the child ever got there.

"Gareki," she said, pinching her nostrils, "you really do smell, my boy."

"It's not me," he concluded, after fanning himself for a while. "It's a smell that's in the air, actually. A smell of death, Miyuki-*san*. After all this, eh, it was bound to happen – had you not noticed this smell before? It was there from the first day, but you weren't there on the first day. It will disappear when it starts to rain, when the rain will make it go back underground."

"If the rain can get rid of this stench, the river can too."

"Ah, no, I won't go into the river! The river's too cold, it's much too cold to wash in it: just before the earth shook, it was full of blocks of ice. I saw them: so big that they were blue in the middle."

"There's no need to take a dip in the Kusagawa. You sit on the bank, I'll make a cup with my hands, I'll take a little water and I'll pour it over you, and I'll rub you gently with sand from the river, and then, once again, I'll take some water in my hands, and . . ."

"You know," he said, "you don't smell very nice either."

Miyuki smiled.

"After I have washed you," she said, "you must wash me."

They walked along the riverbank, looking for a suitable place. Night had fallen. The reflection of the full moon glided over the now-darkened waters. Little Gareki walked in silence so as not to disturb the birds that had been troubled enough by the earthquake. Were it not for the sugary-sweet smell of corpses that came to her in waves, Miyuki would have believed that she was walking by the water's edge one winter evening with her husband (for different reasons from Gareki, Katsuro also liked to walk in silence; lost in his thoughts, he could cover considerable distances without uttering a single word).

All of a sudden, there was the sound of a splash, as if a frightened frog had dived in.

It was Gareki, who had just thrown himself into the water. He swam to and fro, from one bank to the other, creating two small waves that ran from each side of his chin, cleaving the water like a duck's wishbone.

Miyuki had not realised that the little boy knew how to swim. In Shimae so few people did. Even Katsuro, the prince, the king, the emperor of the river, did not know how to swim. Moreover, he had made it a matter of pride: no-one should stretch out on their belly in the Kusagawa's presence, or appear before it in a recumbent position, still less imitate the frog; one should confront the river standing up, both feet firmly planted.

"It's not at all cold," the child said. "The water is warm, come, Miyuki-*san*, come with me!"

The violent friction of the deepest rocks, near the source of the tremor, must have produced a release of heat that could warm the subsoil of the river and the water that flowed over it.

Gareki slid both his hands over the moon's reflection, opened his mouth wide and pretended to be sinking his teeth into the bluish halo as if eating a cake.

Miyuki, in turn, entered the water. Her intention was to immerse herself up to her navel, to hop about on the spot, making shrill little cries, and emerge very quickly to run around and shake herself dry.

But, the river, at this juncture, was far deeper than she had imagined, and she was deceived by the ease with which Gareki had made his way in. Although she pedalled wildly to regain her footing, Miyuki felt that the Kusagawa was clasping her, shaking her, trying to jostle her to make her fall. But she stood firm, casting all her energy and power into her lower back and thighs.

And it was then that she saw it.

Such a deep black, so fierce, so shimmering that it stood out even in the gloomy waters of the Kusagawa, a giant carp had escaped, probably as a result of one of the tremors of the earthquake, from the riverbed, where it had lain flat without anyone noticing it, half concealed in the mud and silt that it had stirred up.

And it rose to the surface, stretching out its mouth framed by four soft, tactile barbels. Over a metre and a half in length and weighing surely a hundred kilos, it had a massive, somewhat conical head and was equipped with prominent eyes capable of looking in opposite directions.

Hoisting itself and wriggling its way onto a ledge of moist clay, it looked like a wretched old man whose back no longer supports him, and who has no other option than to slither along.

Miyuki remembered hearing Natsume state that a ghost broke loose from a human being whenever he or she experienced a violent trauma, just as the best fruit falls from a tree when it is

303

shaken by a storm. These wounded creatures, these still-living spectres, were reputed to remain in the place where the shock had occurred; and there they matured, until they rotted, until they liquefied, and eventually melted into the earth.

Was it not in the vicinity of the Kusagawa, just where the riverbed widens and is pitted with rocks that accelerate its path to the sea, that Katsuro had drowned? And might not the huge black carp be his ghost, completing its farewell and metamorphosis?

What is certain is that the large black carp did not shy away when Miyuki (for this irresistible urge was more powerful than her) reached out her hand to touch it just where the four noses were situated, between its two eyes.

When the touch became a caress, the carp seemed even to enjoy it.

It was Miyuki who was the first to withdraw contact, removing her hand. One of the fish's eyes remained stubbornly fixed on her, as if it were summoning this hand to come back and lavish more caresses on it, while the other eye, more pragmatically, greedily watched a drowning insect.

Miyuki had never seen a fish of this size, and certainly not one that had inspired such great trust in her, even though the black carp would have been capable of swallowing one of her arms up to the shoulder in its excessively wide jaws.

She knew that certain rivers harboured giant carp that came originally from China. Katsuro used to say that over there they swam up a great river, the Huang He, which, by narrowing suddenly, generated enormous waves that plunged from the top of the Hukou falls with a sound of thunder so loud that the birds made wide detours to avoid flying too close to it.

Carried along by a whirlpool of reddish waters, the black carp of Huang He hurtled down the waterfall and disappeared behind the curtains of foam from where, through a miraculous effect of transference, some of them found themselves conveyed to lakes and rivers in Japan.

This, at least, was what Katsuro had heard people say, and what he had told his wife while making it clear that he had never seen any of these tremendous fish himself, and that he even doubted whether they existed.

Miyuki removed the red silk sack that she carried. She emptied the contents at the boy's feet. The gold gleamed softly, the fluffy grey paper of the promissory notes fluttered as they crackled like the thick wings of a moth.

"You go on your own, Gareki. I'm staying."

She pointed to the carp still sprawled on the clay bank, with its thick lips gaping so widely that they looked as though they had been pulled apart, and its mouth from which spurted a light haze of insipid water that was about to get caught in a spider's web, just in front of it, between two bamboo canes. Miyuki explained that she had to try to get it back into the river: that is what Katsuro would have done. But, given the weight of the fish and the lack of any grip, it would be long and laborious work, and while she would do everything she was capable of to save the carp, a repeat of the earthquake could occur which, in an instant, would rip through the plain of Shimae again, opening cracks in the banks through which the Kusagawa would rush, dragging along in its wake everything that was not solidly rooted. Now, Miyuki was not rooted at all. And neither was Gareki. Nobody could see how matters would turn out, of course, but she was determined that the boy should get away as quickly as possible.

"All this is for you, Gareki," she said, pointing to the contents of the basket. "I shall not need it anymore."

Having just explained what the sea was, Miyuki now had to explain gold to him, and the various uses that could be made of it. As for the promissory notes, since she did not understand much about them herself, she simply tipped them into the river with her foot.

The child gathered up the treasure and put it back in the basket which he covered again with the red silk cloak, securing the basket on his back. Miyuki placed a silent kiss in the hollow of her right hand, and, with this kiss, without his realising, smoothed down the boy's stiff, bristly hair.

"Go," she encouraged him. "Go, Gareki."

He took a few steps, turned around, and gazed at her with his expression of a young god.

"It's alright!" he shouted. "I'm going back to my old name of Hakuba."

She waited until he had disappeared. The gods had created nothingness to persuade men to fill it. It was not presence that controlled the world and filled it; it was space, absence, emptiness, disappearance. Everything was nothing. The misunderstanding came from the fact that, from the beginning, people had believed that living meant having control over something, and yet it was nothing of the sort, the universe was as insubstantial, subtle and intangible as the passing wake of a girl walking between two clouds in an emperor's dream.

A floating world.

A fine rain began to fall, arousing the happy croaking of a few frogs. Miyuki looked at the black carp. She thought how marvellous it would be to capture it, to dig a pool for it where it could splash about, while she herself, sitting on the edge, with her feet in the cool water, would have all the time to observe her guest, to tell it about her life, until one day the Office of Gardens and Ponds sent some emissaries to Shimae (the village would have been rebuilt, of course) to ask for a new delivery of carp.

The rain intensified, the sky darkened. Something rumbled, still far away but growing closer. Miyuki took no notice of this: she was thinking of what the journey to Heian Kyō would be like with a carp of that size. One would have to weave it a very long net, at least the size of a man standing up – and of a well-proportioned man at that. Carrying it would necessitate two strong bamboo rods, shiny black, preferably, to be in harmony with the fish's scales, one length of bamboo on the right, one on the left, resting on the shoulders of two strong bearers scampering along, one behind the other. She was smiling, imagining the face of the Director of the Office of Gardens and Ponds on discovering the existence of such a fish, when she heard the whistling sound, the sound of torn silk made by a fissure running beneath the ground like a small dog wild with joy, which was coming towards her as a deep fault opened in the earth.

She lay down by the carp, protecting it with her body.

The creature smelled of the silt, the mucus, the decomposing leaves, the crushed algae, the mouldy wood, the damp earth, the same muted, low, slightly greasy smell Katsuro had when he came back from the river; and beneath Miyuki's breasts, the carp's heart beat at the same calm rhythm, truly majestic, as Katsuro's did

307

on certain mornings, just after he had made love to her. Then he would open the door of their house, and she would see, framed in the doorway, the outline of the man covered with nets, with bamboo poles, with lumps of cork and with balls of still-knotted fishing line that he would have to disentangle beside the Kusa-gawa, because the previous evening, instead of looking after his equipment, Miyuki and he had made love slowly, for a long time.

DIDIER DECOIN was twenty when he published his first book, *Le Procès à l'amour*. It was followed by some twenty other titles, including *Abraham de Brooklyn* and *John l'Enfer*. He is currently Secretary General of the Académie Goncourt, has been Chairman of the Écrivains de Marine since 2007 and is a member of the Académie de Marine. He spent fourteen years on the research and writing of *The Office of Gardens and Ponds*.

EUAN CAMERON's translations include works by Patrick Modiano, Julien Green, Simone de Beauvoir, Paul Morand and Philippe Claudel, and biographies of Marcel Proust and Irène Némirovsky. His debut novel, *Madeleine*, was published in 2019.